The Visitor

Jenna Ryan

Harlequin Books

TORONTO • NEW YORK • LONDON
AMSTERDAM • PARIS • SYDNEY • HAMBURG
STOCKHOLM • ATHENS • TOKYO • MILAN
MADRID • WARSAW • BUDAPEST • AUCKLAND

To Bill and Kay, my parents. To Kathy, my sister.
To Alice, my aunt. To Shauna, my fourteen-year-old
cat. To Mary Shelley, for writing *Frankenstein*. And to
all the wonderful people I met in the Black Forest and
Harz Mountains of Germany.

Harlequin Intrigue edition published August 1993

ISBN 0-373-22239-4

THE VISITOR

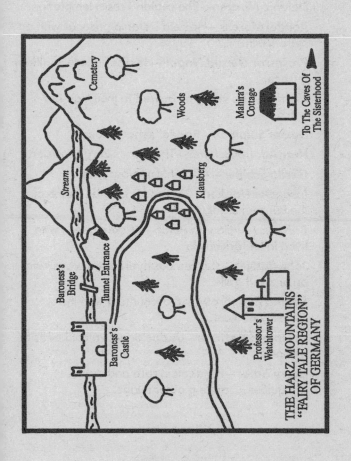

THE HARZ MOUNTAINS
"FAIRY TALE REGION"
OF GERMANY

CAST OF CHARACTERS

Delanie Morgen—She couldn't resist temptation.

Rondel Marcos—He held Delanie prisoner with a mere touch.

Professor Gerald Nagel—He disappeared without a trace.

Mahira—The villagers bowed to their age-old witch.

Dexter Solomon—Rondel's shady cousin.

Herr Adolph Schiller—The town's Bürgermeister.

Gerda Schiller—Adolph's nervous wife.

Inspector Haaken—He lived under the thumb of the Bürgermeister.

Baroness Alicia von Peldt—Wicked queen who lived in a black castle.

John Kessler—This famous hypnotist always wore an amused smile.

Roland Popporov—An accountant with the curiosity of a cat.

Dr. Ingrid Hoffman—A doctor with a cold bedside manner.

Harry Bates—He dealt in rare and dubious antiquities...among other things.

Prologue

The Story of The Visitor

Sisters, hear me, gather near.
The time of evil winds and fear
born of the devil's fiery hand
approaches, darkness sweeps the land
where soon The Visitor will rise
up from the flames of hell, disguised.
But in what form shall not be known
to we of flesh and blood and bone.
The angel only sees the horns
of Lucifer, cast out; reborn
to rule the Underworld of fire
and brimstone, to commit to pyre
all those who seek to find this place,
who call to Satan, desire to face
the tests, temptations of the beast
and servile demons. To the east
and west they flew and south and north,
six demons called and four sent forth.
But two remain in Satan's lair,
this earthly world of wind and air,
of woods and mountain caves and lore
and somber superstition. More
than myth begins to unfold here.
Walpurgis breaks, the night of fear.

For so the ancient Story tells,
four demons will return to hell,
sent there by one from heaven's door
who'll catch these demons one to four.
But not the demons five and six,
and not The Visitor whose tricks
cannot be faced by one so pure.
Two humans must these trials endure.
And if before Walpurgis ends
and May Day dawns, the angel sends
the chosen two, and if they pass
the tests, the six temptations cast
before them, they will then receive
the mandragora. If they cleave
to their beliefs and persevere,
do not submit or bow to fear
for five tests; if they play the Game
and that survive and win, defame
the devil's demons six and five,
they'll find the angel still alive.
Held captive by The Visitor,
removed from sight to thus ensure
that two alone not pure of soul
will make their choices, play the role
of savior to the one divine
whose power cannot cross the line,
who must not seek to intervene,
to guide the chosen two. The scene
is set, the devil waits,
The Visitor in guise whose fate,
whose power on this earth shall be
decided for a century.
But only if the demons lose,
and only should the angel choose
the proper two, defeat the four,
then set this pair at Satan's door.
If The Visitor should win,
a reign of darkness will begin.
But if the angel chooses well,

The Visitor returns to hell,
there to rule the souls who came
of their own wills into the flame.
So this is it, the Story told,
related to us long ago.
Of Lucifer, the devil or
the evil one: The Visitor.

Chapter One

Lightning crackled in the black night sky. Rain streamed down, splashing onto the windshield of the battered Vauxhall, the only car on the thin ribbon of road that wound through this somber section of Germany's Harz mountains.

"Frankenstein," Delanie Morgen murmured, hunching deeper in the cracked passenger seat. "I thought this was supposed to be fairy-tale country, professor. You know, pretty woods and ponds, little Snow Whites playing with deer."

"You're mixing your stories, and it is." Professor Gerald Nagel kept his eyes focused on the road, such as it was. It must be out there somewhere, Delanie reasoned, otherwise they'd be stuck in the mud beside some gnarly oak tree.

"It doesn't feel like a fairy tale," she said, jamming her hands into the pockets of her long black jacket. "And I'm not mixing my stories. This is where Frankenstein's monster was born and Snow White ate a poisoned apple." She dug her feet in as they crashed through a series of water-filled potholes. "I don't understand. Why is it so barren and dead-looking here? Aren't forests usually more lush?"

"This is the forest of sinister fairy tales," the man beside her reminded. "And The Visitor."

"Damn, I knew you were going to bring that up again."

"I have to bring it up now, don't I?"

He sounded impatient, but Delanie was used to the professor's quick mood swings. It wasn't so much temperament with him as it was speed of thought. Although he looked like a cross between a lanky Saint Bernard and a mad scientist, the man was an absolute genius.

So why didn't he see that he was playing with fire by coming to this place, the domain of the legendary Visitor?

"You know," she reminded him, "even that detective at Interpol thinks what you're doing is dangerous."

"It is."

"So why are you doing it?"

"We, Delanie. We're doing it. And the reason should be obvious. We're trying to catch The Visitor. I've exposed his four demons, now we're after the top demon, so to speak."

"The devil." Delanie sighed, running restless fingers through her heavy fall of blond hair. "All right, you say you're chasing Satan, but The Visitor's Story is only a myth, an ancient bit of folklore. No devil came up from hell with four demons—"

"Six."

"Whatever. You're on the trail of a psychopathic killer whom we know has recruited at least four people to do his killing for him."

"Or her."

"But the only connection anyone can see is that there is no connection."

"Oh, there's a connection, Delanie. Quite a sinister one. A lawyer in Edinburgh, a trash collector in Madrid, a grocer in New York, a prostitute in London, the list goes on and on. Yet they were all wearing upside-down pewter crosses around their necks when their bodies were found. Same cross, same chain—"

"And all killed in different ways."

The professor shook his head. His mop of loose brown curls danced in the eerie flashes of lightning that filled the car. "The hows aren't important. It's the crosses that connect them. It ties them to The Visitor."

"Okay, so why doesn't Interpol do something, or the German police?"

"Because I didn't tell them my latest theory, that's why."

"What?" Delanie snatched her head around. "What do you mean you didn't tell them? Who was that woman we talked to in Frankfurt?"

"An old friend. Ours was an unofficial chat. She understands what's at stake here, what I hope to achieve." The professor wore a long tartan scarf about his neck. He used the end of it now to wipe beads of perspiration from his forehead. "Think of it as a game, Delanie. The Visitor against me. One intellect battling another."

Delanie set her teeth as they bounced through another rut. "Your Visitor's a lunatic, professor. I can't believe you didn't tell the police we were coming here, or that you thought he'd be waiting for us."

"Oh, I told them we were coming, I just didn't tell them why. I have my laboratory in an old watchtower near Klausberg, you know."

Yes, she did know that. She also knew that the professor was familiar with every single detail of what the people in this spooky German region called The Visitor's Story. It was a game, he said. His mind against a maniac's. But maniacs could be brilliant, too.

"Maybe you're wrong," she suggested, then grabbed her seat as the front tire hit a large stone. "You can't be sure your mastermind murderer will come to Klausberg."

"Oh, but I can."

She recognized that profound tone right off. She hadn't spent five months in the professor's company without coming to know a few of his many quirks.

She released a heavy breath. "Okay, I give up. Why can you?"

"Because the Story's being played out, don't you see."

She grimaced at the gloomy landscape. "No, I don't see," she said. It was only half a lie. "Explain it to me." She sent him a meaningful sideways glance. "And this time, try to make sense, will you?"

"I always make sense." His tone sounded more impatient as a sharp flash of lightning split the sky ahead. The rain seemed to fall in buckets now.

"This person," the professor began, "our killer—let's say it's The Visitor—is playing out the legend, or as it's better known in Klausberg, the Story. For whatever reason, he knows the Story well. And since over the past twenty-eight months I've managed to help various police forces capture four of The Visitor's hired helpers, or demons, The Visitor must also be aware that I'm equally familiar with the Story. Clear so far?"

Delanie gave him a warning look. "Go on."

"The Story was born centuries ago in the area around Klausberg, oh, maybe as far back as the eighth century A.D. when Charlemagne marched across this part of Europe."

"That's an awfully old legend, professor."

He sent her a toothy smile. "Isn't it though? At any rate, The Visitor chose this spot as his earthly habitat, then called up six very nasty demons from hell. Four of them were sent out, to the four corners of the world. Two remained at The Visitor's side. Now, in terms of what's been happening lately, we know that the first four symbolic demons are gone."

"Those demons being the people you tracked down who had the upside-down crosses actually tattooed on their bodies."

"Precisely. Of course they're all dead now."

"Not the last one," Delanie interrupted. "He's in a coma in a London hospital."

The professor's face brightened. "Yes, he is, isn't he? Well, at any rate, the demons are essentially gone, enough to provoke The Visitor into going on with the Story. They've been eliminated by the so-called angel."

"And that's you."

He smiled. "Very good, Delanie. You're catching on. Now, according to the Story, it's time for The Visitor and the angel to meet."

"Here. In the Harz mountains."

"Yes."

"And then what?"

"Well, then I can't say for certain. If we go strictly by the Story, and if you concede that I've been cast in the role of the angel, then by rights I should be preparing to sacrifice myself to The Visitor in order to save the lives of my chosen two."

Delanie squinted through the windshield. She could no longer see the road. The headlights couldn't begin to cut through the rain and the blackness, let alone the deepening patches of bare-limbed trees. It figured the devil would feel at home in such a spooky place.

"Who—?" The car gave a sudden lurch and she had to clutch the dashboard with both hands to keep from being thrown out. "Who are the chosen two?"

"Oh, you for one, I should think. I'm not sure about the second. However, were there a second, and were I to sacrifice myself..." He paused, gnawing on the inside of his cheek. "Hmm. I'll have to give that a bit more thought. But my point is this, The Visitor will be here, and he'll know I'm coming."

"That doesn't sound very promising, professor."

"It isn't intended to," he snapped, then softened his tone. "Don't worry, Delanie." A quick smile lit his face. "After all, you've been assisting me with my experiments and whatnot for almost half a year now, and I haven't gotten you killed yet, have I?"

"Not yet," she agreed, then pried her fingers from the dash. "How much farther to Klausberg?"

"Ten miles or so, but we'll stop at the watchtower first. I'm expecting a call from Scotland Yard."

"About the condition of the fourth 'demon'?"

"Yes." He made a doubtful motion with his mouth. "He might pull through. If he does and we're lucky, we may get our answers that way."

"And if we're not lucky?"

The professor kept his imperturbable eyes on the road. "Oh, then I should think we'll be taking on The Visitor."

A FIRE FED BY bits of dried moss and twigs burned in the center of a small human circle. Six gray-robed women formed this circle, two of middle age, three old, one positively ancient. The first five called the ancient one Mahira and spoke to her in low reverent tones.

"The flames, Mahira, what do they say?"

Her faded blue eyes studied the tongues of orange and red, watching as a snap of burl caused a small shower of sparks to light up the stone walls around them.

"He comes," she said at length. "The one to whom we call heeds our cries. It is the time of The Visitor. The Story unfolds yet again."

Her head tipped back. Her powdery eyelids fell slowly closed. She began to chant in the old Germanic tongue.

"Come to us. Let us serve you as our forebears did. We are your servants. We are the Sisterhood of Klausberg, witches all. We offer our souls to you."

THE PROFESSOR LAPSED into silence for a long time after his remark about a confrontation with The Visitor. He did that a lot, Delanie reflected. Offered some chilling statement, then refused to elaborate on it.

"It can't be The Visitor," she muttered. "Not the devil, or Lucifer, or the horned beast. We're dealing with a person who kills, professor. A person who's insane and who employs equally insane people to do his killing for him. Or her."

There was no answer, only a violent clap of thunder that made Delanie shudder.

But she couldn't complain about any of this really. She didn't have the right because she didn't have to be here.

She'd met the professor six short months ago at the hospital where she'd been working in Portland, Maine. Dr. Farrell from administration had introduced them.

"Delanie's one of our very best radiologists," he'd said with a smile. He flattered her because he wanted to go to bed with her. He liked tall, blond women with cool, distant attitudes.

Not at all like her father, she recalled with a pang.

She shuddered, returning her thoughts to the hospital. "The professor's a scientist," Dr. Farrell had explained to her. "A combination biologist, physicist and chemist, on staff at Cambridge University in England."

"On sabbatical at the moment," the professor put in.

He had a charming British accent and an appealing absentminded manner. Delanie liked him immediately. There was a sort of a patchwork look about him, too. He wore a shabby gray wool coat, baggy corduroy trousers, scuffed oxfords and he always had that blue and green and black tartan scarf wrapped about his neck. His hair was a mass of rumpled brown curls that fell carelessly about his narrow features. Sometimes he topped them with a limp gray fedora, sometimes with a cricket cap, but never with anything you'd expect.

"You seem bored, Delanie," he'd remarked when Dr. Farrell was gone and they were alone outside the hospital morgue, though why he'd specifically requested that she be the one to take him there was a mystery to Delanie. "Are you bored?"

She shoved her hands into the pockets of her lab coat, standing carefully apart from him. "Not really. I don't much like the atmosphere down here. Maybe that's what you're noticing."

He placed a finger alongside his thin nose, as if suspicious of her answer. A smile curved his lips. "You work with X rays all day long, never with people. Why is that?"

"I don't like people," she said without hesitation.

"Nonsense. If you didn't like people, you wouldn't care that we're standing outside a morgue."

"I don't like touching people," she clarified. She motioned at the double doors. "Do you want to go in?"

He studied her for a few more seconds, then nodded, obviously amused. "There's a body here that I've been asked to examine."

"Asked?"

"By the FBI." He pulled a dog-eared notebook from his coat. "A man by the name of Leland Carruthers. Single, no family, shot in the chest while trying to escape after the stabbing death of a pet shop owner here in Portland."

"I heard about it."

"Did you?" He smiled. "What else have you heard, Dr. Morgen?"

"Delanie. I don't have anywhere near Dr. Farrell's credentials."

"But you are a doctor."

"Of course. And to answer your question, I heard that this Carruthers person is, or rather was, responsible for the deaths of at least eleven people besides the pet shop owner. His list of victims stretches from San Francisco to Bangor. What I don't understand is why you would want to examine his body."

Bending slightly toward her, he whispered, "Professional curiosity." Then he pushed open the door, and while Delanie struggled not to recoil from the chemical smell of death, said, "Shall we have a look at the demon's face?"

Well, he'd had his look, while Delanie paced back and forth doing her best not to see any of the corpses.

Only at his sudden gasp had she turned her head. Good Lord, was he actually examining the dead man's neck with a magnifying glass?

"Did you see this?" he asked. "This tattoo he has is an inverted cross."

Giving a little shrug, Delanie focused on a trolley of sterile instruments far across the room. "So Mr. Carruthers was a devil worshiper. There are lots of them on the East Coast."

"No. This man's a demon."

"Same difference."

The professor ran his thumb lightly over the tattoo. The action brought a shiver to Delanie's skin. "Not quite. Demons are rather worse than devil worshipers. They're in service to the Master."

"I still don't see the difference."

"Carruthers wasn't making sacrifices to Satan, Delanie. He was recruiting souls."

"I see." Delanie paused, inching closer in spite of herself. Then she frowned. "No, I don't. Are you saying that this man thought he worked for the devil?"

"No... Yes, precisely."

No, yes? For the first time, a smile pulled on her lips. "I get it. You're an eccentric, right? One of those lettered people police forces call in to help on a case when they're baffled."

He seemed amused, but only for a moment. Then he went back to staring at the body. "I've caught three demons so far," he told her slowly. "Three of them in under two years."

"That's an impressive record, professor. But could you please explain some more about these demons? I mean, what do they really hope to accomplish?"

He lifted his head. "I told you. They're looking for souls to please their master."

"But that's crazy."

"Well, of course it's crazy. Nevertheless, it's what they're doing. And there's still one demon at large."

Delanie set her hand on the table, accidentally brushed the dead man's arm and jerked her fingers swiftly back. *Evil,* her senses whispered. She rubbed her hand against her hip. "Why do you call them demons?"

"Because of the Story. You'd say legend." Coming around the table, he put his arm about her shoulders, grinning at her startled expression. "Ah, I see. You're a sensitive."

She overcame her shock long enough to ask, "I'm a what?"

"You get feelings from people when you touch them."

"Not always," she denied swiftly, then she gave him a curious look. "Why don't I sense anything in you?"

"Maybe because you're more finely tuned to evil."

She shivered. "That's what my father used to say. He called me a witch. I think he was right."

The professor smiled and adjusted his battered fedora. "He was wrong. And I should have said negative feelings, not evil. In any case, being a sensitive is perfectly normal."

"Well, I don't know anyone else like me."

"I said normal, not commonplace. You got a feeling from that dead demon back there, didn't you?"

She hesitated, then nodded.

He arched a meaningful brow. "Evil?"

"Very."

"Shall I tell you more about these demons?"

"If you want to," she answered carefully, still rubbing her knuckles. "I have time. I'm working a split shift tonight."

"Splendid." He led her away from the table. "That should give me all the time I need to persuade you."

"To do what?"

"To quit your job here and come with me. To be my assistant."

And what could she have said to that? Surprise had made Delanie listen when she might otherwise not have. That and the fact that he was right; she did find her job boring.

It hadn't taken long for her to conclude that the professor was a very good person, and a very persuasive one. Within thirty days, she'd given her notice to the hospital board, sublet her apartment and packed her bags. As for their ultimate destination, she had no idea where that might be. Cambridge maybe, but the professor tended to be rather vague about details.

In the end, they hadn't gone to Cambridge, or even to England, at least not right away. First, they'd flown to Haiti because, as the professor put it, "There's another demon at work, probably the cleverest of the four."

She still wasn't clear on all that demon talk, the fairy tale-folklore myth spawned in the mountains of Germany, but Haiti sounded interesting. Delanie learned quickly that the best way to deal with the professor's leaps of logic was to simply let him babble, which he did frequently, and more often to himself than to her. From these wandering moments, she snatched up whatever bits of information she could and pieced them all together later.

Then the professor received a call from Scotland. The body of a sheep farmer had been discovered in the Highlands, the body of a school teacher in Aberdeen. One had been asphyxiated, the other strangled, but both had been wearing those inverted pewter crosses around their necks.

"Why pewter?" Delanie had asked the professor after a night spent tramping around Aberdeen harbor in the fog.

He shook the moisture from his hair. "No reason. It's a quirk. The Visitor has many of them. He also lies a great deal. Never trust the devil, Delanie."

She didn't intend to, but then she never planned to actually meet the devil. Even good Catholic girls didn't expect to find Satan wandering about dirty city streets.

On two levels, however, the professor's answer had disturbed her. One, there were no devils or demons, only people gone bad. And two, if she was wrong and Satan did exist, where might that leave her when she died? All things considered this working with the professor might be more than she was prepared to deal with.

She considered carefully her decision to stay with him, yet oddly enough not once did she reconsider it. True, he had some strange ideas, but he also taught two of the major sciences at Cambridge University, the police of no less than fourteen countries knew of him, and even the smallest acts of violence disgusted him. She stayed willingly. And in the end he'd led Scotland Yard straight to their killer, or as the professor insisted on calling him, the fourth demon.

"It's a game. *The* Game," he muttered after that.

Delanie wanted to know what that meant.

"We have to move on," he said in a distracted voice. "The four demons are gone, don't you see. It's the same thing that happened to my sister several years back."

"Your sister?"

"Yes," he said with a trace of impatience. "And my brother after her. My whole family is involved in this sort of work."

"You mean your brothers and sisters help the police catch serial killers, too?"

"In a sense. My father is heavily involved in world affairs."

"Really? Would I have heard of him?"

"Oh, I imagine so, but names aren't important." He dismissed the matter with a wave. "The point I'm making is that my sister played The Visitor's Game several years ago.

She was very good, caught all the demons, selected two exceptional helpers to be her chosen two and in the end won."

"So this is a common game."

"What?" The professor looked momentarily confused. "No, no, not at all. It's quite uncommon."

"I don't understand."

"Well, of course you don't," he snapped. "You don't come from Germany."

Delanie sighed. "All right, professor. Let's start over. Your sister played The Visitor's Game. Against a murderer?"

He nodded. "But I was actually thinking about one of the demons she helped to capture. He went by the name of Aric Bellal. He was a difficult one to catch, the most devious demon she'd ever come up against, according to Anna."

"Anna's your sister?"

"Hmm? Oh, yes. She got him eventually. Well, actually, she had to catch him twice. He cheated the first time around and escaped."

"How?"

"Something went wrong. She missed a loophole, and Aric used it to free himself. Anyway, she had to track him down again. That was several years later of course, long after the Game should have ended. In fact, there was quite a brouhaha over it. Aric's family thought he was dead and blamed Anna for killing him. In point of fact, he was only in hiding. Before he disappeared, however, he swore that someone in his family would avenge his death."

"But you said he didn't die."

"But they thought he did. By the time his family came to realize their mistake, Anna had caught him again."

"And then what?"

"Then he really did die, and all the premature revenge they'd extracted was validated in their eyes."

"So his family was like the mob."

"Well, something like that. Aric Bellal was a psychic, a powerful one, I'm told. And he came from an even more powerful family."

"Was Aric Bellal's death ever fully avenged in his family's eyes?" Delanie asked.

"No."

She frowned. "You mean you think that someone in his family might be setting you up? But that's crazy, isn't it? Why go to such lengths to take revenge on you for something your sister did? Why not go after her?"

The professor smiled. "Anna passed on a few years ago."

"I'm sorry."

"Don't be. She was quite a bit older than me, led a very full life." He looked off into space. "I do think she felt badly about our brother's failure, though. He got caught in Aric's web of deceit."

Delanie stared at him. "Did your brother get killed?"

"Yes."

"This sounds like an awfully dangerous game, professor. And more common than you're admitting."

"No, it's all in the family, so to speak."

"And it started with this Aric Bellal and your sister?"

"No, it started when the Story was first born. What happened with Anna and Aric only made it a personal battle." He paused, then added, "On the other hand, I may be completely wrong. It could all just be a coincidence."

"But you don't really believe that."

He smiled. "No."

"So this person who wants revenge used The Visitor's Story to go after your brother, and now he's doing the same thing to you?"

"Probably."

"Why? If your brother lost, even if it was before Aric Bellal really died, then Bellal's death has already been avenged, hasn't it?"

The professor opened a box of raisins and began to eat. "Maybe one death wasn't enough, since that one wasn't Anna's. They never could kill her."

"This is very confusing, professor."

"Isn't it, though?" he said with a sudden grin. He held the box out to her. "Raisin?"

Delanie remembered feeling overwhelmed for days after that. Revenge, false devils, legends, games, what had she gotten herself into?

To her relief, things were quiet for a while after that. Then, one afternoon the professor barged into her new Cambridge flat with no warning and hauled out her suitcase. "We're leaving, Delanie," he'd said. "Today. Pack for three weeks. Plain clothes, the sort you don't mind getting dirty. The part of Germany where we're going to is a somber place, not like the Black Forest spas you hear about."

"But shouldn't you be lecturing, or doing chemical titrations or something?" she asked in surprise.

"This is more important." He tossed her suitcase onto the bed. "Bring sweaters," he said, clamping his hat on his head. "I'll pick you up at two o'clock."

Which he had, and now here they were at 9:33 p.m. on a waterlogged back road near the old border between the Germanies.

Beside her, the professor squinted into the darkness and the pelting rain. "I wonder," he began, then slammed on the brakes so hard that Delanie almost shot through the windshield.

"What?" she demanded.

"A wolf, I think."

"You could see a wolf in this murk?"

"I have excellent eyesight." He offered her a brief smile and raised his finger to the window on his left. "There's another one. Do you see it?"

Delanie sat up a little straighter, her hand braced on the dashboard, her eyes focused straight ahead. "Uh, professor..."

"I'm surprised to find them this close to the village, though." He rubbed at the steamed window beside him. "I wonder if I got off the main road back there."

"Professor." Delanie leaned forward, straining to see through the sheets of rain. "There's someone out there."

"Where?"

Reaching over, she turned his face until he was looking through the front windshield. She pointed to a black shape some fifty meters ahead of them. Forked lightning split the night sky for an instant.

"I think it's a man, professor," she said. "And one of your wolves is heading straight for him."

Chapter Two

"We have to help him, Delanie."

The professor grabbed his hat and was out of the car in one agile movement. Delanie had a little more difficulty coping with the bent door handle.

She managed to climb out and ran after him. One wolf could mean ten for all she knew, and the professor didn't believe in carrying guns.

Delanie's boots sank into the thick mud at the side of the road. Only lightning and the feeble beam of the car's headlights guided her in the right direction. She brushed water and wet hair from her eyes, felt the mud oozing around her boots. Yes, it was definitely a man out there, and what looked like a stuck car. But did the man see the wolf? Delanie couldn't tell, couldn't see much of anything, until she banged into the professor's back.

"Why are we stopping?" she shouted above the howling wind.

He didn't answer. Instead, a slow smile split his face. "It's Rondel."

Delanie tapped his shoulder. "Rondel?"

"Rondel Marcos."

"That's no help, professor."

"Oh, Rondel's an old friend—well, acquaintance." The professor took her arm. "Come on, I'll introduce you."

Delanie slipped, then caught her balance. "What about the wolf?"

"Part wolf, part German shepherd."

"Tame?"

"Usually." He raised his voice. "Rondel! It's Professor Nagel." He grinned at Delanie. "The 'wolves' are Dexter's pets."

"Who's...?" She sighed. "Never mind."

From a crouched position beside his car's left front tire, the man stood. The words *graceful* and *slender* passed instantly through Delanie's mind, followed by *dark* and *definitely not German*.

Not really dark, either, she discovered as he drew closer. His hair was, and probably his eyes, but his skin was relatively fair.

His clothes were rough and simple, the kind a peasant might wear—black pants, a black wool jacket and a black-brimmed hat on his head. He said a quiet hello to the professor, but his stare locked on Delanie.

His eyes were indeed dark, she realized with a small start, and quite beautiful. She saw the two wolf-dogs close in silently behind him.

"You look half-drowned, Rondel," the professor observed in amusement. "What are you doing out on a night like this?"

"All nights have been like this lately," Rondel said. He had a soft accent; not German, closer to Spanish, but not that, either.

"Portuguese," the professor whispered to her. "Delanie, this is Rondel Marcos. Rondel, my new assistant, Delanie Morgen. You two are going to get along splendidly."

"Are we?" Rondel's eyes shifted to the professor's face. "Why are you here?"

Delanie pulled up her jacket collar. "He's looking for—"

"—a new species of wood worm," the professor inserted.

A tiny smile pulled at Rondel's lips. Nice smile, nice mouth, sexy even in this dim light. "I think he's looking for The Visitor," he said, and Delanie turned away. Not the

Story again, please, she begged silently. Rondel added a faintly humorous, "If it interests you, the club is meeting now as it does every year at the Baroness von Peldt's castle."

"Yes, that does interest me, as a matter of fact."

Delanie frowned, tugging on the professor's soggy sleeve. "What club?"

He looked down at her. "Didn't I tell you about The Visitor's Club?"

She shook her head, feeling decidedly uncomfortable as the rain began to slide down her neck.

"Well, it isn't much really, merely a group of people who get together and play games."

"Devilish games?"

"No one knows except the members," Rondel answered, and again Delanie's gaze was drawn to his face, to his mouth first, then to his eyes. She wondered how he would look dry.

Thunder rocked the ground beneath them. Both dogs' ears went up.

Shoving his hands into his pants' pockets, the professor nodded at Rondel's flat tire. "Can we give you a lift to Dexter's place?"

"Mahira's," Rondel said with no expression. "Dex is at the baroness's castle tonight."

The professor's smile was deceptively amiable. "Joined the club, has he?"

"Five years ago."

"Really? Well." Another smile. "Shall we go then?"

Delanie shoved the sopping hair from her eyes. "Would it do me any good to ask who Dexter and Mahira are?"

Rondel motioned to the dogs, said something in soft German, then watched as they ran off into the woods. "Dex is my father's cousin," he said, again without emotion. "Mahira is my mother's aunt."

The professor gave the brim of his fedora a tug and sent Delanie an ironic smile. "She's also a formidable witch."

RONDEL DIDN'T FEEL like entertaining. He didn't want to talk or be pleasant, not even to the professor and his new assistant, who would no doubt be quite beautiful when she wasn't soaking wet.

She had long blond hair, thick and straight, the color of wheat, he guessed. Her eyes were a soft shade of green, or so the headlights suggested. She was almost as tall as he was and very slender, probably a fine-boned creature under her jacket and jeans. More than that, Rondel couldn't judge, but it wouldn't matter in any event. The professor seldom stayed around Klausberg for long, just enough time to make the villagers wonder about him, and then he was gone.

Rondel sat in the cramped back seat, eyes closed, head resting on the split upholstery. Horrible weather for twenty-five straight days had put him in an irritable mood. That, and he didn't want to take the job that was waiting for him in Lisbon, didn't ever want to go back to the city of his birth.

"There is so much restoration of artwork to be done in our museum, Rondel," the curator at the Gulbenkian Museum had insisted. "And you are so good with your hands, with brushes and paint. Think what you could do if you put your artistic talent to work for us instead of selling it to a pack of thieves and swindlers."

Rondel flinched at the memory, then set it aside. Given a choice at this time in his life, he would rather be restoring paintings in old churches, but a job at the Gulbenkian represented a lot of money. And he liked money. It kept him from having to live in filthy back-alley apartments with people who drank too much and more often than not forgot they had children.

"Right or left, Rondel?" the professor asked from the front seat. "I can't remember."

Rondel opened his eyes. "Right," he said. "Then right again at the fork and down toward the grottoes."

"Grottoes?" Delanie repeated. "Mahira lives in a cave?"

Pushing on the pulse that pounded in his temple, Rondel gave his head a small shake. "No, a cottage. She only conjures in the caves."

"Ah, been up to her old tricks again, has she?" the professor asked. There was amusement in his voice, but Rondel thought it might be a cover for concern. Many people in Klausberg saw Mahira and the Sisterhood as women to be feared, if not as outright witches.

The professor's eyes sparkled in the rearview mirror. "Who is she trying to conjure up this time?"

Despite a nagging headache, Rondel couldn't keep his eyes off Delanie's profile. There was a measure of pride in her features that were at once delicate and strong. She had gorgeous bones and a long elegant neck. She looked German or Scandinavian, yet she talked like an American. He wondered how she would react to Mahira.

Then, recalling the professor's question, he shrugged. "I stay away from Mahira when the Sisterhood gathers, but the villagers believe she's calling to The Visitor."

A bolt of lightning shot through the night sky. The professor glanced again in the mirror. "And you, Rondel?" he asked softly. "What do you believe?"

"I think if she does call The Visitor, she has good reason. Turn right here."

The professor swerved the car down a mud road that was little better than a path for horse-drawn carts.

"Maybe you shouldn't drive here," Rondel remarked. "You might not get out again."

"Nonsense," the professor scoffed. "We can get out of anywhere." He gave the steering wheel an encouraging pat. "Can't we, my dear old thing?"

Rondel didn't argue. Truthfully, he was too tired to care one way or the other. But even exhausted, he could still appreciate Delanie's drying ripples of hair, pale gold as he'd suspected. She looked sideways at the professor as he splashed through deep ruts, but offered no comment.

Mahira's cottage was not an inviting place, either outside or in. Half timber, half plaster and stone, it seemed to have settled at a peculiar angle into the valley floor. Ancient trees rimmed the walls, appearing the embodiment of evil with their contorted branches that looked like clawed hands. The shutters hung straight at the unlit windows, but only because Rondel had fixed the hinges. Storm clouds overhead seemed to welcome the smoke that slithered from the chimney. And why not? He'd heard with growing frequency that Mahira had brewed this gloomy weather in honor of The Visitor, or as the villagers saw it, her master.

The professor parked beside the sagging porch. "Why here?" he inquired when the three of them reached the door. "Don't you usually stay with Dexter when you visit?"

"Dex's place burned down," Rondel said. "A man from Klausberg went crazy one night and set fire to it. We think he got it mixed up with this cottage."

Delanie regarded the door in vague suspicion. "Why are people so afraid of her?"

"They say that The Visitor speaks to her." He twisted the iron ring. "Isn't there anyone where you come from who fears the devil?"

She didn't answer, but then Rondel didn't expect her to, not when in the next second she was faced with the weird clutter of Mahira's home.

Dried herbs dangled from the rafters, along with hairy roots, bunches of mushrooms and several antique lanterns. There was a wooden rocker, a table and four hard-backed chairs in the single front room. Mahira sat in the rocker beside an old-fashioned wood stove, wearing a flannel nightgown and a brown robe. Her braid of long gray hair hung over one shoulder. Her fingers squeezed a tiny green bag.

Rondel let the others go in first. He could guess what Delanie was thinking: relic witch, left over from the Middle Ages. Mahira's skin resembled tree bark, scored with grooves and many finer wrinkles. She wasn't an especially small woman, but in her shrunken bones, bent fingers, hair and skin dry like old leaves, you could see the signs of her advanced years.

Rondel knew her age, though few others did, or would ever guess. She'd passed one hundred more than three years ago. She believed absolutely in the power of the Brocken, a high granite mountain to the east where on Walpurgis witches would fly to celebrate their sabbath. Whether that contributed to her longevity, however, Rondel had no idea.

"Professor." She acknowledged her first guest in a low crackly voice. Then her blue eyes shifted sharply to Delanie. "Who are you?"

"My assistant, Delanie Morgen," the professor replied. "How have you been, Mahira?"

"I am old, professor. Why are you here?"

"Wood worms," Rondel lied. He leaned his back against the door, heard the latch click and saw the trapped look that crossed Delanie's face. "He's come to work in his laboratory."

"He has come to find The Visitor," Mahira snapped, but not at Rondel.

She glared at the professor, squeezing the bag in her lap harder. Her face was only faintly visible in the orange glow from the wood fire beside her. No other lights burned in the cottage.

"There is much danger in such a search," she warned him. "But of course you would know that already."

The professor smiled and crossed to her chair. Rondel held Delanie back when she would have followed. "She doesn't trust strangers," he said. His fingers had closed easily about Delanie's arm. Fine-boned, as he'd thought.

The professor squatted down. "Tell me, Mahira, is The Visitor here?"

Her body went stiff. "I feel a presence," she replied. "More than that I cannot say. What do you want of The Visitor?"

"Professor," Delanie began, but Rondel held her in place. "Let me go," she whispered, pulling on her arm. "This is crazy. The professor's talking about a killer. I don't know what she's talking about, or why he's even asking her. What could an old wi—woman know about a murderer?"

"Maybe more than you think," Rondel murmured.

"There have been many murders, Mahira," the professor continued. "People have been killed all over the world. Real or imagined, The Visitor's here in Klausberg, waiting for me."

"Real or imagined?" Delanie repeated in disbelief. "Now wait just a minute, professor..."

"Shh," Rondel cautioned in her ear, then he glanced back as a set of powerful headlights swept the room.

"It is Dex," Mahira announced. "And that man who is our *burgermeister*."

Delanie stared at Rondel. He translated simply, "The mayor."

The professor stood, a lanky sentinel at Mahira's side, as if she needed one. Rondel pulled Delanie out of the way only a few seconds before Dexter Solomon tromped in, a stocky bear of a man with a sour-faced creature in tow.

Dex spotted Delanie right off, nodded cheerfully at the professor and reached for the pretty female's hand.

"Well now, what have we here? You'd be an angel, I presume."

His Whitechapel accent didn't seem to surprise her, but she didn't like something about the situation. Rondel felt the resistance in her arm muscles as Dex raised her hand to his lips. Maybe she didn't trust big men with beards and caps of fuzzy brown hair. Or maybe it was the *burgermeister* who bothered her. No one took an instant liking to Adolph Schiller.

A man of over sixty years, he was hard and cruel-looking, although tall, well built and extremely well dressed. He wore a scowl on his face most of the time, except when he was drunk or holding court. Flinty eyes and spiky white hair completed the picture.

He snapped his first words at Rondel. "You were supposed to collect Dexter from the baroness's castle forty minutes ago. Instead, I am left to chauffeur him back to the home of a—" He hesitated, then substituted a gruff, "—Mahira, while you entertain a strange woman and an eccentric scientist."

"Hardly eccentric, Herr Schiller," the professor remarked calmly. He leaned against a cabinet, hands in his trouser pockets, hat angled over one eye. A wry smile lit his face. "And it's nice to see you, too."

The *burgermeister* said something rude in German, which only made the professor's smile widen.

"Perhaps we should leave," he suggested to Delanie, who was still eyeing Dex in mild distrust. Her hand was tightly clenched at her side.

Rondel glanced at his uncle and tried not to laugh. No wonder Delanie looked mistrustful. Dexter had an ancient battle plate strapped to one shoulder and a powder keg hung crosswise over his chest, cause enough for anyone to stare.

"What is this trash?" Mahira demanded, pointing to the battle plate.

"A token from the baroness," Dex said with a grin and a small bow. "I was helping her in her wine cellar earlier tonight."

The *burgermeister* snorted and the professor chuckled as Rondel opened the door. His momentary amusement had faded. His head was going to explode in a minute. He wanted to change out of his wet clothes and climb into bed. Maybe tomorrow he'd talk more to the professor about The Visitor, and really look at Delanie to see if she was as beautiful as he suspected.

He ushered her onto the porch, foregoing any goodbyes. Mahira didn't waste time with such trivialities, and Dex would only want to kiss Delanie's hand again.

"Mahira's aged," the professor observed when the three of them were alone outside. "Are you going to stay with her, Rondel?"

"Until May. She wouldn't allow a permanent babysitter."

"Her mind seems sharp enough," Delanie noted quietly. "Is she a white witch or a black one?"

Rondel moved a noncommittal shoulder. "No one knows."

"She's a conundrum," the professor said. His smile was cheerful. Reaching into his pocket, he pulled out Mahira's green bag and tossed it to Rondel. "A poultice for your headache. Mahira says you should soak it in the rain barrel first."

Delanie regarded the bag doubtfully. "Will it work?"

Again, Rondel shrugged. "That will depend on how many aspirins I take before I use it."

"Watch her, Rondel," the professor advised, adjusting his wet hat. "Something's not right here, I can feel it."

Delanie pulled her hair free of her jacket collar. "I wonder why?" she muttered. "Witches, demons and devils. I like the fairy-tale Germany better."

"There are witches and devils in most fairy tales, Delanie," the professor reminded her as he started into the rain. "Unfortunately, the ones in this area are the real things."

"AH, the watchtower. My home away from home."

The professor looked around at the damp inner sanctum of his German retreat. Stone walls, darkness and a chill breeze blowing through the open door behind them gave the place a less than hospitable air to Delanie's mind. Still, it fit the professor.

"Now you may say Frankenstein," he told her, inspecting one of the walls.

"Weird," Delanie murmured instead. Kicking the door closed, she dropped her suitcase and walked over to the crooked stone staircase. "Where does this go?"

"To the bedrooms." He grinned. "You'd call them monk's cells."

"I can imagine."

"Cheer up, Delanie." He pushed his hat back and stared up into the darkness. "Think of it as an adventure."

She hoisted herself onto the round slab at the foot of the staircase. "I am." She paused briefly, then asked, "How do you know Rondel?"

"Oh, I met him a few years back." The professor chuckled. "He's a painter."

"I don't trust that expression on your face. What kind of a painter?"

"A great talent. Rondel could paint the Mona Lisa and you'd never know it from the real thing." Tipping his head back, the professor regarded the high ceiling. "Sounds like the roof's leaking up there."

"Oh, now there's a surprise." Delanie hopped down, dusted off her jeans and followed as the professor climbed.

"I assume from your tone that Rondel has in fact painted the Mona Lisa—and maybe a few other classic works, as well?"

The professor continued to study the shadowy ceiling. "Good girl. But don't judge him too harshly until you know his reasons."

"Which of course you don't intend to tell me."

"It's not my place. I hope that leak's not in my lab.... Hurry up, Delanie," he called to her, and she realized in surprise that he'd already reached the top.

"It's like being with a mountain goat," she grumbled, feeling her way carefully upward.

She found him fifty steps later, past the bedroom level, roaming around under a thirty-foot ceiling that did indeed leak. At least Delanie heard a steady drip somewhere in the huge chamber, the size of which she could only estimate whenever the lightning flashed through the many high windows.

A match flared in the darkness. "Ah, much better." The professor lit a lantern, shielding the flame with his hand. "Now, let's see, I started the generator outside, so all we need to do is flip the switch."

Delanie hovered close to the wall, taking in what paraphernalia she could in the shadowy light. There were plenty of cobwebs, piles of boxes and a long table perfect for creating monsters. She saw gadgets of every shape and size imaginable. Another table stood along the far wall, this one full of beakers, test tubes and Bunsen burners. Beneath that were more boxes.

"There it is," the professor exclaimed. "Behind you, Delanie, on the panel. Give that silver bar a pull, will you?"

Obligingly, Delanie tugged a cold hand from her pocket and reached for the only bar visible. "This one?"

"Yes... No!" he snapped. "Don't touch that bar."

She let her hand drop and made a face at him while he pulled on a pair of battered leather gloves with his teeth.

"No, wait, leather won't work," he said to himself. He snatched a piece of rubber hose from the table and tied it carefully around the offending metal lever.

"The panel isn't properly grounded," he explained, then gave her a gentle push and pulled on the hose. The bar came down with a snap. He untied the hose. "Always put a bit of rubber around it first," he cautioned, then left her to locate the wall switch.

Delanie accepted all of this without comment. She wandered past a stack of metal boxes, testing the locks just out of curiosity. In her mind she saw a man's face, slender with dark eyes and sensual features, surrounded by dark hair. But the Professor wouldn't talk about Rondel so she asked instead, "Do you think Mahira knows who The Visitor—I mean the mastermind murderer—really is?"

The professor's head popped up from behind a small cabinet. "Keep it simple and say The Visitor. And the answer is no."

"So she's not such a great witch."

"Well, as witches go, she's pretty great, but telekinetic power isn't everything, you know."

Whatever that meant. Delanie shivered. She knew her clothes were damp and she should change, but it could wait for another few minutes. The rain was absolutely pouring down now, and the thunder and lightning that had moved east for a time had returned to the area with force.

Releasing a tired breath, she tried another lock. This one fell away, surprising her.

"Hey, professor, what do you keep in these cases?"

"What? Oh, nothing much. Odds and ends. Do you see where the water's coming in?"

"No. I can still hear it, though." She went to her knees. "Can I look inside?"

He made a distracted sound that Delanie took for a yes. She lifted the lid—and a second later jumped back in revulsion.

"My God, what's that?" she demanded, staring at a small bulbous object inside. "Is it alive?"

"Hmm?" The professor glanced down in passing. "Mandrake root," he said and continued to search for the leak. "We call it the mandragora."

"It looks like a hairy puppet."

"It is." The professor peered behind the table and absently began reciting a strange verse. "'And if before Walpurgis ends, and May Day dawns the angel sends, the chosen two and if they pass, the tests, the six temptations cast, before them, they will then receive, the mandragora...' Ah!" he exclaimed, interrupting himself. "There it is!"

Warily, Delanie touched the ugly brown root. It had a dry, scaly texture, like a shriveled potato. "What was that you just said, professor? The Story in rhyme?"

He sent her a quick smile. "Exactly. I have it written down somewhere up here."

"What are the six temptations you mentioned?"

"Tests The Visitor devises for the angel's chosen two. For each one they pass, they receive a mandragora."

"That's some reward."

"Symbol, Delanie, not reward. The Visitor doesn't want the chosen two to pass the tests."

Shivering, she closed the box and stood. "I don't think I like this game very much. Do you really believe this so-called Visitor is out to get revenge on you because your sister killed his brother?"

"It doesn't matter, Delanie," he said over his shoulder. "If the Story's being played out, then we'll have to deal with it, whatever The Visitor's motivation."

"Lovely. How far are we from Klausberg?" She had to shout the question above a deep clap of thunder.

"Four kilometers. Mahira's cottage is about a kilometer due east of here through the woods, should you ever care to visit."

"I'll remember that." Delanie strolled over to the staircase and peered down. "Is there a kitchen in this watchtower?"

"Bottom floor, left of the stairs. Try the phone, will you, there by your hand."

She picked up the receiver. "There's a dial tone."

"Splendid. Well, that about does it." Head bent, the professor walked over to her, his shoes tapping on the stone floor, his wet hat still clamped on his head. Hands in his pockets, he looked down at her. "You stay here while I go to Klausberg for supplies."

"Can't I come with you?"

"Inspector Reynolds of Scotland Yard said he would telephone me here some time after ten o'clock regarding the condition of our fourth demon. I need you to take the call while I see what shops in town are still open." He patted her arm. "There's a good girl. The water will heat quickly. You can take a bath if you'd like. Just don't touch that ungrounded lever while I'm gone."

"Yes, professor."

Another pat, a quick smile and he was gone. Only his voice drifted back to her from the blackness at the bottom of the stairs. "Remember, Delanie, don't open the door to strangers. Don't trust anyone. The Visitor's here, and we've both seen firsthand how deadly this devil can be."

Chapter Three

"Tell the professor his 'demon' is dead. No, he never spoke a word. It was a seizure, the doctors say. All very sudden, you understand."

Inspector Reynolds's words echoed in Delanie's head, louder than the thunder that refused to move on. An hour had passed since the call had come. She'd located the bedrooms—tiny connecting cells with lumpy mattresses—dug sheets and blankets from a chest near the closet, hauled her suitcase upstairs and changed into a pair of dark green leggings and an oversize cream-colored sweater. She'd pulled on clean, dry boots and, flicking light switches all the way, had gone downstairs to wait for the professor.

"Gloomy old dungeon," she muttered as she paced in the one room she hadn't bothered to illuminate, the living room, if old watchtowers possessed such things. Anyway, there was a fireplace—no wood of course—and a few crude sticks of furniture.

The storm hadn't subsided in the slightest. If anything, the lightning was inching closer to the tower. Long, jagged forks seemed to sear the trees beyond the windows.

"Come on, professor," Delanie said out loud, snapping her fingers in agitation as she paced. "Okay, so I don't believe the devil is in Klausberg, but that doesn't mean I like being alone, in the middle of the German woods, in the middle of the night during the worst electrical storm I've ever seen."

She stopped pacing beside the unshaded window, letting the darkness close in around her as she watched the wind lash the driving rain. Maybe she should phone Rondel.

No, of course not. Where had that idea come from? She hardly knew the man. She wasn't sure about his uncle, or whatever Dexter Solomon was, and she certainly didn't desire another meeting with Mahira.

Shivering, Delanie walked back to the fireplace, rubbing her arms for warmth. Did she imagine that the floor had a tilt to it? Probably not. Her sixth sense was too eerily accurate for that. It had scared her father, more and more as she'd grown. Abusiveness had turned to fear in him, she'd seen it. He'd been terrified in the end. And then he'd died...

"No, don't!" Delanie denied the memories in a fierce whisper, pressing her fingers hard to her temples. "I am not evil."

She kept her eyes momentarily closed. Rondel. She would think of Rondel Marcos instead, of his dark curls grown long over his neck, and of eyes too beautiful to be hiding the soul of a fiend. He wasn't The Visitor, of that she was certain. Dex she wasn't sure about yet. And as for Mahira... She shuddered.

Long strides carried her back to the window. No headlights; no professor. A rumble of thunder shook the floor, and she steadied herself on the ledge.

"Calling card of the Visitor," she heard herself murmur, although that was absurd. She didn't believe in the Story. But the professor's theory about this chase having turned into a game between himself and a homicidal maniac did make sense, particularly if there was revenge involved. In keeping with the legend, the symbolic fourth demon was dead. Which only left The Visitor.

"And two guardian demons..."

The words came out of nowhere. Delanie spun around, eyes alert, searching the thick shadows. Her fingers gripped the ledge tightly. Her voice stuck in her throat.

But nothing in the room moved. Nothing.

The words had come from her mind. They must have. There couldn't be anyone here. Unless a thief had snuck in.

She stiffened her spine, fighting fear with reason. A thief wouldn't stop to chat with her. Something scraped against the window and she whirled to confront it. Again, nothing, her eyes told her. Only the trees and the pelting rain.

"The fourth demon is dead, girl. The angel must make the sacrifice..."

She spun back. The words came from the air itself; the voice had a harsh edge, female, vaguely familiar.

"Where are you?" She forced the question out, softly, fearfully, a response to something her nerves might yet have conjured. Would an old witch come calling at this hour?

Cold fingers stroked Delanie's hand, she swore they did. Choking back a scream, she yanked her hand away. She backed up, mindless of the tilted floor. "Who are you?" she demanded.

Her boot heel snagged suddenly on the leg of a chair. She struggled to try and maintain her balance.

It was a vain effort. She landed on the floor with a painful thump, hit her head on the table, and for one brief moment saw the shadows move. Like a black fog before her eyes the darkness began to swirl. Pain ricocheted through her skull, a great wall of pain, slamming down in her mind.

Delanie understood darkness, but not like this. There was a sinister aspect to it, invisible, yet she could feel it pressing in on her, suffocating her. Something in it seemed to smile at her...

A sharp gasp from her own throat brought her around. What was happening? Then it occurred to her. The tower smelled wrong, like damp rock and smoke. But she hadn't lit a fire.

More than the darkness greeted her frightened eyes as they peered deeper into the shadows. In the distance she could hear a chant.

"Dead, dead, dead. The fourth demon is dead."

Female voices hissed at her, disembodied, hostile, hidden from her sight. But there was a fire, she could see it now, orange flames dancing in the center of a stone circle.

Dizzily, Delanie climbed to her feet. The shapes around her were blurred. She tried to concentrate. The voices in her head, whose were they? There was no window in the room, only an odd-shaped opening many meters away. Beyond it raged the storm, thunder and shrieking wind that made a great deal of noise but didn't shut out the eerie cadence.

"Dead, dead, dead..."

Dear God, what was this place!

Her vision began to clear. The chant grew louder. She pressed her palms to her ears and stepped back. She wanted to run but couldn't. Her leg muscles refused to obey. She was frozen in place, a statue. This had to be a dream.

But if it were only a dream, then why was her heart thudding against her ribs? Why was her body reacting as though the terror were real? She appealed to the darkness above. "Wake up," she told herself. "Delanie, wake up."

"Dead, dead, dead..."

She held her palms more tightly to her ears. "Stop it!" she whispered. "Stop!"

Suddenly there was silence. The chant ceased. Only the crackle of flames remained, and several huddled shapes, moving deep within the shadows.

Relief made Delanie's limbs weak. Thank God, a dream. In a minute this would all melt away.

"Child!"

Mahira's face appeared out of the gloom, catching Delanie so off guard that she almost fell again. The coldness of a stone wall behind was all that prevented her from tumbling backward. That and the eyes of the woman who stood before the fire.

No, not before it, *inside* it. Mahira stood within the flames. But she didn't really stand so much as float, an apparition through which Delanie could have put her hand if her body hadn't been riveted with shock and fear.

It seemed then that Mahira solidified, drifting slowly toward her. Her eyes never wavered from Delanie's pale face.

"Leave this place, child," she instructed in the same cold tone as before. "Go from Klausberg tonight."

Delanie found her voice with difficulty. "I can't, Mahira. The professor..."

"Knows not with whom he meddles," Mahira finished roughly. "He is no match for The Visitor."

Delanie felt a scream working its way into her throat. "He knows," she managed to choke.

Mahira drew closer, an ancient hag in a gray wool robe. "Do not argue with me. I say he does not know, but perhaps that is wrong. However, it is not the professor who places himself in direct danger. That is not the Story. It is the chosen two who must face the final two demons."

Delanie swallowed hard. "There aren't any real demons, Mahira, and no Visitor from hell. The Visitor is a psychotic killer who knows the Story. Maybe he wants revenge on the professor for something his sister did, and maybe he is here in Klausberg. But whoever he is, whatever his motives, he's human."

"Is he?" Mahira challenged.

Delanie felt even more disoriented all of a sudden, confused. What were those huddled shapes creeping around behind Mahira? They looked like big rats. *Please, God, I want to wake up. I'm no match for this witch.*

"I warn you but once to leave," Mahira said. Her face began to dissolve, captured by a cloud of smoke. "You will die if you do not go from here."

"Die!" Smoke obscured the witch's face and made Delanie's eyes sting. "What do you mean, die?"

"You will die, Delanie Morgen. And so will..."

"Mahira, no!" A man's voice shot through the blackness. "Stop, now!"

Delanie blinked, startled, and like that, the smoke vanished. The shuffling shapes, the fire and the smell of damp earth were all gone. Only a shadowy void remained in her mind, broken and scattered images slipping soundlessly away, leaving silence in their wake.

"MAHIRA!" Rondel shook her shoulder, a mere strip of bone beneath her robe. "Mahira, stop it."

She paid no attention to him. Her body continued to sway before the wood stove. She muttered phrases in a guttural tongue. Old German. He had no idea what she was saying.

"Mahira!"

Her eyelids fluttered, and the hands she'd crossed over her chest came down as her head dropped forward. "Go from me," she commanded in a low voice.

"Break the trance, Mahira," he ordered her. "You're playing dangerous games with your mind."

"Games?" She hissed at him like a serpent, her head snapping up, her eyes boring into his. "What blood do you have that you would think this?"

It was an old challenge. Rondel drew on all his patience. "I won't practice your craft, I've told you that before."

She called him an unflattering name in German but offered no resistance when his hands about her arms brought her to her feet.

"You are a fool, young Rondel," she warned. "My blood is strong in your veins, and yet you deny it. For your foolishness you might well be destroyed. He has chosen you. And the girl. Do you not see this?"

Rondel stared at her. He couldn't see much of anything right then through the blinding pain in his head. Only a hint of a woman's beautiful face, but that was a memory.

"Don't conjure again, Mahira," he said, running weary fingers through his hair. "And leave Delanie alone. Now stay there, and I'll make you some tea."

He started for the kitchen but her soft cackle of laughter stopped him. "Yes, my blood is in your veins, Rondel," she predicted in a tone that made his skin crawl. "I incant in the old tongue, a language I have never taught to you. How is it then that you know in my mind I think of the professor's young assistant?"

DELANIE AWOKE on the floor of the watchtower, her body ice-cold, her head splitting. Rain streamed down the window, but she didn't care. She was here, it was all right. The whole episode had been nothing but a nightmare.

Pushing herself to a sitting position, she shoved the hair from her eyes. She felt a small bump starting at the back of her head. Big enough to knock her out? Given the alternative, she would accept that.

It seemed very late. Her eyes brought the small courtyard into focus. No car. The professor hadn't returned.

The nightmare rushed back, tying her nerves in knots. What had the dream-Mahira said? The professor was no match for The Visitor...

"I NEED your help."

Rondel opened his eyes to find a woman with long blond hair standing next to his bed. Good God, had she been this beautiful last night? His bleary gaze shifted from her face to the mass of black clouds beyond the window and back again.

"What time is it?" he asked, closing his eyes and searching for pain. Only fragments remained. He could live with that.

"Seven o'clock."

"Did Mahira let you in?"

"No, Dex did. Mahira's chanting. I heard her."

Rondel squeezed his eyes a little more tightly shut. It was too early to think about incantations or any other dark mysteries. How had he known what Mahira thought last night?

"Why do you need my help?" he asked.

"The professor's missing."

Rondel cracked his eyes open, studying Delanie through his lashes. She wore jeans again, tight enough to hug her hips, a mauve cotton T-shirt and long black jacket with the sleeves shoved back. Her pale blond hair was straight yet remarkably thick. Her green eyes watched warily for his response.

In a minute that could be an embarrassing thing. For now, he was too groggy to react to more than her statement. The professor was missing.

"Go tell Dex to make you some coffee," he said with resignation. "I'll be there in a minute."

After she'd left the room, Rondel sighed and stared up at the ceiling. Then he glanced again at the threatening sky. No women, he reminded himself firmly, kicking the quilt from his naked body. He had a temper. He had Mahira's blood in his veins. He had anger in him over his childhood in Lisbon. He had doubts and concerns and deep-rooted fears about what he was, and what he might turn out to be. Because sometimes at night, when he stared into the fire...

He shuddered deeply, stopping the thought.

The air retained its winter chill even this far into spring. Rondel took a fast shower, pulled on jeans and old boots, a pale blue shirt and his black wool jacket. With everything else in his mind, Delanie's words didn't really penetrate until he was halfway to the kitchen. How could the professor be missing?

He threw a suspicious glance at Mahira's closed door, then shook his head and continued on his way.

"OH, I shouldn't concern myself too much if I were you," Dex offered cheerfully over coffee and waffles, which Delanie seemed able to face at seven in the morning but which only turned Rondel's stomach. "The professor's a character." He tapped his temple and grinned. "Bit on the absent side, if you get my meaning."

She did and would have argued the point loudly if Rondel hadn't quickly dragged her out of there. Not so much because of Dex, but because he could hear Mahira moving around.

"The professor's not absent," Delanie defended as they walked toward the Klausberg Road and Rondel's abandoned car. "He didn't come back last night, and I'm wor—" She broke off, hunching her shoulders and finishing with a quiet, "I want to know why."

Rondel decided not to question the switch. She had a light dusting of freckles across the bridge of her nose, faint but noticeable in the daylight. He concentrated on those instead. "Maybe the professor's car slid off the road and he went on foot into Klausberg," he suggested. "Sometimes when the storms are bad, the telephones go out."

"The phone at the watchtower was working."

"All night?"

"Until eleven o'clock anyway. That's when Inspector Reynolds called about the fourth demon—I mean murderer. He died in a London hospital."

Rondel sent her a narrowed look. "Demon?" This didn't sound good. "Why would you call a murderer a demon?"

Her expression showed slight indecision. "Habit, I guess," she admitted finally. "The professor called the four killers he recently helped the police to catch 'demons.' I wish I could stop thinking of them that way. I wish I could stop thinking of The Visitor."

This was going from bad to worse. "What do you know about The Visitor?" Rondel asked.

She sighed, shaking the hair from her face. "Well, the professor said those demons he caught were part of the murderer's plan, and he calls the person behind the murders The Visitor. He says this mastermind Visitor controlled the dead demons, and that the demons did the actual killing for him. He mentioned something about demons collecting souls, but he was a bit vague on that point."

"Is he sure The Visitor is a man?"

She gave a little shrug. "I suppose that would depend on whether or not he thinks the devil's a man or a woman. Not that I believe there's any devil involved. I'm almost positive it has to do with revenge."

"Against the professor?"

"In a roundabout way. Apparently, his sister Anna played The Visitor's Game once a long time ago. Do you know the Game?"

"I know of it. Go on."

"Well, one of the demons Anna caught evidently has a powerful family. When this demon died as a result of her capturing him, his family swore revenge. Only Anna's dead now, too, so the professor thinks that someone in Aric Bellal's family—Aric Bellal is the demon who died—is reenacting The Visitor's Story in order to vindicate Aric's death. Do you understand?"

He nodded, but couldn't think of anything to say right then.

He glanced sideways. Her hair shone pale gold beneath a thickening bank of clouds. The woods struck him as uncommonly black this trip, forbidding, choked with vines and trees and twisted limbs, gloomy, as if the whole forest had grown in on itself.

They wound along a muddy path, a shortcut to the road. Very little stirred in the underbrush, except an occasional crow. All in all it was a witchy day. Mahira would love it.

He pushed that thought away and returned to Delanie's problem. "Revenge is a powerful motive." Then he asked, "Is the professor here on his own or at the request of the German police?"

"On his own. Well, more or less."

She bit her soft, full lower lip. Quite kissable, but not by him. Even a simple act like that could lead to much more. And then what? Rondel could almost feel the flames of Mahira's fire calling to him. Look hard and see . . .

He shuddered again, waiting for the rest of her answer.

"For the most part," she explained, "the professor's been working with the police—the FBI and Interpol—but only where the 'demons' were concerned. In terms of The Visitor, he's pretty much excluded the authorities."

Rondel frowned. "That sounds dangerous."

"I know." Sighing, she looked straight ahead. "I don't like grudge matches. And The Visitor sounds psychotic to me. Killing all those people just to bait one man is sick. I told the professor that, but you know him, he never listens."

Rondel felt a chill crawl down his spine. Something to do with last night and Mahira's warning. "He has chosen you. And the girl." But that was fantasy, a witch's craving. The Visitor as Satan didn't exist.

"Rondel?"

Buried in thought, Rondel glanced over at her. She had indecently lovely features, exquisite bones and skin. "Yes?"

"What's The Visitor's Club?"

He shrugged. "What you'd expect. Many people belong to it who know the Story. Some of them live in Klausberg, others don't. It's more of an underground thing beyond this part of the German Alps."

"Does the club always meet in Klausberg?"

He moved a shoulder. "As far as I'm aware. I don't live here."

"That's right. The professor said you were Portuguese." She cast a quick look over her shoulder in the general direction of Mahira's cottage. "You, uh, certainly have a mixed bag of relatives."

"Mixed bag?"

"A variety. Were you born in Lisbon?"

Rondel knew she asked only out of polite interest, but a lid clamped down hard in his mind. "Yes," he said through tight lips. Then he nodded at the road now visible ahead. "My car's there. I'll change the tire, then we can drive to Klausberg and see if the professor got stuck."

She seemed uncertain. "Rondel, you know the Story better than I do. Do you believe that someone might really be acting it out? The professor mentioned something last night about a sacrificial angel and people he called the chosen two. He said that his brother had also been through this same Game, but that he'd been killed as a result. Now four demons are dead, and we're in Klausberg, and the professor's missing. And right after he went out, I had this really strange dream." She pulled on Rondel's sleeve to slow him. "Am I crazy, or does it sound like something truly horrible is happening here?"

"He has chosen you. And the girl..."

Mahira's words slid with eerie persistence through Rondel's head. He jammed his hands deeper into his pockets. "I'm not sure," he said carefully.

But that wasn't true. He felt something deep down inside himself. No, he didn't feel it; he *knew*. And it bothered him, because like Mahira's chant last night, he didn't understand where such certain knowledge came from.

Chapter Four

"Guten Abend." A dainty creature in a frilly white apron and gray dress opened the door to Baroness Alicia von Peldt's formidable castle. "May I help you?"

Delanie nodded, still in a mild state of shock over the nature of the structure before her. Castles weren't supposed to be dark, wicked places, were they? Prepossessing, maybe. But this one, half-restored, half in ruins, looked like a black palace, a home for the wicked queen from *Sleeping Beauty*.

Behind her Rondel said, "We're looking for the burgermeister, Fräulein Adele. Is he here?"

"I'm not sure." Her eyes darted to the right. Delanie didn't know how the maid could possibly see a thing with all the shadows in there. "The Visitor's Club meets at this time. Only members may enter. Perhaps the baroness..."

"Is it Harry, Adele?" A woman's low, cultured voice reached them from the darkness.

"No, baroness, it is—" the maid smiled shyly "—Rondel Marcos, and a woman I do not know."

Or want to know, Delanie suspected, but she kept her expression a blank.

The baroness came into view. She was a woman of exquisite grace—not a beauty, but close. Her features had too many angles to be considered beautiful. There was a sharpness to her nose and jaw and the barest hint of a slant to her hazel eyes. She wore a long smoky-black robe over a red designer dress. Her hair, a lustrous shade of brown, was pulled up on the sides but otherwise was left to fall in deep curls about her shoulders. She couldn't have been more than forty, maybe not even that much, which was young for a woman reportedly married four times.

"Ah, Rondel, my dark-eyed Druid." Delanie must have looked surprised because the Baroness added a teasing, "It is said that Mahira is descended from the Druids of Scotland." A smile much more inviting than the castle spread across her mouth as she returned her gaze to Rondel. "So, you've come to join our club at last, have you? And you bring us another candidate. She who is fair, of face and hair. John Kessler will thank you for such a gift."

Rondel appeared neither perturbed nor flattered by her banter. "Baroness Alicia von Peldt, Delanie Morgen. Baroness, we would like to speak to the burgermeister or Inspector Haaken if he's here."

The baroness sighed, eyeing with apparent envy Delanie's silky hair. "The inspector is not present today, but of course Adolph is here. Please, come in." She made a small shooing motion to the maid. "You may leave, Adele. Go upstairs and sweep a carpet or something. I will attend to our visitors."

The word set Delanie's teeth on edge, but then the baroness couldn't be expected to know that.

The burgermeister was their last hope, and a slim one at that. None of the shopkeepers in the gloomy town of Klausberg had so much as glimpsed the professor. Neither had the five policemen under the command of Inspector Wolf Haaken, a man who, as the wool shop owner and local gossip put it, "Lives under the thumb of the *burgermeister*."

"Adolph Schiller's a bastard," Rondel had said simply when she came out of the shop and asked him about the man. "You'll like him less each time you meet him."

Something had glinted deep within his eyes, but Delanie decided not to pursue it. She would rather not know or understand too much about Rondel Marcos. He held a dangerous, sexual appeal. She'd felt it last night when she touched him, and it was just that much stronger today.

She sighed. Wouldn't you know he'd sleep naked, and look gorgeous doing it, or that she would walk in on such a picture and then be unable to walk out again without staring for five startled minutes at his healthy young body beneath the sheets, lithe and taut and lightly tanned. He was no more than thirty, she judged, with his dark hair resting like silk on his cheek, his features relaxed, innocent in sleep.

But he was no innocent. Not evil, but definitely not innocent.

Gathering her resistance around her like a mantle, Delanie set her mind back on the professor where it belonged.

They'd combed the town, a dizzying maze of stone streets, learning nothing either time. It was as if he'd vanished, like Mahira in her dream last night.

Now, taking a deep breath, Delanie trailed the baroness through the murky cavern of the great hall. Rondel strolled along behind, studying the tapestries and portraits—which made sense, since the professor had said he was a painter.

The baroness led them to a room full of dark draperies and people wearing loose black robes. God, but they all looked solemn. From the folds of their hoods, thirty or more pairs of eyes turned to inspect the newcomers.

"My guests," the baroness said. She waved her fingers. "Herr Schiller, if you please?"

The *burgermeister* roused himself from a low chair beside the fireplace, scowling as he strode across the floor. "What is it?" he growled at Rondel, "I'm quite busy."

His snappish tone made a blond reed of a woman in her mid-fifties jump.

"Gerda Schiller," the baroness murmured disdainfully to Delanie. "She is Adolph's wife. As you see, she has a small problem with her nerves. Now, if you will excuse me, I must find Harry."

The *burgermeister* glared at her, but Alicia von Peldt merely smiled and disappeared into a circle of black robes.

"Explain this intrusion, Rondel," he demanded.

Rondel shrugged. "The professor has vanished. We would like him found."

"Talk to Inspector Haaken. I am not the police."

"You are not human," Rondel retorted angrily.

"Herr Burgermeister," Delanie interrupted with determination, "the professor left the watchtower late last night. He said he was going into town for supplies, but he never came back. It's possible that someone in Klausberg set a trap for him."

"Using The Visitor's Story as bait," Rondel elaborated.

"Ridiculous," the *burgermeister* scoffed, and Delanie's irritation rose.

"There might be a measure of revenge involved," she said coldly. "That isn't ridiculous, it's frightening. You're the mayor of this village. Surely there's something you can do."

A soft chuckle forestalled the *burgermeister*'s response. "Is this Professor Gerald Nagel we speak of here?"

A slenderly built man with a small pointed beard and dark slicked-back hair joined them. He wore a black turtleneck sweater and pants beneath his robe and an amused smile on his face.

Delanie regarded him warily. "You look familiar. Should I know you?"

The man introduced himself with a quick military bow. "John Kessler," he said smoothly.

"The famous hypnotist from Berlin," Rondel added. "He's known throughout the world."

"And he is delighted to make your acquaintance." The hypnotist would have brought Delanie's hand to his lips, but she managed to politely withdraw her fingers from his grasp before her senses could react to his touch. He acknowledged the action with a nod, then asked, "Now what is this about the professor?"

"He's missing," Rondel said. "Have you seen him?"

"No, hardly." The man laughed. "You say he left the watchtower last night, *fräulein?* Then the answer is simple. He became sidetracked and drove on, perhaps to Magdeburg."

"Do you know him well?" Delanie inquired.

"I would not say well, but—"

"No, I didn't think so. If you did, you'd know he wouldn't do that."

"Of course he wouldn't." The baroness glided past with a heavyset man on her arm. "I cannot find my darling Harry anywhere, but this is Roland Popporov." She introduced her companion to the growing group. "Herr Popporov is an accountant from Vienna. He will be the first of our members to play the Game. I would explain the Game, *fräulein,* but it is for members only, you understand."

Delanie didn't care about the club version of the Game or the fat bespectacled man with muttonchops who stared at her and Rondel as if they were creatures from another world.

"Herr Schiller," she tried again, but the *burgermeister* dismissed her with a sour look.

"Talk to Haaken," he said, then he stalked back to his chair and settled in with his beer stein.

"Old Scrooge," Delanie muttered.

"Yes, he is," Mr. Popporov agreed. He poked at his wire-rimmed glasses. "Is that a cross around your neck?" He crept closer. "Are you of the Catholic faith?"

"Roland is practicing for the Game, I think," a new voice remarked. "Pay no attention to him."

A tall, practical-looking woman with strong features and mousy brown hair pulled back into a tight bun joined them.

"Herr Popporov possesses the curiosity of many cats, I'm afraid." She didn't extend her hand. "I am Dr. Ingrid Hoffman from the Brulen Institute in Oslo," she said stiffly. "We deal in chemical disorders of the brain. I've met your Professor Nagel, *fräulein.* An interesting man, but I agree with Herr Kessler, he is also prone to lapses of concentration. Perhaps you should telephone Frankfurt or Berlin. The authorities in both of these cities will know of him. Possibly they can be of help."

More than any of you, Delanie thought impatiently, wanting only to leave here before someone actually did succeed in touching her.

"Thank you, Dr. Hoffman," Rondel said. He intercepted Roland Popporov's fingers before they could pull the filigree chain from around Delanie's neck. "But I don't think the professor would bring his assistant all the way from England to Klausberg, then drive off and leave her stranded.''

''Then perhaps the question would best be put to Mahira,'' the baroness suggested. She smiled at Delanie. ''Mahira is a powerful witch, you know, the leader of the Sisterhood.'' She slapped Popporov's hand away from her diamond bracelet. ''Sticky fingers. You're worse than Dex. Go away, and save your powers of observation for the Game.'' She turned her eyes to Rondel's guarded face. ''Where is Dex by the way? The Game begins in less than thirty minutes. He should be here for the commencement ceremony.''

''I'm sure he will be.''

Delanie felt Rondel's palm pressing into the small of her back. Time to go, and not a moment too soon for her taste. These people were positively spooky, but then what could you expect from people who made a game out of a story about the devil?

''This was a waste of time,'' Delanie whispered to Rondel as the baroness led them back to the great hall.

''Talking to Herr Schiller usually is,'' the baroness remarked over her shoulder. ''He has no compassion. It is beyond me how he ever got to be *burgermeister*. At any rate, I will speak to Inspector Haaken for you. What was this revenge you spoke of?''

Delanie explained about the professor's sister and his idea that the Visitor was someone connected to the dead 'demon,' Aric Bellal.

The baroness frowned. ''I recognize this name, Aric Bellal,'' she said. ''He belonged to our club many years ago. Adolph speaks of him sometimes. I think they were friends.''

''Did you know him?'' Delanie asked.

The baroness set her fingers under Delanie's chin, bringing her head up until their eyes were level. ''I'm not a vain woman as a rule,'' she said with a smile. ''But do I look between fifty and sixty years old to you?''

A word flashed in Delanie's mind, there and gone too swiftly for her to catch it. "No," she admitted. "You don't. What does your age have to do with Aric Bellal?"

"He was last here thirty years ago, when some relatives of my late husband owned the castle. Then Aric Bellal died and Adolph became a monster, or so Gerda would tell you if she weren't so... Ah, but where are my manners. I have no right to talk about her or Adolph this way. Forgive me."

Delanie knew better than to pry. "Thank you, baroness," she said politely.

Smiling, the woman opened the door. "Do come and see us again, both of you. Perhaps you'll join our club. We are all a little eccentric, but you would not be disappointed. We have a lot of fun at our meetings, and of course the Game is always a great amusement. Myself, I fail miserably each time I play, but then so do we all. You don't understand, of course, but you would if you joined with us."

She took Delanie's hand. Again something slid through her mind. *Selfish. Vain.*

The baroness continued. "In the meantime, my dear, try not to worry about the professor. I've known him for many years. He is very resourceful, rather like my latest male friend whom I can seldom manage to locate. Maybe he and the professor have disappeared together."

Rondel's expression was distracted, as if his mind were miles away. "Harry Bates," he explained to Delanie, "is a dealer in rare and dubious antiquities."

"A member of the Visitor's Club?" Delanie asked.

"When it suits him," the baroness said. "He seldom plays the Game. If you happen to see a tall man, Delanie, with brown hair and eyes greener than yours, looking like he should have a champagne glass in hand, you might send him up here. That will be Harry. Now as I said, do not concern yourself unduly over the professor. I will speak to Inspector Haaken as soon as he arrives."

Delanie nodded, wishing there was more she could do, wondering why Rondel had grown so quiet all of a sudden.

His silence sustained him as far as the Klausberg Road, when he finally said, "How many people did the professor's demons kill, Delanie?"

She regarded the bunched clouds overhead. The sullen black mass seemed to have suspended itself directly over the forest. "Too many to count," she answered, disguising a shiver. "The victims were chosen at random, as far as I can tell."

"There was no connection made between these deaths?"

"Only that all the victims were wearing inverted crosses around their necks when they died, and all the demons had that same inverted cross tattooed somewhere on their bodies." She sighed and looked sideways at him. "What do we do now, Rondel? We don't have any proof of anything. And even if we did, your burgermeister doesn't seem the type to act on it."

"He isn't." Rondel downshifted, nodding at the Klausberg marketplace. "Do you want to buy food while we're here?"

"I suppose." She hesitated, her hand on the door. "You will help me find him, won't you?"

He seemed surprised. "Of course."

Relief slid through her but it was tempered with the uneasy knowledge that someone around here might very well be crazy enough to believe that he or she really was the devil. Revenge could easily be taken to that extreme. She'd heard of similar if less drastic cases many times at the hospital.

"If it is the Visitor's Story," she said softly, "where do we start?"

Rondel's dark eyes gave nothing away. "We check up on Aric Bellal," he told her. "And if we have to, we play the Visitor's Game."

MAHIRA SAW many images in her mind. Smoke from the fire made them blend, overlap.

"Protect he who comes," was the song of the Sisterhood. "Protect, protect . . ."

Mahira let her trance deepen, just enough to clarify the visions. A girl with anger in her eyes came clear to her. The girl had blond braids. Mahira concentrated. Now a man appeared. He was drunk, afraid, in a rage. The man shook a woman, and the girl's anger deepened. Hatred flashed in her young eyes. "I hope you die," she shouted.

The woman took on definite form. She was also blond, also afraid. She pulled away from the man. She whispered, "Baby, don't say things like that."

The madrigal of the Sisterhood took over. "We chant for him. Protect, protect."

"Be silent," Mahira commanded. The picture of the girl faded. Another took its place. Now Mahira saw a small boy. He kicked the man, a police officer, who held him, and tried to bite his arm. "I'm taking you home," the officer said. "You cannot run wild on the streets."

But the boy was not running wild. He was running away, or trying to. His father owned a local bar, and several young women who worked in the back rooms. His mother drank wine day and night. He hated it at home. He wanted to go off and be a gypsy. He wanted to paint.

Mahira watched him, then slowly let the image dissolve from her mind. One picture she knew, the other she did not. The word *witch* came to her, but she pushed it away. There was nothing she could do. The ingredients were there. The choice had been made. She motioned to the Sisterhood with her hand.

"Call to the Visitor," she instructed. "Say to him that all is prepared."

Chapter Five

"How do you know the professor?" Delanie asked politely as Rondel helped her carry armloads of groceries into the watchtower's stone kitchen.

He smiled at her tone. "We met in New York City when I was seventeen. That would be thirteen years ago now."

"That's why you speak such good English. I wondered."

"But didn't want to ask." Rondel glanced around with mild interest. Buildings made of cold gray stone weren't his favorite places. He preferred warmth and texture to medieval harshness. "I think you must be someone with a curious nature that you would very much like to be rid of, is that right?"

She finished unloading her bag of groceries, then turned to face him, pushing her hands into her jacket pockets. "No, that's wrong. I have no curiosity in me at all."

"Then why are you working with the professor?"

She looked away, out a small window and into the black woods. "Because he's very persuasive, and I wasn't too thrilled about my job at the time I met him." She brought her gaze back to his. "I'm not a complicated person, Rondel. I'm not even very interesting. I'm thirty-one years old and I was born in Rapid City, South Dakota."

"Near Mount Rushmore."

"Yes," she said flatly. "I went to college at Vermillion, which is also in South Dakota, then I moved with a girlfriend to Portland, Maine, because that's where her family lived. I've been there ever since."

Rondel loosened his coat, although the old tower was very cold. "Until you met the professor."

"That's right."

"At which point your life became much more interesting."

She studied his features as if unsure what to make of him. "You're a strange man. I don't understand you at all. What do you do for a living?"

Now this he didn't want to get into. "I do different things, Delanie. It depends on my mood."

"The professor said you were a painter."

He leaned against the counter, aware of the granite edge that dug into his hip. "I was. Maybe I will be again. I haven't decided. What time is it?"

"Almost six. Do you have to leave?"

Have to, no. Want to, yes, quite badly. She might think she was uninteresting, but Rondel found her utterly fascinating.

He looked around one last time, grimaced at the cheerless walls, then nodded. "I should check on Mahira."

Delanie didn't move from the crude kitchen sink. Weak beams of light from the window made a silhouette of her head and shoulders, but he could feel her eyes on him even so. And of course that only made his reaction to her all the more disturbing.

She tipped her head to one side. "Will you tell me something?"

"If I can."

"Is she really a witch?"

His smile grew faintly ironic. "Yes."

"You mean she has actual powers?"

"I think she does."

Did she stiffen a little at that answer? Rondel couldn't be sure in the bad light.

"What about you?" she asked almost hesitantly. "Do you have powers, too?"

Now he really did need to get out of here. Pushing off from the counter, he crossed to the sink. "No, Delanie," he lied. "I don't. And neither does the person the professor's trying to find. The Visitor's a myth. Just because people around here believe he's real doesn't make it so."

He reached out a hand to her and slowly she removed her fingers from her pocket. They were ice-cold against his skin.

"I know The Visitor's not really the devil," she said. "I'm not that superstitious. What bothers me is that whoever he is, he's got the professor." Desperation tinged her voice. "I don't know the Story well enough to play The Visitor's Game, Rondel. I don't understand about the chosen two and the six temptations they're supposed to face."

Rondel's long fingers closed about hers, warming them. "Come and have dinner with us, then," he suggested reluctantly.

"Why?"

"Because Mahira knows the Story better than anyone in Klausberg."

Delanie returned her eyes to the forest. "Except for The Visitor."

"AH, my demon jailor." The professor smiled, gripping the bars of his underground cell with both hands. "Wherever here is, it must be a long way down. You're puffing like a steam engine. Not very thoughtful of The Visitor to make you keep tabs on me. Maybe your demon counterpart would be better suited for the job."

The man mopped his face with a handkerchief. "I'm The Visitor's favored helper," he panted. "The other is nothing."

"I see. You're the demon of trust. Popporov, isn't it?"

"That's what I am called."

"And your counterpart is . . . ?"

"Worthless, as I said." The demon used his handkerchief to clean his glasses. "If it's a name you're after, professor, I'm afraid I cannot supply it. I am a demon of utmost discretion."

"And quaking fear. Understandable, of course. I'd take care if I were you. Duplicity is The Visitor's middle name." The professor surveyed the man from under the brim of his hat. "Tell me, Herr Popporov, where exactly am I being held?"

"Where do you think?"

"That's what I'm asking you. Are we in the old tunnels under the ruined part of the castle?"

The demon lifted a pudgy hand. "No need to sound so impatient, professor, the answer is yes."

"Ah, so that means the baroness is either your worthless counterpart, or The Visitor, or completely ignorant of the full purpose of the Club."

The demon smiled. "A logical deduction, but far from clever. The Visitor's Club, as we both know, is a cover for more profound matters, and the baroness seldom ventures into the restored portion of her dungeon, let alone into this slimy place. Tell me, have you seen many rats?"

"Several. I've been naming them to pass the time." The professor kept a straight face. "I haven't decided what to call you yet."

Popporov drew a hissing breath. "Do you think this is a game, professor?" he demanded.

"Not at all." The professor's features darkened. "I think it's *the* Game, and very serious."

Popporov sidled closer like a fat crab, not entirely trusting of the bars that separated them.

"Your chosen two came to the castle this afternoon."

"Really? Looking for me, were they?"

"Yes."

"But you weren't impressed. I'm disappointed. That's one temptation down, you realize. They could have gone off and left me to my fate, but they didn't. They're searching for me. They're putting their safety in jeopardy for me."

"One temptation is not six, Professor. I would not have selected those two people."

The professor smiled. "But then you're a demon, aren't you, Herr Popporov? You wouldn't understand my reasons."

"I don't have to understand them. I maintain simply that they will not survive the next five temptations."

"I think you might be surprised."

"I doubt it." Distastefully, Roland Popporov eyed the professor's tartan scarf. "In any event, it's time they learned what they're up against."

The professor walked over to the far wall. "I assume The Visitor has a plan for filling them in." One eyebrow went up. "Through Mahira, perhaps?"

"That will depend," Popporov replied.

"On what?"

"On whether or not The Visitor would prefer to deal with them personally."

"CHEER UP. You're over the first hurdle," Dex said at the dinner table. "You know that, don't you?"

Delanie didn't know anything right then. Mahira had been staring at her ever since Rondel had brought her here— glaring, actually, through eyes colder than two pieces of blue ice.

"That's how The Visitor's Story goes," Dex continued, spearing a piece of pork. "The chosen two must face The Visitor's six temptations in order to learn the whereabouts of the angel."

Rondel watched Mahira, his expression guarded. "How do you know we've survived one of the temptations, Dex? We haven't been given the mandragora yet."

With his mouth full, Dex couldn't answer, so Mahira did it for him, speaking for the first time that evening. "You have survived the first temptation. The mandragora will come. The girl..."

"Delanie," Rondel said with a quick glance at Delanie and a gesture that she should eat.

Mahira gave a reluctant nod. "Delanie could have accepted what those around her said, that the professor had gone on without her and that she should not worry. She, and you as well, said no to this and continued to search for him. Better perhaps for both of you that she had made the wise choice and gone back to Maine, for now you are in the Game, and from this there is no escape."

Delanie choked on a piece of spinach. "How do you know where I come from?"

"I am a witch." Mahira's eyes didn't waver from hers. "I know more than you will ever be able to accept."

Delanie could have disputed that, but she didn't. Instead she asked, "Can you explain the mandragora to me? I saw one in the professor's lab. I know it's a mandrake root and that it has to do with passing a temptation, but I don't understand how."

"The mandragora is a sign," Mahira said. "The Visitor must leave one for each temptation that is passed. It is that simple."

"Leave one where?"

"Wherever he chooses. The Visitor is not predictable."

Rondel sat calmly back in his chair, as if none of this were even slightly unusual to him—candles for light, a witch in coarse gray robes at the head of the table, a pair of dogs who looked like wolves sitting on either side of Dex, and for two hours now, the relentless hammering of wind and rain outside.

"Tell us the Story, Mahira," Rondel prompted her. "At least tell us the important parts."

The old woman's eyes flashed. "You know the Story, blood of mine."

Rondel gave her a dark look. "Don't, Mahira," he warned in a voice very close to a growl. "I know it, yes, but Delanie doesn't."

Mahira's eyes returned to Delanie. "There are six temptations," she said. "These are tests devised by the Visitor. Fail one and the angel will be destroyed."

Delanie found her voice with difficulty. "Only the angel, not the chosen two?"

The old witch said something unflattering in German. "Of course the chosen two. This is understood. Except for the first temptation, in which the choice is freely offered, failure will condemn both who are chosen to a most unpleasant death. You have five temptations yet to pass." She pointed a bent finger across the table. "I will have more potatoes, Rondel."

He handed them to her. "Go on, Mahira."

"There is no more."

Dex grinned at Delanie. "Eat, girl," he advised. "You'll have to be in shape to take on The Visitor. Leastways that's my philosophy, although for my money, you'd do well to let Inspector Haaken handle the whole mess. You've got some lunatic out there who's playing at being The Visitor, and for whatever reason, he's probably holding the professor hostage. And you have to know that this crazy bird is just waiting for you to trip up so he can knock off three more victims." He shook his head. "You're asking for trouble, the pair of you."

Delanie set her fork down. She didn't like spinach or this conversation. "If we do as you suggest, Dex, then we fail the first temptation, which you just told me we've already passed."

"That's right, I did say that, didn't I?" With his wineglass, Dex saluted her. His eyes glinted in the candlelight. "In that case, here's to luck, Doctor."

Delanie looked up. "How did you . . . ?"

"I told him," Mahira interrupted.

Rondel leaned forward on his elbows. "What are the next five temptations, Mahira, do you know?"

"No."

"You mean we have to guess?" Delanie asked, then wondered why she bothered. She didn't believe any of this anyway. What could Mahira possibly know of a deranged murderer? The old woman thought The Visitor was really the devil. They should be looking into Aric Bellal's background, not talking about temptations.

"I mean," Mahira replied, "that the temptations are not predetermined. You can be certain only that each one will be directed at the weakest part of your character."

"For instance?" Rondel prompted.

Mahira lifted her eyes to the ceiling, then closed them, as if searching her mind for something. "No," she said finally. "This is all I am permitted to tell you."

Dex tapped his temple and grinned. Then he looked over at Rondel. "Enough of this superstition, my boy. What say you and me..." A beam of light cut through the room and he stopped in surprise. "Visitors—sorry, Delanie—guests? In this weather?"

Mahira set her bony hands on the table. "It is Harry Bates. He has come to see you, Rondel."

"Me?" Rondel glanced at the window with a frown. "Why?"

"Well..." Dex stood, indicating that Rondel should too. "Come onto the porch with me, my boy. I'll explain." He draped a heavy arm about Rondel's shoulders. "You see, I had a talk with Harry this afternoon, up at Alicia's castle. One thing led to another and pretty soon..."

The rest of his words were swallowed up by the force of the storm. The door opened, then closed, and suddenly Delanie was alone with Mahira. Even the dogs were gone.

"You didn't eat your greens."

Delanie raised only her eyes from the table, unsure what to make of the remark. "Is that bad?" she asked.

"It is foolish," Mahira said. "You will need strength to face The Visitor."

"Does that matter to you?"

"For you alone, no. But you are not alone in this, and for Rondel I care very much. I did not want him involved." The old woman got stiffly to her feet. Delanie resisted the urge to help her. "Come," she said sharply. "Make yourself useful and collect the dirty dishes. Washing up is woman's work."

"Now wait just a minute," Delanie began, but Mahira banged her fist on the table, halting her in midprotest.

"A test only," she snapped. "You are too touchy. You will get my Rondel killed with your anger."

"I'm not angry."

"Bitter then. Resentful." She made an irritated gesture. "Concern for Rondel clouds my mind. I cannot read you properly."

"Good," Delanie said quietly, collecting the empty plates.

"Don't mutter."

She set her jaw. "I said, good."

Mahira's blue eyes fastened on hers. "You wished your father dead. What do you call that if not bitterness?"

The stack of plates almost slid from Delanie's fingers. "How could you possibly know that?" she whispered.

"I grow tried of hearing this same question, girl. And do not drop my good dishes. Your father was a cruel man, cruel to you and to your mother and to everyone else around him. You hated him."

"I didn't."

"Yes you did. You still think of him with great anger. And great guilt. This is your burden. You are confused. You need religion."

"I have religion."

The old witch laughed. "You believe in God?"

"Yes."

"And yet you fear the devil."

"I—" Delanie paused, then challenged, "don't you?"

Mahira's laugh became a cackle of delight, underscored by a rumble of distant thunder. "Fear The Visitor? Fear? Foolish girl. I, Mahira, lead the Sisterhood of Klausberg. What have I to fear?"

Delanie couldn't think of a single thing. Except...

"Fear for Rondel, maybe?" she suggested in a solemn tone.

Mahira hobbled back to the table where Delanie still stood. Her powdery features looked menacing in the fluttering candlelight. One crooked finger jabbed Delanie's chest.

"If he is harmed and by some miracle you survive, be assured, Delanie Morgen, that you will not live to talk about it. For if The Visitor does not carry your soul off to hell, I, Mahira, blood-tied to Rondel, most certainly will."

"THINK OF IT as an investment in your future, Rondel." Dex rubbed his fingers and thumb together. "Money to save or spend as you see fit."

"With a tidy commission on the side for you and Harry."

The three men had gone to the old icehouse, a small straw-filled outbuilding with a broken trapdoor and a leaking roof. Harry had said he had a "business proposition," which meant another phony art deal. Rondel was sick to death of painting fakes.

"At least think about it, Rondel," Harry urged now.

He was young, only a few years older than Rondel, and cultured, but it was entirely pretense. He'd been born in Haiti, the son of an American fisherman. His British accent, mannerisms and polish were as forged as the paintings Rondel had done in a more desperate time.

From the wall, Rondel regarded Harry's fine features. He shouldn't ask, but habit compelled him. "How much?"

"Five hundred thousand in U.S. dollars."

Rondel almost choked. "For a Goya?"

In a navy blazer and white turtleneck, Harry managed to look elegant even sitting on a bale of hay. "If it's too low, I could try to talk the buyer up."

Rondel sent him a narrowed look. "It isn't too low. What do you get out of it?"

"If I'm lucky, the Baroness's hand in marriage. She'll have a fling with a pauper, but you know the old saying, Rondel. Money marries money. If I'm not fast, there's an old count who'll whisk her off to Bavaria soon enough."

"And there goes the honeymoon in Nice," Dex said. He looked hopefully at Rondel's unrevealing features. "What do you say, boy? Can Harry and I start spending our hard-earned commissions?"

Hands in his pants' pockets, Rondel let his gaze travel to the barred window. "I don't know. I'll think about it."

"Well, don't think too long," Harry cautioned. "Our buyer's a member of the club. Once the fun and games are over, he'll be off. And what you won't do, there are any number of greedy artists who will."

"Then why don't you talk to them?"

"Because you're better," Dex said. "And you've never been caught."

"Yes I have."

"All right then, you never got charged. You chose the wrong deal with the right person."

"I got lucky," Rondel translated, feeling cold and hard. He did not want to relive old times.

"What's your answer, Rondel?" Dex asked.

"I told you, I'll think about it," Rondel said, fighting an irritable sigh.

"I'd prefer something more definite."

Rondel narrowed his eyes, his anger mounting. "Don't push, Dex."

A thick hand went up. "Push? Not me. How about a beer, eh? I have a barrel of dark stashed in the cellar. Stop staring like a mother hen at the cottage, Rondel, and go bring us up a pitcher. Mahira won't hurt the girl. Anyway, I have a feeling that she can take care of herself."

"Girl?" Harry's head came up.

"Woman." Rondel left the wall. His gaze flicked to Harry's hands. Soft and effeminate, with long nails, and no indication that they'd ever done more than lift a champagne glass. He looked away. "Her name is Delanie Morgen. She's the professor's assistant."

"Blond, pretty?" At Rondel's nod, Harry smiled. "I heard about her. American, no money." He gave his head a sorrowful shake. "Too bad. You say she's with the professor?"

"Was." Dex motioned Rondel to get the beer. "It seems he's gone missing." Raising his voice, he shouted above the wind, "On your left, Rondel, the fat barrel marked Hausbach—not that you'll be able to make that out in this murk. I tell you, Harry, I've never seen weather like this . . ."

Away from the lash of the storm and the two men above, Rondel closed his eyes, pressing his forehead against the damp wooden ladder. Delanie, he thought tiredly. He should go back and rescue her from Mahira. But he could scarcely deal with his own problems right now, let alone a cranky witch.

Do it, his brain kept telling him. Grit your teeth and paint the damned picture.

Then something happened that had never quite happened before. An image appeared in front of him. It was hazy at first, the outline of a misshapen body formed in shades of red and black and orange. It flared to fiery brilliance, settled and finally spoke to him.

"Money, Rondel," a long mouth whispered. "For you. For Mahira. How fitting that you should paint The Witches' Sabbath. Take the deal. You'll never get another like it. Never."

Rondel tried to clarify the vision, but couldn't. He looked away sharply, then back.

Gone, both image and voice. But it hadn't been a product of his imagination, he was sure of that.

Shoving himself from the ladder, Rondel felt his way to the barrel. He turned the spout and filled the pitcher under it, hesitated, then set his mouth on the spigot and drank down several mouthfuls. It wouldn't help to get drunk, but it couldn't hurt.

When he'd had enough, he wiped his mouth with his wrist and sat back on his heels. What did he believe in? he wondered. In the devil? Probably. In The Visitor's Story? Not really. In himself? Not much.

He shuddered, recalling the fiery image. He had Mahira's blood. Did he also possess her talents?

He let his head fall back, eyes closed. "If this is a temptation," he murmured, "and the Story's unfolding with me as one of the chosen two, then we're in big trouble, Delanie. You, me and the professor. Because I don't know what I'm going to do."

"THAT MAN is a monster!"

Gerda Schiller jumped at the sound of the baroness's angry voice. She looked up guiltily from her seat in the corner of the shadowy grand salon. "Are you speaking of Adolph?" she asked.

"Who else?" The baroness shook her wrist, then pushed back the sleeve of her robe. "He grabbed me. Look, I'm bruised already."

"I'm sorry," Gerda murmured, lowering her lashes. "He's been very violent lately. I don't know why."

The baroness rubbed her wrist. "Don't be sorry. He's always violent, and the reason is obvious. The man is evil. You should leave him before he kills you."

"I can't leave," Gerda said. She stole a glance at her husband across the room. He was talking with Ingrid Hoffman, laughing with her and Roland Popporov.

"Now there is a rare sight," the baroness said scornfully. "He threatens me because I will not..." She stopped then substituted a smooth "...give him the key to my wine cellar, and yet he makes jokes with a woman like that."

Gerda sighed, ignoring Alicia's near slip. Of course Adolph would want her. He enjoyed a conquest, and Alicia had never been interested.

"He is unpredictable," she said, then cringed as Roland Popporov said something that evidently angered her husband. Only Ingrid's hand on his arm prevented him from jumping up and following the little man out of the room.

"I should bar him from my home," the baroness declared. "And that woman, too. John Kessler told me earlier that she is a neurotic manipulator. I think he's right."

Gerda watched in fear as her husband patted Ingrid's hand. He stood, scowled, then started toward them.

"What are you saying to my wife?" he snapped at Alicia.

The baroness tossed her hair, but her body had gone quite rigid. "I told her that you are evil," she said. "You are more cold and cruel than even The Visitor would be."

Adolph's lips drew back. "You will pay for that remark, Alicia."

She trembled but retorted, "You would not dare to touch me. I have powerful friends."

"So do I. You have heard the name Aric Bellal?"

She hesitated. "Yes."

"Then I need say no more. There is no friend or family on earth more powerful than his."

Gerda would have laughed if Adolph hadn't been reaching for her. He put too much store in old friendships. Aric

Bellal had used him to meet other more important people. Gerda knew that, because she had also known Aric. Intimately.

"Get your coat," her husband ordered now, and obediently she rose and left the gloomy salon.

"Good night, Frau Schiller," Ingrid Hoffman called to her in a mocking voice. "Herr Popporov didn't upset your husband too much, I trust."

Gerda closed her eyes. She hated so many of these people, hated her husband, her life.

When Gerda arrived, Roland Popporov was standing outside the cloakroom, lighting matches and blowing them out.

"Your husband is a very sensitive man," he observed. "I tell him that he will fail the Game miserably, and he becomes angry. I confide that I am privy to certain secrets about the Game this year, and he begins to foam at the mouth. Why is that? I wonder. Does he think that no one should ever best him?"

Gerda said nothing. Alicia had called Adolph evil. Yes, he was evil. And Gerda would pay dearly for all that had been done to incite his temper tonight.

Pulling on her coat, she hurried out, but not fast enough to avoid Roland's plump moist hand on her wrist. "Don't worry, Gerda," he consoled with a patronizing smile. "The Visitor is watching all of this. He will deal with your husband's arrogance. He will deal with your husband."

DELANIE SMELLED BEER on Rondel's breath when he returned to the cottage, but he wasn't drunk. Too bad. She could have used a stiff drink herself right then. Mahira had been watching her all through the cleaning-up process, which she'd insisted was Delanie's responsibility.

"Do not chip my great-grandmother's china," was all she'd said, then she'd sat down in her rocker and stared.

"Mahira..." Rondel slid her a warning look when he saw the stack of clean dishes on the sideboard.

She continued to rock. "The girl will not suffer for a little labor."

Delanie handed him the dish towel. "Washing up is woman's work," she said with a perfunctory smile. "Rule of the Sisterhood, I'm told."

Rondel swore softly, then took her aside and said, "Do you want to go to the watchtower now?"

She tried to ignore the feel of his fingers on her arm, the damp scent of his skin and hair, but it was impossible. "I think so."

"Do you understand the Story?"

"I'll figure it out."

"And you're sure you would rather sleep in the watchtower than here?"

She gave him a look that made it plain she'd rather sleep in a ditch, and he sighed, raking his fingers through his hair and grimacing. "Would you like me to stay with you?"

Only if she was very, very foolish. She bowed her head. "If you wouldn't mind."

Her answer seemed to surprise him. It didn't really surprise Delanie. That it was a sensible choice, however, didn't necessarily make it a wise one. Rondel was much too attractive for her liking. He was quiet, extremely reserved and disturbingly sensual. And for some reason, his ascetic lifestyle appealed to her. He made her want to touch him, and she never, never felt that way about men. She tolerated contact; she couldn't remember ever wanting to initiate it.

"Should you leave Mahira alone, though?" she asked with a quick look at the glowering witch.

Amusement pulled on Rondel's lips. "There is a telephone, Delanie." He released her arm. "I'll get a few things and be right back. Ignore her if she starts to chant."

Delanie waited until they'd said their goodbyes and were in the car before she inquired, "What does she chant about?"

He concentrated on the muddy road. "I don't ask."

"Why not? Are you afraid of her?"

"Hardly. She wouldn't hurt me."

Delanie recalled Mahira's warning, shivered and hunched down into her seat. "I'm sure, but don't you ever wonder whether she's good or bad?"

"Not particularly "

His response baffled her. "Why?"

"I told you, she wouldn't hurt me. I see that as good. The rest isn't important."

She sighed. "I was right. You are a very strange man."

"Am I?" He shrugged. "Maybe I am. I stopped labeling things good and evil a long time ago. I accept Mahira for what she is, and she accepts me."

Delanie slid him a hesitant sideways glance. "Why did you go to New York when you were seventeen?"

She thought his fingers tightened slightly on the steering wheel, but she couldn't be sure. There was no lightning tonight, only the rain and the wind—and if she looked very hard, she could see an eerie blue glow suspended over the mountains far to the east.

"I wanted to see it," was all he would admit. Then he noticed the direction of her gaze and said, "The Brocken."

She sat up. "The place where witches used to meet?"

"You know of it?"

"The professor mentioned it on our flight to Frankfurt." She paused, then asked in a worried voice, "Do you think we'll find him in time?"

A cord on Rondel's neck stood out, as if he was under some sort of strain. "I don't know," he said. "I hope so. It depends on the temptations The Visitor devises for us."

"But how will we recognize them?" She twisted sideways in her seat. "What I mean is, how will we be able to separate those five things from the temptations that people face all the time in their everyday lives?"

"We won't," he replied simply.

"That's not very helpful." She thought for a minute. "For instance, what would happen if you decided you didn't want to be chosen?"

He glanced sharply at her. "Why would you ask me that?"

"Because Mahira doesn't want you involved."

"I know that. But the choice isn't hers to make. According to the Story, the angel makes the selection."

"And the angel, or in this case the professor, chose us."

"Apparently."

"But what would happen if you said no, right now, to-night?"

"The angel would be destroyed."

She huddled deeper into her seat, watching the raindrops that splashed against the windshield. "In other words, we have no choice. We either play the Visitor's Game and win, or the professor dies."

He looked over at her but said nothing. What could he say? It was true.

For the first time since she was eleven, Delanie felt a surge of protectiveness rise up inside her, a fierce instinct that both strengthened and angered her.

She stared into the rainy German night, and vowed, "I won't let the professor die, Rondel. I won't."

Chapter Six

There was a light burning outside the watchtower when they arrived, a thin silvery beam bobbing in the darkness. Or was it a reflection from the car's headlights?

Delanie blinked, scanning the surrounding trees. "Did you see that?" she asked Rondel.

"What?"

"A light or something. There!" She touched his arm. "To the right of the watchtower."

He stopped the car and cut the engine. "Someone's out there," he said, doing up his coat.

Her heart lurched. "The professor!"

"Creeping around his own watchtower?"

Delanie's elation vanished. "No. Then who?"

"A prowler, maybe."

A chill ran down her spine. She shook his arm. "Rondel, would The Visitor come here?"

"I don't think so." He pushed open his door. "Wait here," he said, then disappeared into the darkness before she could object.

Delanie considered her options for a moment. But then something else moved, and she knew it couldn't be the same thing as before because it was on the other side of the old tower. No one, not even a person who thought he was the devil, could get around the building that fast.

Cautiously, she slid from the car. The wind and rain pelted her but she ignored it. She also tried to ignore the frantic pounding of her heart, but that was more difficult to do. Where had Rondel gone?

She saw nothing except that flash of movement again, a shadow that didn't linger long enough to take on definite form. Picking up a mud-soaked branch, she crept forward. The branch was heavy. It would hurt if she needed to use it.

The rain saturated her clothes, making her cold and miserable, but she refused to crawl away and hide. She was not a coward, never had been. Let The Visitor tempt her, let him try to trick her...

Maybe he was trying to trick her right now!

She paused nervously, her hand resting on the watchtower's rough outer wall. What if this was a test, something to do with the weak spots in her character?

Out of the blackness, a light suddenly flared. The starkness of it momentarily blinded her. She ducked, but knew she'd been seen. She could hear feet squelching in the mud and then a man's grunt of displeasure.

Then, as quickly as it had appeared, the light was extinguished. The muddy footsteps headed away from her, moving swiftly toward the rear of the tower.

It was crazy for her to follow, but Delanie wanted the professor back, and this man might know where he was. She ran after him, shoving at her sopping hair, certain she could catch him before he reached the woods.

The very last thing she expected was for the ground to open up and swallow her. But it did. One second she was running, the next, she was tumbling through the darkness to God only knew where.

A scream broke from her throat. Her hands flailed at the air. At first, they found nothing, but then, miraculously, her fingers caught a ledge, something hard and wooden and solid enough to support her weight.

The resulting jolt almost tore her arms from their sockets. Pain sliced through her shoulders and neck, followed by an odd sort of euphoria that made her feel numb and faintly giddy, as if the light had returned to shine directly into her brain.

"Rondel!"

She cried his name, though she wasn't really aware of doing it.

There was something clamoring in her head, some invisible force pulling on her body. She swore someone's fingers clawed at her from below. She arched herself away, then stopped and ordered herself to stay calm.

But the roar in her head was so loud, words overlapping, snatches of pictures pouring through her mind. Demon, she thought and almost saw a face. The word vanished. She struggled to maintain her grip. It felt as though someone was trying to pry her fingers free.

She closed her eyes. More words rushed in. *Demon. Evil. No soul.* All those things came to her. A man had been here tonight. She couldn't see his face. He'd touched the wooden frame that she now clung to. She felt his presence running through her.

"Serve The Visitor," she murmured, only half-aware of the rain that soaked her.

Her fingers had gone numb. She couldn't think. Where were these words coming from?

"Deceit," she whispered. "Duplicity." A shock ran through her, jolting her out of her trance. "Professor!"

Her eyes focused on the shadows, and the wall of the watchtower high above.

"Rondel!"

The wind whipped her cry away. Delanie concentrated. She had fallen. Ignore the sensations, she told herself. Climb out. There must be a way.

She shifted her grip. The wood sagged dangerously. The wind roared in her ears. Her fingers tightened, then froze as a new word flashed in her mind. *Covetous.* She saw teeth and a charming smile. She felt a hand on hers. Limp, moist.

She shuddered and searched for a foothold. Nothing. Where was Rondel? Who were these people whose presence she felt? Two of them at least, separate entities. One evil, one covetous.

The invisible force seemed to drag her down again, like the current in a black whirlpool.

Fight it, she ordered her muscles. It isn't real.

It felt real.

She dug her nails in, her body tensing. Was the wind laughing at her? She shoved the idea away.

Delanie!

The impression of her name being spoken startled her, but she continued her upward struggle. Only the wind, she told herself.

"Help me, God," she prayed, then wondered if God would hear her. She'd said, "I hope you die!" once, and her wish had been fulfilled. That couldn't have been God's doing.

"Delanie." This time the voice had substance. There was a sense of urgency to it.

Her arms ached. The blackness below beckoned to her.

"Give me your hand, Delanie."

Slowly, her mind cleared. The roar subsided, and the flow of words. A man was reaching for her.

"Rondel," she whispered. "It's—no, it's too far. I can't reach you."

"Yes you can. Trust me, Delanie. Let go and grab my wrist."

Water from the sky and his hair dripped onto her face. She could see his eyes above her now, dark and concerned. He had beautiful eyes. Trustworthy.

Her fingers slipped as her arm muscles weakened.

"Let go, Delanie."

Swallowing a sob, she took a deep breath and gave herself a determined upward thrust. At the same time, she released her left hand. He caught her firmly about her wrist, and she knew right then that it would be all right. He wouldn't drop her. The angel had chosen very well.

"You FELL into the old cellar," Rondel explained when they were inside and more or less dry. "Someone left the doors open."

"Considerate," Delanie remarked, frankly annoyed by the incident now that she was back on solid ground.

The two bedrooms in the watchtower were connected. Rondel had to pass through hers to get to the hall. He stood in the doorway of his own room, wearing a pair of black sweatpants and a red T-shirt. His feet were bare, his hair was drying and beginning to curl around his neck and cheeks.

"I couldn't catch them, whoever they were," he said. His eyes were fixed on her window and the twisted trees beyond. "They must have gotten in through the cellar doors. The lock would have been easy enough to pry open. I'll board it up for you in the morning."

"They?" Delanie repeated. She sat on her bed and gave the belt of her yellow terry cloth robe a tug. "So there were two of them."

"Two that I saw."

Two people here tonight, two demons left to serve The Visitor. Delanie regarded him doubtfully. "Should we call the police?"

"Inspector Haaken?" Rondel ran his fingers through the ends of his hair. "Probably not, for the professor's sake. I checked the cellar. I can't believe the professor would have kept anything valuable down there, and you said his laboratory looked untouched."

"But if those were The Visitor's so-called demons, why would they come here? To set up a temptation?" She stood, tapping her fingers together. "Well, anyway, I'm going to call Interpol in the morning about Aric Bellal. There isn't much we can do until then. Do you want some coffee?"

He smiled a little. "It might be a good idea." At her uncomprehending look, he added, "Get us away from the beds."

She glanced at him in surprise.

His smile widened. Whatever was bothering him had obviously been set aside. "A temptation, Delanie." He motioned at the lumpy mattress. "The professor's the angel, not me."

She set her hand on the door frame, unsure how to respond. He came toward her, but she wasn't ready for that. She turned and started down the stairs to the kitchen.

"Mahira thinks I'm going to get you killed," she said over her shoulder. "Now you tell me that I'm a temptation. Put those two things together and I come out as a treacherous temptress.''

"Not as far as the professor's concerned.''

He was too close to her, but she paused anyway. "That's true. He chose me, didn't he, so he must trust me. I wonder why?''

"Maybe he saw something special in you.''

"Like Mahira did?'' An eerie tremor passed over her skin. "I hope not. I'm really not a forbidding...'' Her eyes landed on the table, and suddenly widened. "Rondel, look!'' she exclaimed, grabbing his arm. "It's a glove, a worn-out brown leather glove. Oh, God!'' She recoiled at the second thing she saw. "And a root.''

"The mandragora,'' Rondel murmured. "The sign. We've passed the first temptation.''

Delanie avoided the obscene little root and picked up the glove beside it. "This belongs to the professor,'' she said. "He had it in his pocket the night we came here. I remember because he said the leather wouldn't protect him if he touched an ungrounded metal bar up in his lab.''

Rondel took the glove from her. "Then The Visitor does have him,'' he said so quietly that she almost didn't hear. Closing his eyes, he bent his head to hers. She felt his breath on her cheek and an unexpected surge of heat in her limbs as he whispered a soft "Damn'' into her hair.

THE MORNING had a deep gray cast to it, but then all mornings did these days. Rondel breathed the cold air into his lungs and let his eyes roam the black tangle of forest beyond Mahira's cottage.

"I can't do it, Dex,'' he said. "I'm sorry.''

Dex let a sack of barley, probably pilfered, drop to the ground, then sat on it, breathing hard. "That's a contradiction in terms, boy,'' he panted, wiping a film of sweat from his broad forehead. "You're sorry, but you can't do it. Therefore, if you did do it, you wouldn't feel the least bit sorry as I see it.''

Rondel gave him an ironic look. "You would see it that way.''

The remark didn't faze Dex. "I'm a soldier of fortune, Rondel, self-made and always on the lookout for a new angle. This is an awfully good angle. You sure you won't reconsider?"

"I'm sure, Dex," he said, wishing he meant it.

The older man heaved himself to his feet, patting the two dogs that followed him. He didn't seem offended. "Well, the offer will stand for a few more days, so if your conscience decides to take a vacation—"

"It won't."

"—you'll still be able to accept."

Rondel gave up. You couldn't talk seriously to Dex. Bending down, he picked up the discarded sack.

"You're a good lad." Dex clapped him hard on the back, and Rondel grimaced. Delanie didn't weigh much, but she was tall and hauling her out of that cellar had strained his muscles.

He was loading the grain into Dex's battered pickup when a thought occurred to him, a sudden inexplicable sensation that Mahira and the Sisters were up to something.

Straightening, he asked Dex, "Where is she?"

"Mahira? In the cave. But you can forget it, boy, you'll never find her."

"What's she doing there?"

"Calling The Visitor?" Dex's eyes sparkled. "Come on, you're taking this far too seriously. Let her throw her powders on her fire and mumble old German poetry. Words can't hurt us."

Rondel didn't respond, merely slid his gaze to the caves. There was no point going down to look. Dex was right, he'd never find her.

Jamming his cold hands into his jacket pockets, he fought a shudder. "Talk to Harry for me, will you, Dex?"

"Righto. I'm on my way up to the castle now." His face broke into a broad grin. "It's Harry's turn to play the Game, today. I reckon he'll fail as badly as old Popporov did." With his head, he gestured to the watchtower. "You and that pretty doctor going to keep looking for the professor?"

Rondel nodded, hopping from the truck. "He's got to be around here somewhere."

"Don't count on it," Dex said with uncharacteristic gravity. His face creased into a frown. "I tell you, Rondel, I've seen things up at the castle that would curl your hair. It's a hellish meeting this year."

"What do you mean?"

Dex shrugged. "I can't explain it. Something just doesn't feel right. There's no sense of fun, if you take my meaning. The baroness has noticed it. Harry and Gerda, too."

The castle wasn't visible from here, but Rondel looked in the general direction. Suspicion darkened his eyes. "Do you know what's causing it?"

"No idea, but I'll tell you, that burgermeister's not helping things any. He grabbed Alicia last night, then all but tore poor Gerda's arm off as they were going out the door. Alicia would like to oust him from the club, but unfortunately, cruelty to fellow members isn't an official taboo."

A shiver born of memory and something much deeper crawled through Rondel's body. "The bastard should be hanged," he muttered.

"Burned," Dex said. He climbed into the cab, motioned for his wolf-dogs to stay, then sent Rondel a meaningful look. "For my money, if there is a real Visitor, that man had better be it."

Rondel frowned. "Why?"

"Because if there's worse than him in this world, there isn't a person alive who'd stand a chance of beating him at the Game."

DELANIE WALKED in slow circles around the professor's laboratory, hugging his glove to her chest.

"Maybe I shouldn't have phoned Interpol," she said to herself and the absent professor. "But I have to find out about Aric Bellal and his family. And I want to know who broke in here last night and left the mandragora."

She kept pacing in circles. Movement made it possible for her to think and not fall prey to the gloomy weather. It was a monstrous day outside. Even dressed in black stretch pants with two layers of T-shirts under a cable-knit sweater and lined leather boots, she was cold.

She was also frightened, unnerved. Those men she and Rondel had seen last night, had they broken in here solely to leave the mandrake root and this glove? Was the glove a warning of some sort? Would the men come back?

She wished Rondel would show up. When she heard a car engine below, she ran to the window.

A black BMW was rolling to a stop. Someone stepped out. Not Rondel, Delanie realized in mild disappointment. A woman. Still clutching the glove, she went downstairs and waited on the porch for the woman to approach.

"Hello," she said politely, then caught back a breath of reaction. Her visitor was the burgermeister's wife, Gerda Schiller, complete with a black eye and a split lower lip. Delanie knew from experience what those things signified.

"Are you all right?" she asked, reaching for the woman's arm. "Can I help you?"

"No." Gerda held up a gloved hand. She was a tall woman, extremely thin, with pale gray eyes and a defeated look about her. "Please, Fräulein Morgen, I only need to use your telephone. My car isn't working properly, and I must get to Mahira."

"Mahira?" Delanie pushed opened the front door. "But she's—I mean, I'm a doctor. Don't you think...?"

"Please, no." Gerda laid a hand on Delanie's arm. "The telephone only."

The unexpected contact sent a jolt through Delanie's body. Hatred, her mind whispered. Hatred and bitterness. Also a glimmer of helplessness, but that was fading. In its place was emerging a strong desire for revenge.

The last word chilled Delanie's blood. She removed her arm unobtrusively from Gerda's grasp. Revenge against whom? she wondered. Her husband—or someone else?

Delanie rubbed her arm, motioning to the living room. "The telephone's by the hearth. Are you sure I can't help you?"

Gerda's eyes were perfectly calm, a bad sign. "My husband has a foul temper. There is nothing you can do about that."

"But the police..."

"Are under his control." The woman drew off her gloves and sat in one of the low chairs. "I appreciate your offer, *fräulein,* but you don't understand what it is to live with a truly evil man."

Yes she did, Delanie thought, but held her tongue. She was still grappling with the emotions she'd sensed in Gerda.

She looked down at the woman from a discreet distance. "What can a witch do to help you that the police can't?" she asked, not really expecting an answer.

Gerda laughed, surprising her. "An ordinary witch, very little. However, Mahira is not ordinary." Her tone challenged Delanie to dispute that. "She sees the future. She has great mental strength. She can make things happen."

Delanie's fingers curled into fists. "Making things happen through mental force is no gift," she said in an even voice. "It's a curse."

"You would not say that if you were in my position."

I *was* in your position, Delanie wanted to retort. She didn't. Instead, she asked, "What makes you think Mahira has powers?"

Gerda smiled. "Because Adolph fears Mahira, and no one else."

Delanie eyed her speculatively. "Tell me, did he ever fear a man named Aric Bellal?"

Gerda gave a small start of recognition. "You know of Aric?"

"The professor mentioned him."

"Ah, yes, I heard the professor was missing. I'm sorry." She bowed her head. "To answer your question, I don't believe that Adolph had any fear of Aric. There was no reason to. Aric had a malicious side to his nature, so in this way they were alike."

"Did Mahira know him?" Delanie asked.

"I don't think so. Aric had no time for witches. He had his own mental powers, much stronger than those of a witch, he claimed. But then, he was known to brag a lot. And his powers didn't help him in the end. He died thirty years ago, you know."

"You mean his real death?"

"I beg your pardon?"

Delanie waved the question aside. "It's not important. Can you tell me anything else about him?"

"Nothing except that he would never play the Game at the club. He said it was for amateurs."

"How did he die, do you know?"

"I believe he got arrested. Something happened while he was in jail. I don't know the details." Gerda's pale eyes regarded Delanie suspiciously. "Why are you so curious about Aric?"

Delanie hesitated. "I heard somewhere that his family was very powerful. The professor seemed to feel they might bear a grudge against him. I wondered if his disappearance could have anything to do with that."

Gerda fumbled with her gloves. "I couldn't say, *fräulein*. I have my own affairs to deal with."

"Yes, I know," Delanie said. "You want Mahira to do something to your husband, don't you?"

Gerda didn't deny it. "My husband has evil in him. Perhaps Mahira has evil in her, as well. I know she understands the nature of evil. She helped Rondel when he was young. Perhaps she'll do the same for me."

"Helped Rondel?" Absently, Delanie drew on the professor's glove. "How?"

Gerda's smile was distant. "He had an unhappy childhood, I'm told, although you will never get him to say a word about it."

"Then how did you hear about it?"

"I know people who are connected to him. My source is unimportant. What matters is that Mahira did things to make life better for him."

She shouldn't pry, Delanie knew that. But she couldn't resist. "What kinds of things?"

"She was related to Rondel's mother," Gerda said softly. "Both Rondel's mother and his father are now dead. In the village, they say this was Mahira's doing. She traveled all the way to Lisbon to get Rondel when he was young, and three months after she had returned with him, they died. It was a road accident. They were killed instantly in the crash, but what caused their vehicle to crash, the villagers wonder.''

A ripple of alarm slid through Delanie. ''What about Rondel?'' she asked. ''How did his parents' deaths affect him?''

''I don't know. He was thirteen by then. When he was fifteen, he went to live with Dex in London for a short time. Soon after that, his life became his own. He often comes here to visit Mahira. His visits soften her, which is why I dare to approach her now. He is of her blood, you know.''

Delanie stared uncertainly. ''What does that mean?''

Leaning forward, Gerda lowered her voice to a conspiratorial level. ''They say the blood of the witch did not appear in Rondel's mother. But it is supposed to be strong in Rondel.''

Delanie pressed her gloved hand to her throat. ''Are you telling me that Rondel's a witch?''

''Of course not,'' Gerda denied hastily. ''You simply have to be careful around him, that's all. Because of Mahira. Hurt him and she will hurt you.'' Her head came up. ''Someone is driving past on the road. Maybe I won't have to use your telephone after all.''

Delanie restrained her when she would have risen. ''What would Mahira do, Gerda?''

At that moment, Gerda's eyes looked more opal than gray. ''I believe she has the power of The Visitor on her side, *fräulein.* Such witches, it is said, can kill with a mere thought.''

MAHIRA PEERED far down into the flames. Why could she see nothing inside them?

''Be silent, Sisters,'' she commanded. ''The fire defies me today.''

One by one she separated the tiny points of flame. From within, images began slowly to coalesce. The blond-haired girl took shape again, but for the moment Mahira dismissed her.

"Rondel," she commanded. "You are in there. I would see you."

A young boy appeared. This was not the picture she wanted, but she would accept it.

He was running in the streets, a wild creature. His mind and his will were strong. Not once in those unhappy early years had he called to Mahira for help.

The old witch sighed. "Enough," she said. "Show me what lies ahead."

The flames refused to obey, so she used her most powerful chant on them. "I will see tomorrow, now!"

Never in all her many gatherings had the fire been so stubborn. Never had it roared up to full human height. But it did so now, and the Sisters fell back in horror.

"Mahira, what is happening?" one of them cried. "What have you done?"

Mahira remained unmoved by what she saw. "We are visited," she told them. "Be still."

But they went on murmuring among themselves.

Two flames rose higher than the others, like horns on the head of a misshapen beast. Mahira waited until they had achieved their full height, then brought her eyes up to them. No face emerged for her to see, and only the familiar voice of the fire spoke into her head.

"What is done cannot be undone. He is chosen, and now twice tempted. No future will you see for him. Be warned, Mahira, do not interfere again . . ."

The voice left, the fire settled back to its original size and the horned flames vanished. With great care, Mahira passed her hand through the smoke.

"Return, Sisters," she said, weary to think of the ordeal that lay ahead. "There is much work to be done."

RELIEF SWEPT through Delanie's body. It was Rondel on the road, and Dex close behind in a blue pickup truck.

Kill with a thought!

Gerda's words echoed in her head. She tried to shut them out, but she couldn't. Had she killed her father with a thought? Trembling, she shoved the dark memories aside and followed Gerda outside.

"I must see Mahira," Gerda said to Rondel when he got out of his car.

He glanced at Delanie, who explained, "Her car broke down. She wanted to use the phone."

"Oh, I don't think you should be driving, Gerda." Dex joined them. "You come with me. I'll take you home."

"No. I must see Mahira."

"Later," Dex promised.

"No, now. Rondel, please." She appealed to him. "She's my last hope."

Rondel stared at her for a minute, then he said, "She can't do what you want her to, Gerda."

"She's a witch."

"She's an old woman. She can't solve your problems."

"I still want to go to her."

Rondel gave Dex a silently expressive look, and Dex nodded. "Right you are, into my truck then, Gerda. We'll see if Mahira's up from the caves yet. I'll come back later and have a look at your car."

Delanie waited by a gnarled chestnut tree until Dex and Gerda had driven off, then she looked at Rondel. "Up from the caves?"

"Don't ask." He sounded tired of the subject, so she dropped it.

"I thought we could..." She broke off with a frown. "Is that the phone?"

"Sounds like it."

Delanie ran for the door. Maybe Interpol had found something on Aric Bellal.

She snatched up the receiver with a breathless, "Yes?"

A man's voice replied, "If you wish to see the professor alive, come to the Cemetery Rocks this afternoon at four p.m."

"What?" She motioned to Rondel. "Who is this? What are the Cemetery Rocks?"

"Be there at four p.m.," the voice repeated. "If the chosen two are not present at precisely that time, the professor will die."

ROLAND POPPOROV hung up the telephone with a click and a satisfied smile. "I'm so good at this," he congratulated himself, then buttoned his coat and hurried to where the professor was being held.

He was puffing by the time he arrived, but still delighted with his ingenuity. The boring other, the one called number six, would never have come up with such a fiendish plan.

"Ah, Herr Popporov, come for another chat, have you?"

The professor was stretched out on his cot, his hat covering his face. He sounded amused, which annoyed the demon.

"You find humor in your situation, professor?" he inquired.

"Two temptations down, four to go," the professor responded. "And the answer is no. The situation is quite serious. It's you I find humorous."

Roland's cheeks became mottled. "Perhaps you'll change your tune when I tell you that I've arranged a surprise for your chosen two at the Cemetery Rocks this afternoon."

The professor lifted his hat a fraction. "*You* have, Herr Popporov?"

"With The Visitor's permission, of course."

"Ah, yes, The Visitor. I do hope you're watching for tricks."

"What does that mean?"

"Oh, nothing. What kind of a surprise have you planned for my chosen two?"

"Something quite frightful, I assure you. You see, The Visitor is finding the Game a little boring. He thought we should do something to make it more interesting."

The professor sat up. "You're deviating from the Story, Herr Popporov," he warned. "That won't be tolerated, you realize."

Roland smiled. "Not to worry, professor. We know the Story as well as you do. We know which rules can be broken and which ones may only be bent. Now, if you please, I'll take your other glove and your scarf."

Rising with deceptive grace, the professor strolled up to the bars. Obligingly, he handed out his second leather glove and his tartan scarf.

The serenity of his expression made Roland's nerves twitch. As soon as the items were in his possession, he scuttled swiftly backward.

"Good," the professor said calmly. "You understand that I'm not as helpless as I seem in here. Remember that, Herr Popporov. Harm Delanie or Rondel in any way and these bars will mean nothing. Even The Visitor won't be able to stop me from destroying you."

Chapter Seven

"I feel like we should be leaving a trail of bread crumbs," Delanie remarked as they walked through the eerily silent woods. She looked up through gnarled branches and a webwork of vines that seemed to be strangling them. "Isn't it awfully dark for this time of the afternoon?"

Rondel followed her gaze. "It's a black overcast. Don't worry about it."

He felt her press closer to him and had to set his teeth against the reaction of his body. He had little resistance left in him right now. Her skin was so smooth and creamy, her hair a pale sheaf of gold. Long bangs drooped slightly over one eye, making her seem even more vulnerable than he suspected she already was.

Maybe it was fortunate that they had only a short distance to go before they reached the Cemetery Rocks. If he thought forward to that moment, he'd stop thinking about Delanie, or at least he wouldn't be thinking of her in any sexual way, only of her safety.

"Are those the rocks up there?" she asked, breaking his concentration, which was fine because his mind was on a dangerous path.

He halted at the edge of the forest. His gaze rose up a steep granite hill. "There are thirteen rocks that look exactly like headstones at the top."

"Thirteen headstones. Charming. No wonder The Visitor came to Klausberg." He felt the shiver that ran through her. "I don't suppose there's a tranquil blue lake on the other side?"

He smiled a little. "No, it's more like a black heath, only not quite so inviting. Beyond that, there's another stretch of forest."

"Frankenstein and the destruction of the old queen in *Snow White* all rolled into one?"

"You could say that." His eyes remained fixed on the peak and the juts of stone barely visible from where they stood. "Something's not right here," he murmured.

"You mean it's a trap? We did discuss that possibility earlier."

"I don't like it." He rubbed the back of his neck where his skin prickled. "We know the professor can't be here. It's not part of the Visitor's Story, so why bring us to this spot?"

"The man on the phone said we had to come or the professor would be killed. Maybe this is one of the temptations."

She moved closer still. It had to be fear, Rondel thought with an inward grimace. She wasn't the touching type.

"Maybe it is," he agreed, taking her hand and pulling. "One way or the other, let's get this over with. What time is it?"

"Three-fifty-three. Rondel?"

"What?"

"You don't think the burgermeister could be the Visitor, do you?"

"Because of the way he treats Gerda?" Rondel stopped and turned her to face him, pushing the hair from her eyes and tucking it behind one ear. "Lots of people are cruel, Delanie," he said. "That doesn't make them the devil."

It surprised him that she didn't pull away, but she didn't. She simply set her hand on his wrists and stared at him through unsure eyes. "Aric Bellal," she said at last. "That's what I really keep coming back to. And revenge. How could anyone justify killing a hundred people just to bait one?"

"It's been done before."

"I know, that's what scares me. But how would this insane Visitor know that an 'angel' would come so he could play the Story out properly?"

"He wouldn't. But the point is one did come. The professor recognized what was going on with the four so-called demons and he tracked them down. Then he came to The Visitor's earthly home."

"So if the professor hadn't become the angel, the demons would have gone on killing until they messed up and got caught?"

"Possibly."

She looked away. "What about all those inverted crosses the victims wore and the tattoos on the demons' bodies? Would Aric Bellal's family go that far?"

Rondel began drawing her upward again, over clumps of stone and rough brush. "We don't know anything about Aric Bellal or his family. They might go that far. It might also be revenge against the professor from another source."

"For a reason we don't know." She frowned. "I don't think so."

"Why not?"

"Because nobody's nicer than the Professor."

"Nice people can do evil things without meaning to, Delanie."

He felt her stiffen and looked sideways at her, but all she said was, "Not the professor. I don't believe tha-at."

She slipped as she uttered the last word. Rondel steadied her. Then he saw a flash of movement ahead and halted so abruptly that she banged into his arm.

"What?" she demanded.

"I saw something."

"Man or animal?"

He didn't answer right away, but waited until he saw it again. A rueful smile curved his lips. "Animal," he said. "One of Dex's dogs."

Delanie dropped her forehead against his shoulder. "Are they really part wolf?"

"Mostly wolf."

"Lovely." She halted abruptly at the top of the hill. "My God, what a creepy place."

They'd reached a plateau of sorts. Enormous boulders dotted the ridge, interspersed with a scattering of thin trees and thirteen crooked rocks shaped like tombstones.

Delanie hung on tightly to his hand. She was wearing the professor's glove, he noticed. He didn't blame her. He could use a security blanket himself, right about now.

"There aren't any actual graves under those stones, are there?" she asked in an apprehensive voice.

"Not that I know of. Time?"

"Three-fifty-nine."

"Close enough." Rondel squinted through the collection of curved stones. "There's something over there."

He picked his way carefully across the uneven ground. There was a sharp drop off the north side of the hill, a fall of at least thirty meters into a rocky chasm. The ledge here was unstable, which was no doubt why they were being lured to this particular spot.

"It's the professor's scarf," Delanie exclaimed. She shook free of his restraining hand and ran forward to scoop it up. "And his other glove."

Rondel caught her, yanking her resisting body back into his. "It's dangerous," he hissed. His eyes circled the area, distrustfully. "I don't see the professor."

Something crackled under his feet and he looked swiftly down. "Dry brush," he murmured, then gave Delanie a small push. "Come on, we're going back."

She pulled away. "No."

Why was she staring at the second glove in her hand, feeling it with her fingers? "Don't argue, Delanie. There's something wrong here. Can't you feel it?"

"No—yes! I mean I feel something." She looked again at the glove. "I'm not sure what it is." She touched the leather back. "Demon," she murmured obscurely, then frowned. "Evil. Sadistic." Her head came up. "A trick!" she whispered. "You're right, Rondel. We should go."

He eyed her in suspicion. "What do you mean, evil? What trick?" His fingers curled about her arms. "What do you know, Delanie?"

"Nothing." She squirmed, trying to free herself. "It's a feeling, that's all. Please, let's just get out of here."

She slipped when he slackened his grip, caught her balance, then looked down at the twigs under her feet. "What is this stuff?" she said "You'd think a witch was about to be—"

In the next second, Rondel detected the strong odor of gasoline and a familiar male voice inserted the word, "Burned?" to finish Delanie's statement.

Rondel spun toward the voice. He heard Delanie's soft, "Oh, no," of dread, and his own hissed breath.

"Gasoline, matches, ropes, gun." A man with pale brown hair, glasses and muttonchops growing on his cheeks and jowls cheerfully ticked off the items on his stubby fingers. "I'm holding the gun, as you see. Now if you'll please move apart from one another, I would be so grateful. There, that is much better." He poked at his spectacles. "You remember me, I think. Roland Popporov. We met at the baroness's castle."

"And talked on the phone?" Delanie added with polite sarcasm.

She had draped the professor's scarf around her neck and looked amazingly calm, but her pale cheeks betrayed her to Rondel. That and the tiny quaver in her voice. Rondel's body tensed in a protective reaction.

"Yes, we did, *fräulein*," Popporov agreed.

The gun was pointed at Rondel's chest, although the man himself never looked away from Delanie.

"Please do not move, Rondel, or I will shoot you."

Rondel quieted his straining muscles and the fear that wanted to rise in him. He'd learned a long time ago how to deal with all forms of fear.

"Shoot, or kill?" he asked, watching the man closely.

"The choice is mine to make," Popporov said with a smile. "Would you care to find out what it will be?"

"Not especially." Rondel continued to stare. The man was sweating heavily, but it was cool up here, with nothing except the boulders to break the wind. He seemed to want to pull the trigger quite badly, and yet he held off.

"Did we fail a temptation?" Delanie asked, and Rondel closed his eyes, thanking God for his decision that morning.

Popporov's leer deepened. "What do you think, *fräulein?*"

"I think if you kill us, you'll be in a lot of trouble," she replied, lifting her head in a gesture of defiance.

From The Visitor, Rondel wondered, or a closer source?

There was something peculiar about the way she'd been examining the Professor's glove. He'd seen Mahira do things like that. And the words she'd spoken—demon, evil, sadistic—where had they come from?

He shuddered, shoving the unfounded suspicions away and returning his mind to Popporov. The gun barrel wavered as the wind gusted up, plucking at the man's collar and the lapels of his baggy wool suit.

"Maybe *I'm* The Visitor," Popporov said in response to Delanie's remark. "In which case, I can break all the rules I want to."

"Then why bother with the Story in the first place?" Delanie retorted coldly. "You're not The Visitor, and you know it. Why did you bring us all the way out here? Are you related to Aric Bellal?"

Popporov's cheeks reddened. He blinked at her. For one brief moment, he appeared to lose his focus.

Rondel didn't stop to reason. He lunged for the man. But the dried twigs under his feet crackled just enough to alert Popporov, who swung the gun up at the last second and caught Rondel hard on the jaw.

Maybe it was a lucky hit, or maybe good reflexes, Rondel didn't know. But the pain that shot through his head and neck was certainly real. He felt a second blow, this one a sharp crack on the back of his skull. He heard Delanie scream, "No!", and saw flashes of a scuffle somewhere far

above him. Finally, there came the chilling echo of a gun-
shot.

"Delanie..."

He fought to remain conscious, to keep his body in motion. But that time was past. He felt himself slithering to the
ground. His muscles went limp, his mind drifted slowly
away.

"Rondel!"

Delanie shouted his name. He detected the distant sounds
of a struggle.

"Oh, that the other should dream up such a plan," Popporov chortled.

Delanie grunted. "Let go of me, you little creep!"

Yes, a fighter, more angry than afraid. One final shudder tore through Rondel's body, then he caught a fleeting
glimpse of a young blond girl with braids, an image that
made no sense to him at all.

"I hope you die!" the girl shouted.

Through the swirling darkness in his head he saw Mahira's ancient face and smelled gasoline. Something rough
and brittle scratched his face, but he couldn't see it. And
then the darkness rushed in completely.

THE GASOLINE FUMES were the first things to penetrate the
black pain in Rondel's head. He felt something wet splash
on his ankles and forced his eyes open. Focusing them was
another matter.

Popporov hummed as he poured fuel from one of two red
cans onto the dry twigs.

"Welcome back," he said quite happily. "You're tied up
to one of these most appropriate Cemetery Rocks. *Fräulein*
Delanie is behind you. I had to gag her, I'm afraid. She was
calling me names, and as the baroness's castle is not terribly far away, I thought it unwise to let her carry on." He
squatted down, his fat fingers pinching Rondel's cheeks,
and checked his eyes. "Are you awake now?"

Rondel mumbled something unintelligible.

Popporov sat back. "Half-awake, I would say, and angry, from the way you're glaring at me." His smile was a

taunt. "I trust this kindling you're sitting on isn't too uncomfortable."

"This isn't part of the Story," Rondel managed to say, wishing he could twist his head around to see if Delanie was all right. But for now it was all he could do not to sink back into unconsciousness. "Wasn't the art deal part of it, Popporov? Didn't I pass the Visitor's test?"

The man blinked. "I have no knowledge of an art deal."

"No?"

"None at all. However, I believe this is for you." He motioned to the mandrake root in Rondel's lap. "Mandragora, I think it's called."

"Tell me about Aric Bellal, Herr Popporov."

Again a flush rose in Popporov's cheeks. "I'm afraid I don't know that name." Smiling now, he stood. "Shall we get on with the fun?"

Rondel couldn't think properly. He should pump the man for information, he knew that, but his mind was still so fuzzy. Yes, the art deal was part of The Visitor's plan, the second temptation. The proof was in his lap. But who was Aric Bellal to Roland Popporov? Was there a connection? Rondel sensed one, though he suspected it might be indirect.

He half closed his eyes. "Mahira!" he whispered under his breath, then he brought his head up sharply. For a second, he could have sworn he saw her, standing at the edge of the cliff. But no, it was only a gray boulder.

He let his head fall back against the slab of rock behind him. Without appearing to, he tested the strength of the ropes about his wrists and ankles. There was no slack.

Popporov circled them. "The demon and the chosen two," he declared. "Such a lovely sight."

He smiled broadly, then stood back, producing a box of wooden matches from his vest pocket. With theatrical exaggeration, he struck one of the match tips. The wind caused the flame to flutter wildly but didn't extinguish it.

"Goodbye, chosen two," Popporov said with a light laugh. "We will meet again. In hell!"

Leaning forward, he dropped the match on the gasoline-soaked brush.

THERE WAS NOTHING at that awful moment for Delanie to do except squeeze her eyes closed and pray. She did both, not wanting to see the flames that would soon become a funeral pyre.

Words still flashed in her head. Popporov had touched her with his damp, demon hands. She'd seen him through sensation. *Evil. Twisted. Soulless.* He liked to torment people, that came very clear to her. He thought he was clever. He feared The Visitor. He viewed the 'other' with contempt.

What other?

Other demon maybe? The impressions were cloudy. Who was this man? She sensed nervousness in him where the name Aric Bellal was concerned. Were they related?

Her senses told her that the fire had been lit.

Please, God, she begged, let this end quickly.

She waited, breath held.

Instead of the pop and crackle of flames, however, she heard only the howl of the wind, and then beneath that, the soft resurgence of Roland Popporov's laughter. Behind her, Rondel swore. At Popporov? Slowly, Delanie inched her eyes open.

A tiny stream of smoke rose from the brush. She stared, astonished. The match had gone out! It lay across a wet twig still making a sizzling sound.

She snatched her head around, accusing Popporov with her eyes, because her mouth was tightly gagged.

He clasped his pudgy hands. "A mere jest," he said in obvious delight. "It was water I put on the kindling. I spread gasoline around the other rocks."

Rondel said something, probably in Portuguese and probably not very flattering.

"Oh, come now," Popporov reproached. "What right have you to deny me my pleasure? You've passed two temptations. You should be pleased with yourselves. Of course, there are four more to come, and The Visitor is notoriously devious..." He faltered, then shook the lapse off to continue. "But then, that is all part of the Game, is it not?" He approached Delanie. "Promise you won't scream?" he asked, then without waiting for an answer, he yanked the scarf from her mouth. His finger grazed her cheek. Evil, her mind whispered. A fool. A fiend.

Calmly, he began gathering up his gas cans. "I must be going now. But in case you were thinking of mentioning any of this to the police, there are two reasons why you might reconsider. One, both the burgermeister and Inspector Haaken are members of The Visitor's Club—and need I say more than that, since we all know that The Visitor and two guardian demons are also members. And two, we are dealing with The Visitor's Story here. Any interference from parties unconnected with that Story will be deemed a breach of rules, the professor's life and your own to be immediately forfeited." His smile broadened. "I trust we understand each other? Good. *Auf Wiedersehen* then."

The wind gusted up again, blowing bits of dirt and bark into Delanie's eyes. She closed them, twisting her head to the side until the breeze died down.

When she opened them again, Roland Popporov had disappeared.

Chapter Eight

Rondel knew his perception was off, that he kept slipping in and out of consciousness, but he swore he actually saw Popporov dissolve into the air.

"No, can't be," he muttered, unable to keep his eyes open. "Got to be a dream."

He heard Delanie's urgent voice through a fog. "Rondel, are you all right?"

He tried to make his mouth work, but no sound came out. Or maybe it was only that he couldn't hear himself above the roar of sound in his head. It rose, then died off. He told himself to be still, to relax, breathe normally and concentrate.

"Think of one thing," Mahira always said. "Let nothing else interfere."

He focused on Delanie's voice, imagining that it came from the baby willow several meters in front of him.

"Are you all right, Rondel?" she repeated.

"Not quite," he said. "My head . . . Keep talking."

She complied instantly. "Where did Popporov go? Did you see him?"

"Into the shadows." Rondel's gaze rose to the black sky. The stone was cold on his back, the circulation all but gone in his hands and feet. An unpleasant surge of memory helped him stay awake. "He didn't hurt you, did he?"

"No, only you. He got lucky with his gun."

"I heard a shot before I passed out. What was that?"

"We were fighting for the gun. He won. The bullet didn't hit anything." She paused. "What did he mean we've passed two temptations, and what was all that about an art deal?"

"The second temptation. I passed. He left the mandragora sign."

"Someone wanted you to paint something?"

Fierce shafts of pain sliced through Rondel's skull. "A fake Goya," he said, feeling oddly short of breath. "Dex and Harry offered me the deal last night. I turned it down this morning. The Visitor must have found out."

There was silence for a moment, then she said, "Maybe The Visitor found out because Dex and Harry are involved in The Visitor's plan."

"Not Dex," Rondel maintained. He took a deep breath. "Besides, The Visitor's too devious to be caught that easily. The offer was anonymous, made to a dealer who's a member of the club. He offered the deal to Harry and Dex, who offered it to me."

"You're sure."

"It's always done that way. The club member wouldn't even be able to tell you who the real buyer is. It's not good publicity to let it be known that you're planning a robbery."

"I can imagine."

Rondel's mind began to wander. He brought it back with difficulty. "Anyway, Delanie, if a painter agrees to do a copy, he does it, no questions asked."

"But you turned them down. Why?"

"Because I'm tired of crooked deals. And because it sounded wrong."

"Like a temptation."

"Something like that."

"What about Aric Bellal? Do you think Popporov was telling the truth when he said he didn't recognize the name?"

"I doubt it, since he's working for The Visitor." The tree doubled up as Rondel stared at it. For a second, it looked almost human. Thin-limbed, with a tail and horns... He closed his eyes, shutting the illusion out. "Can you scream, Delanie?"

"Of course."

"Then do it, or we'll be here all night." Unless Mahira had seen this in her flames, but Rondel didn't hold out much hope of that.

Behind him, Delanie began to shout for help. Yes, she could scream, and she was angry enough at Popporov to do it with a vengeance.

The willow began to float in his head. The sky grew darker, which either meant it was going to rain, or they'd been here for a very long time.

"Is anybody there?" Delanie shouted wearily, and for the first time, more than the wind responded.

"Hello? Who's up there?"

Rondel's head dropped back against the stone. "John Kessler. Tell him to hurry the hell up, will you?"

The hypnotist's black cap of hair was unmoved by the wind that roared around the plateau. Again today, he wore black pants and a black turtleneck sweater, and over them a gray cape-coat with a high collar.

"He looks like the devil," Delanie whispered. "Right down to his beard. All he needs are horns."

Rondel smiled, once more closing his eyes. He didn't care what Kessler looked like as long as he released them.

"Well now, this is an intriguing sight, I must say." The hypnotist picked his way with graceful care through the stones. "I'm almost afraid to ask how it happened."

"Then don't," Rondel said. "Just please untie us."

"Of course. I will start with the *fräulein.*"

"What are you doing out here, Herr Kessler?" Rondel asked.

"I am bird-watching with Ingrid Hoffman. A tiresome sport as far as I'm concerned. Somehow, we became separated."

"You mean she's lost in the woods?" Delanie asked.

"She told me she saw a fat warbler, and ran off to find it. I thought I saw a man, but she said no, it was a bird. And to answer your question, *fräulein,* it is not she who is lost, but me. There, is that better?"

"Thank you," Delanie replied.

She used her polite tone on him. That meant she didn't trust him.

Rondel forced his eyes open to John Kessler's narrow face. "You said you saw a man. Do you know who it was?"

"No, only that is was not Adolph Schiller." Kessler chuckled. "He was in a foul temper after the Game today. Said he should have followed Aric's lead and never played."

"Aric Bellal?" Delanie asked. "Did you know him, too?"

"My mother and his sister were friends, but of course that was many, many years ago. Of Aric himself, I know very little. I was only beginning to hone my craft when he died."

"Your hypnotic skills," Rondel reflected.

"Aric Bellal was a psychic," Delanie added.

John Kessler smiled enigmatically. "Yes, I have heard that about him. I believe he was deemed authentic by a number of noted physicians in Stockholm. Or was it Oslo? No matter, they say his talent was genuine."

On her knees beside him now, Delanie leaned over Rondel to whisper, "Ingrid Hoffman comes from Oslo."

Whatever that might mean.

Rondel set his bleary eyes on John Kessler. The man had long white fingers, quite mesmerizing to watch. Would The Visitor have such hands, perhaps be a hypnotist by nature? Were his mother and Aric Bellal's sister more than friends? Relatives, possibly?

Delanie had untied his hands. He rubbed the blood back into his wrists. "Tell me, Herr Kessler, how do you feel about the Visitor?"

"I think the Story is fascinating." The hypnotist lifted his head and sniffed. "Is that gasoline I smell?"

"Do you think The Visitor's real?" Rondel pressed.

Kessler sat back, stroking his short beard. "I suppose so," he said. "Evil is everywhere, all over the world. You need only look to the town or city where you live to see that." He gestured at the kindling. "Is that what this is all about? Your version of the Visitor's Game?"

"More like a practical joke," Rondel replied, not at all sure what to make of this man.

Kessler rose and looked around. "What a dreary spot for a joke. Do you know the way out, Herr Marcos?"

"I think so." But right then, Rondel didn't think he wanted to leave. Delanie's hair was brushing his cheek. He liked the feel of it against his cool skin, and the touch of her fingers on his arm.

Before he could stand, Ingrid Hoffman's voice reached them from the edge of the forest. "Herr Kessler, are you there?"

"Yes, Doctor, we'll be right down." The hypnotist regarded Rondel, his hand outstretched. "You seem a bit muzzy. Can you manage?"

Rondel hesitated, then took the offered hand. He wanted to test something out, old advice Mahira had given him.

"Open up your senses. Let what will come, come."

Kessler's fingers wrapped themselves firmly about his. From her knees, Delanie watched, curious, Rondel knew, but saying nothing. He let himself be pulled up. He opened his mind and waited, but no strange vibrations passed through him, no pricks of fear or doubt. So much for Mahira's advice.

Or maybe that wasn't his talent. He glanced back at Delanie's observant features.

"My goodness, what is this?" Dr. Hoffman declared from the rim of the hill. She sent Delanie a smile that didn't quite reach her eyes. "I thought you had run away," she said, sidling up to the hypnotist. "What is happening here?"

"A bit of sadistic fun," Delanie answered from her knees. "Herr Kessler rescued us."

"How fascinating."

The woman pulled on a pair of orange mittens that didn't match the pink muffs on her ears. The rest of her clothes were drab. A study in contrasts, Rondel reflected. He remembered Delanie's comment. Dr. Hoffman worked in Oslo, at the Brulen Institute. They dealt with chemical disorders of the brain. Had Aric Bellal's psychic ability been excited by a chemical imbalance? Had Ingrid Hoffman known him? She was in her late forties, so she could have known him. She could have been related to him.

Her brown eyes turned to his, so fathomless in their depths that he thought of a shark. "No soul," he murmured under his breath, then shook Delanie's inquiring look away.

"Did you locate your warbler?" Kessler inquired.

The woman's gaze left Rondel. "It was only a pigeon, I'm afraid. A fat, stupid pigeon. I let it go."

"I don't think pigeons are stupid," Delanie said, watching her. "Passive, maybe."

"This was not a passive pigeon," Dr. Hoffman maintained. "It flew right into the coils of a snake. Fortunately, the snake was in a sluggish way today. It is very cool for late April."

And this was a very strange conversation, Rondel decided. Double-edged, possibly full of innuendos. Reaching down, he took hold of Delanie's hands and brought her to her feet. "It's getting late," he said. "We should be going."

Kessler's eyebrows went up. "What about your sadistic joker?"

"Oh, he's long-gone by now," Delanie said with an eloquent smile for the doctor. "Snake-hunting."

"What do you mean, she went back to the cave?" Rondel demanded forty minutes later of Dex.

He'd dropped Delanie off at the watchtower, assured her that he did not have a concussion and that he'd come back as soon as he checked on Mahira. But Mahira wasn't around to be checked on, and his head actually did hurt, very badly, and Dex was the only person in the vicinity upon whom he could vent his frustration.

"Why did you let her go?"

Dex grinned, and, mindless of the pouring rain, began unloading his truck. "You ever tried to stop her?"

Rondel massaged his aching neck muscles. He kept seeing snakes and pigeons in his head. "She's stubborn, not immovable. You should have locked her in the cottage."

"No thanks, lad. I don't want my head served up for a witch's dinner."

Shoving the hair from his face, Rondel grabbed Dex's arm to get his attention. The wind was blowing hard now. Full darkness was less than an hour away.

"Which cave?" he shouted above a heavy gust.

Dex heaved a pouch over one massive shoulder. "The one down by those dwarf trees. Leastways, that's her favorite. But mind you don't slip and fall in the poison oak. Give you a nasty rash. You wouldn't be able to paint—should the mood suddenly strike you, that is."

Rondel set his jaw. "Did you talk to Harry?"

"I tried to, but he and the baroness were together for most of the day. I'll try again tomorrow, unless of course you change your mind."

Rondel turned. "I'm going to the cave. If Delanie calls, tell her I'll be back at the watchtower in an hour."

The dogs watched but didn't follow. Who could blame them, Rondel thought as he slipped and slid down the muddy incline to the place where Mahira and the Sisters were probably chanting.

Something nagged at him. He didn't want to acknowledge it, but the idea haunted him. Dex had tried to talk to Harry. Tried, but he hadn't done it. So how had Popporov known that Rondel passed the second temptation?

Maybe Dex had told someone else at the club that Rondel had turned down an art deal. Rondel doubted that Dex would do that, but it was a straw to cling to for now.

Rain dripped into Rondel's eyes. He raked back his hair and squinted farther down the slope to a gloomy patch of rock and earth and a squat, ugly growth of trees. There were thirteen of the dwarfs, which resembled ancient humans, malevolent, waiting for innocents to pass.

From the corners of his mind, a memory emerged, one that momentarily slowed his progress. His father used to 'wait' for him sometimes. Once he'd discovered that Mahira was a witch, he'd figured that maybe Rondel was a witch, too. And that being the case, maybe there was money to be made on his son's talent...

Rondel pushed the memory away. He didn't want to see things in his mind, never had. Mahira had accepted that about him—well, more or less. At least she hadn't forced him into anything. He'd always managed to avoid seeing mental pictures, until now.

He recalled the image he'd seen in the icehouse. Something sinister. Then he remembered the tree at the cemetery rocks this afternoon, his impression of horns and a tail, and for a moment the idea that Mahira was there. Illusions or something else? He didn't know, but he didn't like the uneasiness he felt.

And what about Delanie?

He blocked the questions with an effort. The rain was unceasing, the murky twilight creeping steadily into night. He stepped carefully over the poison oak and pushed through a tangle of dead vines into the cave.

He smelled the burning wood at once and then saw the huddled shapes of the Sisters. They moved like hobbits through the smoke.

"Pray to him," they chanted. "He is among us. His agents are among us. Pray to make them strong. Pray to him who has come."

"Mahira..."

Rondel spoke her name under his breath, tired but determined to remove her from this place. He went all the way in and quietly approached the circle.

She saw him at once, and motioning to the Sisters to continue, watched as he drew closer to the fire.

"You should not have come," she said, her eyes returning to the flames as he sat down beside her. "You are chosen. I can tell you nothing."

Rondel was cold and miserable, but he held fast to his temper. "I didn't come here to argue with you. I came to take you home."

"Where is the girl, Delanie?"

"At the watchtower."

"You are hurt," Mahira spat out. "I knew this would happen." She sounded angry. "It is the girl who has hurt you."

"No." Rondel set his hands on her shoulders, turning her to face him. "It had nothing to do with her. It was someone else. Mahira, what do you know about all of this?"

She stared at him without expression. "I know that it is the Story and that you are in great danger, both of you, but I do not care about her."

"I do," Rondel said softly, surprising both of them. "And I care about the professor. Do you know where he is?"

"No."

"Would you tell me if you did?"

"No."

"Do you know if he's alive?"

"It is the Story. It is The Visitor's promise that the angel should remain alive."

"Why?"

"Because that is a rule."

Rondel wasn't sure how to put this. "Mahira," he said carefully. "The Visitor is a murderer, not Satan. Do you understand that?"

Her face was stony. "That is what you choose to believe, but you are wrong. And do not give me that look of exasperation, Rondel. You are wrong, and that is that. What else would you have me tell you?"

Exhaustion swept through him. "Nothing," he said, rubbing his eyes. "Come on, I'll take you home." He glanced at the shuffling Sisters. "All of you."

"We are not finished yet," Mahira said. She took his hand in her dry, bony ones. "What more can I tell you that you do not understand?"

It wasn't a question she expected him to answer. Rondel kept still and indulged her. The fire was warmer than the rain, and she liked to do this. His thoughts turned to Delanie, who was waiting for him.

"Oh, that girl again." Disgust filled Mahira's tone. "I see her in your mind. Why do you care about her?"

He smiled. "Does there have to be a why?"

"Not always, but you are special to me. She is not."

His frustration rose. "You talk as if Delanie and I were involved. We're not. You know we're not, and you know why we never will be."

"You fear your emotions too much, your nature, things you do not understand." She turned his hand over so she could look at his palm. Or was it the rope burn she examined on his wrist? "You are now and have always been my child."

"I know," he said evenly. "That's what scares me."

"The word *witch* scares you."

"Not the word, the concept."

"Delanie Morgen is a witch."

A feeling of vague horror swept through him. "What?"

"You heard me."

And wished to God he hadn't. He closed his eyes. He could hear Delanie's voice in his head. *"Evil, Rondel. Sadistic. It's a trick!"*

She'd been holding the Professor's glove, "feeling" it. Popporov must have touched that glove. He'd brought it to the plateau. He was a demon, evil and sadistic. He'd played a cruel joke on them. Delanie had gotten a sense of him from the glove. It all fit.

Rondel opened his eyes, and sighed. There was no point denying what he knew to be the truth about Delanie—and maybe about himself as well.

"How did you know?" he asked, looking at the flames rather than at Mahira.

"I felt it in her. Her mind is shielded but not impenetrable. Had you let me teach you my craft, you would have sensed the truth yourself. The professor knew, that is why he chose her. And you."

"Then why don't you like her?"

Mahira's shoulders stiffened. "I do not dislike the girl. It is her mental abilities I mistrust. She does not command them. Because of this, they can be used against her."

"Aric Bellal was a psychic," Rondel murmured, distracted. "Whoever wants to avenge his death might be one, too." He looked up. "Could a psychic affect her?"

"Possibly."

He hesitated. "Did you know Aric Bellal, Mahira?"

"I knew of him."

"Is someone in his family behind all of this?"

A bitter smile touched Mahira's lips. "I would say yes to that, but do not ask me how I know or who this person is. I have no answers for those questions."

"Then tell me more about Delanie."

With great deliberation, Mahira set more twigs on the fire. "There is no more to tell. She is not in control of her powers. This frightens her. It should frighten you."

Smoke rose from the stone circle in a thin stream. Rondel watched it spiral up, then billow out as it hit the roof of the cave. "Did it frighten her family? Do you know?"

Mahira stared directly into the fire. Her features were rigid, fathomless. "Her father was a cruel man, abusive."

Rondel snapped his head around. "To Delanie?"

"Maybe, for a short time. But then he grew nervous of her. She hovers on the line between good and evil. Do you understand this?"

"No."

Mahira's fingers curled.

"In death, souls like her father's go straight to The Visitor's world of fire. That is accepted. There is no challenge in such an acquisition. But to take the soul of the angel to hell, this is most desirable to The Visitor. To take the girl would also be a pleasing thing. It would mean that she has been drawn over the line. Do you understand the difference?"

Rondel nodded. "But what does that have to do with her father being nervous of her?"

"The Visitor uses people such as he was. They are bait, to lure and trap those souls who might otherwise choose a different path."

"God over Satan?" His mind resisted this conversation. "I can't accept that, Mahira."

She took his hand tightly in hers. "You will," she predicted with a certainty that momentarily unnerved him.

He let the dizziness rush through his mind, not fighting it. His eyes traveled to the fire and the greenish-gray smoke that rose from it. In the flames he saw her, the blond-haired girl he'd glimpsed just before he'd passed out at the Cemetery Rocks.

Her eyes flashed hatred. "I hope you die," she shouted, and the man she spoke to took a faltering backward step.

"Go away," she told him. Her anger was so strong that Rondel could feel it. "Stay away!"

A shudder swept through him. He pulled free of Mahira's iron grasp.

"Don't," he warned, wanting out of here quite badly. "Stop."

A cunning smile flickered across her lips. "It is you who must stop, Rondel," she said. "I did nothing. What you saw in the flames did not come from my mind. It came from your own."

Chapter Nine

The rain made a dull drumming sound on the ground outside the watchtower. It was six p.m. and dark, but it shouldn't have been. Delanie shivered and hugged her arms tightly about her chilled body as she paced before the fire. She wore jeans and a long peach-colored sweater. The professor's tartan scarf was draped about her neck. It was the only security blanket she'd ever accepted.

She wished she could blanket her thoughts as easily, but of course she couldn't.

Roland Popporov is a demon, her mind kept whispering. What if he was a real demon from hell? That was impossible. But Mahira disagreed, and she was a witch. Delanie knew her powers were real because Mahira had told her about her father. A cruel man, she called him. She saw the truth. What else might she have seen?

Delanie's fists clenched. "Nothing," she declared to the fire that crackled in the hearth. "There's no more to know. I am not evil."

The flames jumped a little, startling her. She turned away, shutting her eyes and bending her head. "Where are you, professor?" she said softly. And Rondel, where was he? Where was anyone she could trust?

She hugged her arms, turning again. The wind blasted the outer walls, driving rain against the window. She had all the lights on, but they were flickering, and she didn't want to go up to the lab to check on the faulty electrical panel.

Beside the telephone, she noticed an ivory wallet. She set her fingers on it, testing herself. A name came to her. Gertrude Schiller. Logical. It didn't take special powers to figure that out. She flipped it open anyway and looked. Gertrude Schiller, the license read.

Then she looked closer. Stuffed in behind the license was a tiny plastic bag with a lock of white hair, some nail clippings and a picture of the burgermeister. Delanie hesitated, then opened the bag and touched the hair.

Adolph Schiller, her mind told her. She frowned, snatching her fingers back and pressing them to her throat. What had Gerda planned for her husband?

"Mahira," Delanie whispered uncertainly.

A loud banging on the door intruded on her thoughts. "Let it be Rondel," she begged, heading for the great door. "Let him tell me this is nothing, that Mahira doesn't cast evil spells."

But it wasn't Rondel creating the racket, it was the burgermeister, and he appeared to be in a barely controlled rage.

Delanie refused to open the door all the way. "What do you want, Herr Schiller?" she demanded, bracing her shoulder against the edge.

"My wife has lost her wallet. She told me she came here today." He pushed on the door with one gloved hand. "I will come in, if you please, *fräulein,* out of the storm."

Don't do it, she told herself, but he looked so bedraggled that she relented.

"Thank you," he said curtly when she stepped back. He smoothed down his pointy white hair and scowled. "Have you seen her wallet?"

"I'll get it for you."

"There was money inside. I will count it of course."

"Be my guest," she said, aware that he was following her. She picked up the wallet and threw it at him with no pretense of politeness. "Count the money and leave."

His black eyes glinted in the firelight. "You are most inhospitable, *fräulein.*"

"I know."

He pocketed the wallet smoothly, not budging from the hearth. "Why did my wife come here?"

"To use the telephone. Her car broke down."

"That is what she said."

"Then we're all agreed." Delanie's voice was cold.

The burgermeister took a menacing step closer. His features had a brutal cast in the glow of the fire. "You're thinking something, I can tell."

Delanie said nothing.

"She has accidents, my wife," he continued. "She lies about them."

"I see."

He took another step, and this time Delanie edged backward. She was brave, not stupid.

"Do not patronize me, *fräulein*," the burgermeister warned. "It makes me angry."

"Go to hell, Herr Schiller," she said suddenly. Her searching fingers found the fireplace poker behind her and wrapped themselves about the handle. "That's what the Visitor's Club's all about, isn't it? Hell and the devil. You must fit right in."

His eyes were hooded and hard. "I am a man of God, *fräulein,* whatever else you might think of me."

He continued to advance, his expression so malevolent that Delanie yanked the poker free and brought it up two-handed before her. "Go away," she repeated. "And don't come back. I had a father like you. He's dead now."

She saw him hesitate. "What are you saying?" he demanded.

"Figure it out, Herr Schiller."

He kept his distance, but a horrible smile slowly split his face. "And you tell me to go to hell? I have never killed anyone, *fräulein.*"

She glared at him. Don't think it, she ordered herself. Don't wish him dead.

He regarded the blackened poker as if measuring his chances against her anger. "You would not use that," he decided.

"Don't test me," she warned. Her palms were damp around the metal. "There are worse things I could do to you than hit you with this."

For a long moment, neither of them moved. Only the fire and the force of the storm broke the silence in the old watchtower. Finally, just when Delanie thought she was going to scream, the burgermeister straightened with a tremendous show of restraint.

"I will go," he agreed. "Not because you command it, but because it is what I choose to do." He held up a threatening finger. "But do not talk to me ever again of hell. And do not talk of my wife to anyone. She has accidents. No one will tell you differently."

Delanie motioned. "The door's that way."

"Do not forget..." he began, then broke off sharply and sniffed the air. "What is burning?"

Delanie glanced around. "I don't..." Her eyes widened in alarm. "Your coat!" she exclaimed, dropping the poker. "Get it off."

He immediately began to fumble with the sleeves, but for some reason his hands became tangled in the fabric. Delanie clawed at his collar as flames crept along the hem. *Cold,* her mind said of his nature. *No soul!*

A pair of headlights cut across the wall, but she scarcely noticed them.

"Unbend your arms," she shouted, fighting the words in her head.

He continued to flail about. Finally, in a burst of frustration, Delanie tore the coat from his shoulders, almost pulling him over in the process. She tossed the burning wool onto the stone hearth, then stood back and watched as the flames consumed it.

The burgermeister spun around, his features contorted with rage. "How did that happen?" he cried.

"You must have gotten too close to the fire." Delanie avoided the hand that would have grabbed her arm. It had been bad enough touching his coat. "There's no screen, Herr Schiller. Your threats made you careless, that's all."

"What's going on?" Rondel demanded from the doorway. "What are you doing here, Adolph?"

"I am watching my coat burn to ashes," he snarled. He stabbed a finger out into the storm. "This is her doing, the witch!"

Delanie started, then realized where he was pointing away from her and relaxed.

Rondel took a deep breath, as if controlling his temper. "Mahira's at the cottage, Adolph."

"What does that matter?" he challenged. "Aric could read minds across vast distances. Why should it be different for Mahira?"

"And yet, you weren't afraid of Aric Bellal," Rondel remarked. "Why not?"

"He was a psychic. She is a witch. Witches can kill with their minds."

Delanie gnashed her teeth. "That's not true," she denied in a fierce whisper. "It can't be true." She fixed her eyes on the burgermeister's face, steadying her voice. "Tell me, Herr Schiller, do you know any other psychics?"

Her question seemed to distract him. A ghastly smile worked its way across his mouth. "So curious about Aric Bellal, *fräulein*," he said. "You introduce his name to the people at the club, and suddenly everyone is talking about him again. He would be flattered at your interest. But of course my old friend is not here. He is dead, and his death was the fault of a woman named Anna Nagel."

"How do you know that?" Delanie asked, her suspicion deepening.

"Aric was my friend," Schiller said. His expression grew ugly. "And you have the nerve to come to me and say that I must help you find Professor Gerald Nagel, brother to the woman who took away Aric's life. No, *fräulein*, I will not help you. The professor can rot in hell for all I care. I only hope that is where he goes." His voice rose in triumph. He turned for the door. "For a man such as he, The Visitor will show no mercy."

"I SEE WORDS, Rondel," Delanie said later in a monotone. "I touch people and sometimes objects and words come into my head. I touched the burgermeister's coat, and right away I sensed coldness. He has no soul, or very little. On some level, he already belongs to The Visitor."

Stunned, Rondel watched her kneel before the fire. He still stood in the middle of the living room, hadn't even taken off his wet jacket yet, and here she was blurting out all the things he'd been wanting to ask her, but hadn't known quite how or where to start.

"The burgermeister was a friend of Aric Bellal's," she went on dispassionately, her eyes on the fire and the pieces of Adolph's wool coat that hung like smoldering cobwebs on the higher logs. "And Gerda knew Aric, and John Kessler was connected to him through his mother, and Ingrid Hoffman works in Oslo where Kessler thinks Aric's psychic powers might have been tested. And even if she didn't know him personally, relatives of the baroness's last husband did. She could be older than she looks and trying to bluff us. Any of them could be related to Aric Bellal, or close friends of the family. We know Popporov's involved, but there must be others."

Carefully, Rondel started toward her. He made no mention of Dex. Let her talk. He wanted to hear this.

"I got a sense of Popporov from the professor's glove," she confided with a quick glance over her shoulder. Lightning flashed outside, illuminating her delicate features. "But you knew that already, didn't you?"

He nodded, still advancing.

"When I almost fell into the cellar last night I felt something there, too. Two separate things, actually. One was evil, the other was covetous. And charm." She frowned. "I think there might have been charm to go along with the greed. The evil, I don't know. It could have been Popporov. It felt demonic, strong, but not centered in him." She shook her head as if to clear out the confusion. "Anyway, someone broke in and left the professor's glove and the mandragora." The lightning flashed again, out over the woods. He heard her sigh, then saw her smile wanly into the fire. "Do you believe any of what I'm telling you?"

He studied her from above, his troubled eyes sliding down the pale gold length of her hair. "Every word," he said.

She looked up sharply at him. "Just like that?"

Thunder rumbled far away over Klausberg. It seemed a sign of some sort. "Mahira told me that you were a witch," Rondel admitted.

Delanie's head fell back. "Not a witch, a sensitive. At least that's what the professor said."

Rondel smiled, going to his knees beside her and taking her hand in his. "The professor would probably know." He waited a moment, then asked solemnly, "Do you see things when you touch me?"

The lightning revealed a smile on her lips. "No, but then I didn't when I touched the professor, either. He said I was more finely tuned to negative emotions than to positive ones. I don't like the idea, but it's probably true."

"You're scared, aren't you?" Rondel said, wishing he hadn't talked to Mahira earlier. "You don't know how to control what you can do."

There was a hint of fear in her eyes, and defiance. "Did Mahira tell you that, too?"

He grimaced and ran a hand through his damp hair. "She's a very strong witch, Delanie. She knows things about people that they don't even understand about themselves."

It seemed to him that Delanie drew down deeper into herself. The thunder underscored her barely audible, "Does she know whether or not I can kill?"

Rondel refused to be shocked. There was pain in her features.

"You think you can kill with your mind?" he asked her gently, then set his hands on her shoulders to stop her when she would have turned away. "Answer me," he said. "Do you think you could kill someone with a thought?"

She faced him, her expression mutinous. "No," she said flatly. Then she lowered her lashes and whispered a reluctant, "Yes." A sigh escaped her. "I think maybe I could. I think maybe I have. Would Mahira be able to tell me?" Her eyebrows went up. "Would you?"

Lie, he ordered his mouth. Don't admit it. It isn't true if you don't acknowledge it.

He took a deep breath. "I don't know. Sometimes I see things. Then I deny them, and they disappear."

"You have visions?"

"In a way." A piece of bark snapped and he glanced at the fire. Strands of the burgermeister's coat still hung on the logs. Below that, in the coals, lay what appeared to be a wallet. "I don't see words, or get a sense of people from touching them. What I see are the beginnings of pictures in my mind. Sometimes they're projected outward so they appear three-dimensional, but usually they're more like mental impressions, flashes of things that can either have a voice or not, depending on how strong they are."

She stared in amazement, her eyes a beautiful shade of green in the firelight. "So you do understand," she exclaimed softly.

"Understand, yes. Want it, no." His thumbs massaged her shoulders through the fine knit of her sweater.

She set her hands on his wrists, choosing her words with great care. "Gerda said some things about you when she was here this morning."

His muscles tightened. "Only about me?"

"About Mahira, too, and your parents."

"About how their car crashed right after Mahira took me out of Lisbon?" He forced the tension from his body. "Mahira wouldn't kill for me, Delanie. She knows how I would respond to that. Don't listen to Gerda. She's easily affected by gossip, by just about anything, in fact."

"Maybe she has a right to be affected. Her husband's a monster. Rondel?" Delanie's fingers dug into his wrists. "It was my father. He was a horrible man. I told him I wanted him to die. That same night, he drove his car into a ditch."

Rondel said nothing about what he'd seen in the fire in the cave. "Was he sober?"

"No."

"Then you probably didn't do it."

He got no reaction from her, nothing except an unbelieving stare from her gorgeous green eyes.

The lights fluttered around them. He felt his hands tighten on her shoulders.

Don't, he thought, but it was no good. He wanted to know what it was that he could never have. Two witches? The ramifications were too gruesome to consider. But one small kiss, what could that hurt?

She didn't move or try to free herself. He almost wished she would. The lights flickered again. The fire sizzled to his left. He swore under his breath, then lowered his head and brushed his lips against her hair.

Like silk. He'd known it would be.

A small sigh came from her throat. She watched him, but now there was something else in her eyes. Curiosity?

He smiled to himself. Two witches making love. Would it be all visions, or pure sensation?

He slid his lips to her neck and she shivered, swaying closer despite the heat of the fire and his body. No, this was dangerous. He should stop.

But before he could draw back, she'd cupped his face in her hands, pulling his head firmly forward in a kiss so deep and arousing that a ripple of shock ran through him. She seemed as fascinated as he was by the sudden contact, and just as unwilling to end it.

There was no light teasing of lips, no coaxing or testing of responses. There was only his mouth open and hungry on hers, and a highly erotic sensation passing between them. No shape, only concept. Maybe it was the idea of danger, of a forbidden relationship. Or maybe it was just that he had wanted her almost from the moment he'd met her.

His tongue was hot in her mouth, wet and deliciously thorough in its exploration. Her skin smelled like the rain, her hair like the flowers after it. Yes, very dangerous.

He saw the more immediate danger out of the corner of his eyes, a glimmer of something that didn't belong here. The lights flared briefly, faded, then died. A sudden, unnatural hiss from the fire made him drag his mouth away and look.

A clap of thunder rocked the old stone floor. The reverberation sent a chill down Rondel's spine. Why? He had no fear of storms.

"What...?" Delanie began, but he pressed his fingers to her lips.

"I'm not sure."

She kept absolutely still, turning suspicious eyes to the flames.

What were they waiting for? he wondered. There was nothing...

A piece of the burgermeister's coat ignited with an unexpected snap. The flames shot up and out. At the same time, a shower of sparks landed on the hearth.

Delanie jumped back, bringing Rondel with her. He scarcely noticed the movement. Something had formed within the flames. Did she see it?

Her hand rested on his back. He crouched on his hands and knees, mesmerized by the blaze and the film of green smoke that surrounded it. He felt dizzy, unbalanced. What was happening?

More thunder reached them and then a flash of lightning. But Rondel's gaze was riveted to the center of the fire, to the image materializing deep within the smoke and coals. It was solidifying, fanning slowly outward, taking on color and definition as it grew.

Delanie didn't make a sound, but he knew she saw it. Her eyes were wide with a mixture of wonder and fright. Her hand was balled into a hard fist against his spine.

Limbs appeared in the smoke, long and sinuous, like scarlet threads with claws for fingers, and slanted yellow eyes. The colors shifted, overlapped. The serpentine limbs began to fluctuate. Rondel's lungs felt seared, but he couldn't back away.

A mouth appeared, and two curved horns. A spiked tail snapped down on the logs, causing a whiplash of sparks and cinders to fly overhead.

The yellow eyes focused on Delanie's startled face. "You," it hissed in a hideous snake's voice. "Delanie Morgen. You are the one. Yes... You are almost mine."

A clawed arm emerged from the fire to point at her. Was the thing still growing?

Rondel stared at it. Why couldn't he move? "Not real," he said through his teeth, but it was more a prayer than a statement.

Another wave of dizziness swept over him, and the monstrous vision laughed. "Denial will not save you, Rondel," the snake's voice warned. "And nothing can save Delanie. You are *my* chosen ones now. Come to me. Come..."

Delanie uttered a choked cry. Rondel had difficulty managing that much. But he had to make his throat muscles work.

"Go back to hell," he ordered the image. Through sheer willpower he forced his eyes away from it and closed them. *Not real. Can't be real. Mahira...*

He heard a *whoosh*, then felt hot air and smoke on his face. He opened his eyes. Yes, it had grown. The limbs flexed, then actually seemed to step out of the fire. The figure hovered on the hearth, a mass of connecting sinews.

It leaned over, its blurred features contorting into a malevolent mask. "My brother is dead," it snarled. "And soon you will be, too. Dead and trapped in my domain."

The slanted yellow eyes filled the room and Rondel's mind. The voice dropped. Thunder broke over the watchtower. The bloodred color of the limbs deepened as two clawed arms reached down.

Rondel swore he actually felt one of those claws scrape lovingly down his cheek.

"I am The Visitor," the thing whispered above the roar of the wind. "I am here. I have your angel trapped. Soon all three of you will be mine."

"WHERE'S MAHIRA, Dex?" Rondel demanded, bursting into the icehouse twenty minutes later. "She's not at the cottage."

Dex leaned heavily on a large burlap sack. "Well, she's not here, that's for sure." He grinned. "Evening, Doc."

Delanie nodded, but her eyes were on the darkened cottage. God knew where her mind was. Probably remembering the apparition, which she'd seen as plainly as Rondel had.

He shivered in the dampness of the outbuilding. Had a claw really grazed his cheek? He could still feel that, along with Delanie's hand on his back. Was that how she'd seen it? Through him?

It didn't matter. It had happened. The Visitor, the thing had called itself. But that was impossible, a trick. It had to be. Something planted in the burgermeister's coat. He'd let the coat burn on purpose. Or maybe it had been a hallucinatory powder tucked into the wallet Rondel had noticed.

But the wallet was Gerda's, Delanie had informed him on the way here.

So what did that mean?

Rondel had no idea. Had the effect been real or illusion? His head swam. He needed Mahira for this.

"She could be with the Sisterhood," Dex was saying now. "They like to incant at night. Not in the caves, of course, that's a dangerous climb after dark. You might phone the other Sisters. Before you do, though, I could use a hand." He winked at a silent Delanie. "Beer in the cellar, Doc. Take your mind off your troubles fast enough. Here you go, Rondel. Mind you don't break anything. That's valuable stuff in that sack."

"Scavenger," Rondel muttered, hoisting the bag onto his shoulder.

"Collector," Dex corrected.

"Are you sure Mahira didn't say where she was going?"

"Positive. Don't slip in the mud."

Rondel grimaced, but obliged. Maybe physical exertion would wipe the macabre image from his mind.

It didn't. Fifteen minutes and four loads later, he wiped a film of rain and dirt from his face with the back of an old work glove and accepted the beer Delanie held out to him.

"You look like a chimney sweep," she remarked. She sounded calm, almost amused. He knew it was a facade. Taking the lantern Dex had lit, she wandered over to an old rotted door. "What's this?"

"Underground tunnel to the cottage," Dex said, heaving his body down the ladder. Rondel could hear the rungs groaning above the storm. "We can't use it anymore. It's all caved in."

"Completely?" She sent him a disappointed look. "I've never been in an underground tunnel before."

"Well, if it's tunnels you want, the ones up at the baroness's castle are the best in these parts. You could get lost for a week and never cross the same passage twice."

A glimmer of an idea formed in Rondel's head. "Can you get into the castle through the tunnels, Dex?"

"'Course. Why? You and the doc here thinking of sneaking in, maybe watching us poor unfortunates play the Game?"

Delanie smiled. "Doctors don't sneak, Dex."

His eyes sparkled. "Then doctors don't have much fun."

"Where are the entrances?" Rondel interrupted.

"Well, there's one in the woods by the old briar hollow, another by the stream out behind the ruined part of the castle, a third by the Cemetery Rocks and three others you'd have to be shown before you'd be able to find them."

"The Cemetery Rocks," Delanie repeated. "Maybe that's how Popporov disappeared."

"It's possible," Rondel agreed. With his gloved fingers he felt the bump on his head where he'd been hit. A very real hit from a very hard gun. But out there, his eyes had played tricks on him. There were no dissolving demons, only deranged killers. As for the fire tonight, well, he still had to talk to Mahira about that.

He saw Delanie watching him and wanted very badly to take her in his arms. Then he remembered what they probably both were and his body gave a convulsive shudder.

"We'll look tomorrow," he said, taking a drink instead. "The answers must be in that castle."

Chapter Ten

"Hold still, Delanie," Rondel said as he fastened the last snap on her borrowed green raincoat. "There's no point wearing this if you're not going to do it up properly."

It was three o'clock in the afternoon on another day of pouring rain and cold winds. The only break in the storm had come about half an hour ago. That's when they'd left the watchtower, loaded with rain gear and Dex's dogs, just in case.

Brushing her hair back, Rondel set a matching hat with a wide brim on her head, then smiled as she absently began rolling up the sleeves of the coat. It was reversible and hung down almost to her ankles. She looked like a wood nymph under all that yellow and dark green fabric.

When she was finished, she looked around at the forest clearing and the stream with its arched stone bridge. "Pretty," she murmured. "Are you sure we've come to the right place? I don't see a tunnel entrance."

"It'll be in one of the caves," Rondel told her, pulling on a pair of black rain gloves with his teeth. "Dex couldn't remember which side of the hill the cave we need is on."

Delanie surveyed the dark clouds overhead. "The rain's going to come down in buckets any minute." She looked sideways. "Why are the dogs' ears up like that?"

"Thunderstorm's coming." Rondel's gaze ran along the stream, which currently resembled an angry river. Gray-green waves roared over the rocks and bulging tree roots, driven more by the wind than the current. "Do you have your flashlight?"

"Yes. I'll check the two caves behind us, okay?"

He nodded. "I'll look on the other side of the hill." He gave her hat brim a warning pull. "Remember, Dex said the entrance is about twenty meters inside. It's a trapdoor on the ground. If you find it, call me. I'll leave one of the dogs with you."

He hesitated, then bent his head and kissed her before starting off.

He'd spent the night in the watchtower, a long, horrible night of sandwiches and beer and no fires. No power, either, and no help forthcoming from Mahira, who'd returned to the cottage before they left but refused to tell them anything.

"It is not permitted," she'd said in a stony voice. "You must proceed alone."

So they'd proceeded to the watchtower and not spoken once of visions in the fire.

They'd talked about the paintings he'd done when he was younger instead, and about the time he'd almost gotten caught. He told her about the Gulbenkian Museum, which Delanie had heard of, and then she told him about her time with the professor.

The wolf-dog preceded him into the cave just as the first drops of rain began to fall. It barked softly at the thunder that resounded far in the distance.

Rondel scratched the animal's ears, then, playing his flashlight beam along the muddy floor, counted off twenty meters. It seemed almost too easy that the door should simply be there, but it was. Even covered with moss, he couldn't mistake the heavy planks.

Shoving the flashlight into his pocket, Rondel crouched and worked his fingers into the narrow groove that was the opening. The heavy door was rotted and warped, but it opened after several strenuous attempts that left him winded and questioning his stamina.

The dog peered into the blackness, sniffed and started down.

"Down what?" Rondel wondered out loud, pulling off his glove and holding it between his teeth while he dug out his flashlight.

He got down on his stomach and aimed the beam into the hole. There were steps into the tunnel, carved out of the earth and overlaid with flat stones. Cobwebs clung to the raised door and the walls, but enough of them were broken to make him realize that this entrance had been used recently.

By whom? For a moment, he pictured the professor's face.

Shaking that puzzling thought away, Rondel started down. He'd go a hundred meters or so, then double back and find Delanie.

The dog sat waiting at the bottom of the stairs, ears up, tawny eyes on the opening above. Rondel wasn't sure why, but the animal's alert attitude disturbed him. What didn't the dog trust?

At the base, he stopped, accepting the chill that ran through his blood as natural. The tunnel was cold and black and slimy, thick with the smell of decay. But more than that, some deeper instinct warned of imminent danger.

He heard the warning groan far too late to do anything about it. It came from the trapdoor overhead, which he'd forgotten to secure. He closed his eyes, envisioning the scene in his mind, knowing there was nothing he could do to change it. The crash of wood echoed loudly through his brain, then slowly died off. Only then did he look.

The door had fallen, all right, aided by the wind that had been funneling into the cave in icy blasts.

He glanced down at the dog. "Sorry," he murmured. "My fault."

With a sigh, he started up the stairs. Using all his weight, he pushed upward on the wood, and kept pushing until sweat ran down his neck and back.

It was no good. The force of the slam had wedged the door in deeper than ever, sealing the edges completely.

Rondel rested for a minute, pressing his damp forehead to the wall. He had visions, but he was no magician. There was only one way out of here now.

"NO TRAPDOORS in either cave," Delanie told the dog who waited for her at the overgrown entrance to the second cave. "Nothing but dirt and mold and little mice bones."

Her eyes roamed the overgrown embankment. No Rondel. She dusted off her gloves and stomped the mud from her boots. The sky had gone from gray to black. More rain coming, she realized, and by the sound of the thunder that was creeping over the woods, this squall would be highly electrical. She decided to forget waiting and find Rondel.

Rearranging her hat, she started away from the cave, toward the old stone bridge that crossed the stream, which currently resembled a torrent with a lethal-looking whirlpool in the center. Her boots slipped on the muddy path, but the thunder and flashes of approaching lightning kept her moving. That and the memory of the thing in last night's fire. No matter how hard she tried, she couldn't forget that.

Sinuous red limbs, horns, a spiked tail—it had to be The Visitor, didn't it? But it couldn't have been real. Rondel was right. The burgermeister must have arranged it. Something to do with the burning of his coat.

Of course, Gerda's wallet had burned, as well.

Shivering, Delanie glanced back at the ruined portion of the castle that towered above her. Were they all up there in their robes? Were some of them watching? "For killing my brother," last night's Visitor had warned. Had Aric Bellal been brother to one of the club members?

Delanie hunched her shoulders. From here, the castle looked doubly sinister, a medieval watcher that brought to mind a huge stone dragon.

Resolutely, she shoved aside vines and weeds and prickly bushes. Several times she had to stop and untangle her clothes from long thorns and branches. She was almost to the bridge when she spotted Gerda Schiller sitting on the arched wall.

The woman was wrapped in a gray coat and kerchief. With her, holding her hand and patting it, was the baroness, dressed in navy blue silk that didn't look as though it would stand up to a good soaking. Delanie couldn't hear their words, but it was obvious from her bent head and shoulders that Gerda was upset.

Thunder rolled through the forest. With a quick look in that direction, the baroness stood. She tried to bring Gerda to her feet, but Gerda wouldn't budge.

Then the baroness stilled her motion and straightened. Her eyes fastened on some forward point that Delanie couldn't see. But then, she didn't have to. The burgermeister's disagreeable tones probably carried for miles.

"I have told you not to interfere, Alicia," he bellowed. "This is not your affair."

He was drunk, slurring his words, staggering. Delanie crouched quickly in a patch of bushes. The dog sat obediently beside her. More thunder sounded over the forest.

The baroness's response was inaudible, trapped in a clap of thunder, which made Delanie tremble.

A gust of wind brought more of the burgermeister's harsh words to her ears. "Gerda is my wife." He snatched up the woman's limp arm, nearly tipping over in the process. "She has nothing to say to you."

Delanie inched closer. The sky was pitch-black now, the wind a roar in her ear. The fire image reformed in her mind. *"Delanie Morgen,"* it hissed. *"You are almost mine."*

She shrank from the words. "No," she whispered. "You're not real!"

The burgermeister's face was the personification of the thunder. "Come now," he ordered Gerda.

The baroness folded her arms. The rain started again, changing from a few drops to great driving sheets within seconds. "You are a beast, Adolph," she accused. "You will go to hell for the things you do."

He ignored her, yanking his wife to her feet.

A bolt of lightning overhead lent an eerie aspect to his sharp features. He looked maniacal, possessed. Delanie's heart beat faster. Who was this horrible man?

With the dog behind her, she crawled carefully forward. The wind blew hard in her face, like invisible hands pushing her back. Even the vines looked black now, shadows of the sinuous Visitor. "My brother is dead!" the image had hissed.

She forced herself to keep moving. The burgermeister stood between the two women.

"Let her go!" the baroness cried. But Adolph merely slapped her hands away.

Gerda appeared to be in a zombie-like trance. Even the forked lightning didn't rouse her. She watched unaffected as her husband seized the baroness's wrists.

"Foolish woman," he shouted. "Do you know who I am? You dare to defy me?"

He laughed, and his laughter was amplified by the thunder. Delanie flinched but refused to stop. Something was going to happen. She could feel it.

The baroness wrenched free of his grasp and reached for Gerda. So did Adolph. The rain blurred Delanie's vision. A vine wrapped itself around her throat. She choked and stopped to pry it loose.

But all it did was tighten. The snake's voice in her head whispered, *"See to your own predicament, Delanie."*

Her fingers clawed desperately at the vine. She was facing the bridge, hidden, but even struggling she could see that Gerda was facing her. Her zombie eyes looked up from under her hair.

"Gerda, help me," the baroness screamed.

Gerda didn't move. Gasping for air, Delanie worked her wet fingers under the vine and tore it free. She scrambled to her feet, tossing the vine aside. She'd imagined the voice. She wasn't imagining the struggle taking place on the bridge.

Delanie moved out of the tangled underbrush. The wind drove rain and wet leaves into her eyes. A fork of lightning shot through the sky down to the bank of the stream. On its heels came the thunder. The ground shook. The baroness slipped past Adolph and reached for Gerda. But the burgermeister was faster. He grabbed his wife's arm and dragged her aside.

"Let her go," the baroness shouted.

Delanie saw his teeth pull back. With his free hand, he hit his wife across the cheek, then threw back his head and laughed.

Again the lightning flashed, and this time Gerda did move. Snarling, she threw off his hand.

Delanie shoved back her hair. She couldn't see. What was Gerda doing?

The rain swirled around Delanie's head. Beside her, the dog growled. She squinted through the downpour, shocked to suddenly see the burgermeister tumbling from the bridge. He screamed Gerda's name as he fell, then the baroness's.

"Alicia, help!" he cried. He hit the water hard, while Gerda looked on, her eyes dull and listless once more.

Delanie's first thought was to run into the water, to see if she could save him. Her second was a more vindictive desire to let him drown.

"Gerda!" The baroness shouted in alarm, but she got no response. She knelt on the wall. "Adolph, are you there? Can you hear me?"

Delanie ran as far as the bank. The burgermeister lay facedown in the water, unmoving. He must have hit his head.

The wind pushed at her, harder than ever. "Go back," it seemed to urge.

The baroness ran from the bridge. She screamed for help, but no one at her castle would hear her above the storm. All Gerda did was stand and stare.

Let him die, a voice in Delanie's head commanded. The rain and hair in her eyes blinded her. She saw the fiery Visitor, heard the snap of his long tail. *"You are almost mine!"*

She pressed her hands to her ears. The wind poured over her.

To her left, the baroness kicked off her shoes and waded in. The wind tore at her clothes and hair. "Adolph!" she called again. She lost her balance but caught it with the help of a boulder. Her uncertain eyes suddenly found Delanie. The skies darkened. The thrash of the rain increased. "Will you help, *fräulein?*"

"No!" A hand shot out to grab Delanie's coat. Gerda's white face appeared through the murk. "Please do not!"

Delanie hesitated. The baroness waded in deeper. Gerda's grip tightened. She pulled on Delanie's arm. "Let him die," she said angrily. Thunder underscored her words.

"Go to hell," Delanie had shouted to the burgermeister last night. Then the Visitor had appeared in the flames.

"I'm a doctor," she said to Gerda, shaking free of the woman's hand. "I'm sorry. I can't let him die."

She felt Gerda clutching at her raincoat. A bolt of lightning almost struck the bridge.

"He's caught," the baroness shouted.

"She cannot do it alone," Gerda hissed in Delanie's ear. "And she will not sacrifice herself for him. Turn away!"

No, Delanie told herself. The six temptations. The professor. Maybe this was connected to the Story somehow.

But it couldn't be. It was too dangerous.

A curtain of rain pelted her now. All she could see was the gray water, and the baroness reaching for Adolph Schiller's wrist. Thunder crashed directly above them. The stream looked lethal.

She closed her eyes. "I should let him die. But I'll do it for you, professor." She forced her feet to carry her out into the water. The mud sucked at her ankles.

The baroness was still tugging on Adolph's wrist. "He is stuck," she shouted. "I think perhaps he is dead."

Delanie struggled on. How could this possibly be a test?

The baroness was panting with exertion when Delanie reached her. "It is too late. His face is blue."

Delanie could hardly see the man. The current dragged her backward. She peered through the wall of rain. No, he wasn't breathing.

"What now?" the baroness gasped.

Delanie touched Adolph's neck, then quickly recoiled. *Evil!* "Take his other arm," she shouted. "We'll drag him out."

It took forever, but they managed. Delanie collapsed on the shore beside him. Gerda did nothing, just sat there with her knees drawn up, a blur behind the slanting rain.

The baroness shoved her sopping brown hair from her eyes. "I'll—find Ingrid Hoffman," she said, fighting for breath. "She is a doctor."

So am I, Delanie thought, but didn't have the strength to explain that. She hauled herself up, exhausted. Her eyes landed on the burgermeister, his white face illuminated by a streak of lightning. "Die," she whispered, then immediately retracted the word. "No, don't die."

She grabbed his head, fixing it in position. She had to clear the tracheal tube.

Delanie felt Gerda's eyes on her, heard the thunder and the wind in her ears. She released a heavy breath, her numb fingers working automatically. *Evil,* her mind told her again and again. *Cold. No soul.*

She applied the necessary pressure to his chest and watched in stony silence as he began to choke up the deadly water.

"It wasn't enough," Roland Popporov muttered as he descended to the old tunnels. "Not enough and improperly handled."

Ahead of him in the darkness, he saw the professor's smiling face.

"Very nice try, Herr Popporov," he applauded. "Of course, I knew she would pass."

"She almost didn't," Roland said in a testy tone. He had begun to hate these visits. Even behind bars, the professor unsettled him. "I think she knew it was a temptation. I watched, you see. There was interference also, and that did not help our cause." He sighed. "As I said, a poorly conceived plan. My counterpart is not as meticulous as I am."

The professor raised his head, adjusting his hat so that he looked out from under the brim. "You've offered your I-told-you-so's to The Visitor, I assume."

Roland shrugged. "I'm not a fool, professor. I make suggestions. Sometimes my master listens, sometimes he doesn't. In any case, your chosen two will never pass the final temptation, however many they may survive up to that point. Perhaps you should consider making peace with your creator.''

The professor's smile retained its air of confidence. ''Don't you worry, Herr Popporov,'' he said. ''I made my peace long ago.'' From his pocket, he produced a pack of worn playing cards. ''Care for a game of gin rummy?''

''You are most erratic,'' Roland said. ''I don't trust you.''

With great deliberation, the Professor shuffled the cards. ''That's very wise of you, Herr Popporov.'' The light in his eyes caused Roland to step back a pace. His smile widened. ''Very wise of you indeed.''

Chapter Eleven

The baroness's castle was in a minor state of pandemonium when Rondel arrived.

"Dead as a door knocker for a minute," Harry said under his breath as he dragged him through the cellar.

Rondel had emerged from the tunnel into the decaying vaults of the castle. Another ten minutes of blind searching had brought him to the wine cellar where Harry was selecting the evening's wine—and talking to someone, Rondel thought at first. But Harry said, no, he'd just been muttering to himself, and what was Rondel doing down here, anyway?

Rondel would have explained except that Harry had cut him off. "Never mind, old boy. I bet you haven't heard about Adolph, have you? Delanie and Alicia fished him out of the stream an hour ago."

They'd gone upstairs to find the club members milling about like curious monks.

"She should have let him die," one of them said.

"But that's murder," another pointed out.

"It would be his just deserts," the baroness remarked. "I don't know what I was thinking when I went in after him." She came over, rubbing her wrist and shaking back her damp hair. "How did you get here, Rondel?"

Harry grinned. "I ran across him in the cellar."

"What?"

"I got lost in the tunnels," Rondel told her. He looked at the staircase. "Where's Delanie? Is she all right?"

"Perfectly. She is with Ingrid Hoffman—excuse me, Dr. Hoffman. The woman is most picky on that point." With a frown, the baroness indicated the bruises on her wrist. "He is a brute, that man. No wonder Gerda pushed him in."

"Gerda pushed him?" Rondel asked in surprise.

"Well, it looked that way to me, but then it was raining very hard and I was falling backward at the time." She shrugged and pulled down her sleeve. "Why didn't you tell me that Delanie was a doctor?" She knit her brow. "Or did you tell me, and I forgot? Oh well, it's not important, I suppose. We pulled him out. It is done. I only wish that Gerda would stop staring at me like that. She has the expression of a zombie, don't you think?"

Rondel followed her gaze to the corner of the salon where Gerda sat in one of the baroness's dresses, head slightly bent, looking up at them through cold, unblinking eyes.

"Maybe she's in shock," Harry suggested.

"Delanie thought she might be, but Dr. Hoffman says it is some form of psychosis, and what would Delanie know of such disorders, seeing as she has never worked at a facility as prestigious as the Brulen Institute. If you wish to find her, Rondel, she is arguing with the doctor on the second floor, fourth room on the right."

With a final glance at Gerda, Rondel left. He could feel her lifeless eyes trailing him to the door.

"I do not practice simple medicine," Ingrid was saying flatly when Rondel located them in the upstairs sitting room. "You revived him, he is your patient."

"He's your friend, not mine," Delanie retorted.

Her hair was damp and rumpled, her green eyes angry in the pale light. Rondel smiled a little, leaning in the doorway to watch.

"You have the compassion of a snake," Ingrid charged. "What kind of a doctor are you?"

"A tired one."

Ingrid pursed her lips. "All right," she said finally. "I will attend to him, but if anything happens, it will be on your conscience."

"Nothing's going to happen. The man has the constitution of an ox."

"A fine attitude, I must say," Ingrid remarked with a bitter laugh. "It is fortunate, *fräulein*, that you do not belong to the club. You would have no chance at all of winning the Game."

Delanie gave her a sharp look. Rondel straightened from the door frame. Ingrid's laughter grew mocking, heightened by the thunder beyond the castle walls.

"Pretty like an angel, John Kessler called you. But I see you for what you are, Delanie Morgen." Thrusting her stethoscope down on the table, she clamped an unrelenting hand onto Delanie's arm. "You have no feelings. You say you care about the professor, but do you really? No. Women like you care only about themselves. I've met your type before, many times. But I console myself with the knowledge that one day you will actually be forced to confront The Visitor." Her teeth flashed in the grim light. "We play his Game at the club for amusement. But you, *fräulein*, one day I think you will play it for real."

"VINDICTIVE," Delanie repeated to Rondel thirty minutes later at the cottage. "Hostile. Consumed." She frowned. "I'm not sure what she's consumed with, but it's something unpleasant. And it was all so clear, so immediate, as soon as she touched me."

"Shh," Rondel cautioned, handing her a cup of coffee. "Mahira."

The old witch hobbled across the floor in her coarse gray robes and rope belt. "My hearing is better than you think, Rondel," she snapped. She focused her attention on Delanie. "What was clear and immediate?" She held up a warning finger. "And do not lie to me. You get feelings from people, I know this already."

Delanie wrapped her hands around the warm mug. The baroness's maid had dried her clothes for her, but she still felt chilled, right down into her bones.

"Tell her," Rondel advised from behind her chair.

Delanie took a deep breath. "Ingrid Hoffman," she answered.

"What about her?"

"I felt...vindictiveness in her. And something more cloistered. An obsession." She clenched her fist in frustration. "The right word's there, but it's elusive. I can't quite see it. Maybe it's jealousy."

Mahira's hooded eyes bored into hers. "You saved Adolph Schiller's life today. Why?"

Delanie's head came up. "How did you..." At Rondel's gentle nudge, she broke off. An eerie feeling fluttered in her chest, but she overcame it and said, "Because I had to."

"You did not want to save his life?"

"No."

"Why did you do it?" Mahira repeated, and this time Delanie's temper flared.

"Because he's a human being, Mahira. And I am a doctor."

"You did not think about the temptations, that this might be one of them?"

"Yes, that occurred to me."

"But?"

"It seemed too farfetched, impossible to arrange."

"Too many variable factors," Rondel supplemented.

Mahira's fist hit the table. "Nothing is variable where The Visitor is concerned. Do you think you are dealing with a child?"

"I don't think we're dealing with the devil," Delanie said, but she knew her voice lacked conviction. Well, whose voice wouldn't after what she and Rondel had seen in the fire last night?

Delanie trembled under the weight of Mahira's glare. "The Visitor is real," the old witch maintained. "Believe that or you will die."

"But Aric Bellal's family..."

"Forget this man, or if you cannot, then think of him as a demon with a powerful demon family."

" 'My brother is dead.' " Delanie repeated the words the fire-Visitor had uttered. She turned to Rondel. "It did say that."

He stared at Mahira, who stared back. "You're not going to tell us any more, are you?" he asked.

"Read the Story," she said. "All you are permitted to know is there. 'And if before Walpurgis ends, and May Day dawns, the angel sends the chosen two...' "

"Walpurgis?" Delanie interrupted.

"May Day Eve," Rondel told her.

"You mean there's an end to this nightmare? A time limit?"

"You did not know this?" Standing, Mahira picked up Delanie's raincoat and thrust it at her. "Go to the watch-tower and read the Story through. Both of you. The professor will have it written there."

Delanie slid her arms into the sleeves. "Walpurgis," she said again. "That's only a few days from now." She dipped into the pockets, wondering where she'd put her gloves. Then she spied them on the table. "I didn't know there was..." She choked off the sentence, snatching her hand back out of her coat and balling it at her throat.

"What?" Rondel asked, looking around.

"In my pocket," she whispered.

She saw him glance at Mahira, whose expression gave nothing away. Reaching in, he extracted the hairy root her fingers had accidentally found.

"The mandragora," Mahira said dispassionately. "You have passed the third temptation."

"I'LL GO BACK to the cottage and talk to her alone," Rondel said as they entered the watchtower. "Maybe she'll tell me something." His eyes roamed the shadowy gray walls of the entryway. "Will you be all right here?"

"Of course," Delanie lied. She nodded toward the hearth. "I'll start a fi... No, I won't. I'll take an electric heater up to the lab and look for the Story. The professor did say he had a copy.''

Rondel's eyes studied her face. His features were sensual in the weak glow from the car's headlights. Delanie wanted to touch his cheeks, his eyes, his mouth, just to feel the warm texture of his skin. Maybe if she tried very hard, held herself very still, she would be able to reach inside his mind.

A faint smile hovered on his mouth. "Two witches," he said obscurely. Then he pressed his thumb to her lower lip, bent his head and kissed her. "I'll be back in an hour," he promised, and was gone into the rain before Delanie could recover her composure and stop him.

She stood for a moment, bemused, then shook the odd sensation aside and headed up the stairs for the lab.

"Use a rubber hose to pull the panel lever," the professor had said, so she did, and soon there were lights. Well, one or two, anyway. She couldn't locate the main switch.

Turning on the heat, she shed her raincoat. Shuddering, she recalled the root she'd found in her pocket. She pushed the memory aside and started going through the professor's metal boxes.

It took her five minutes to discover the right box, and five more to read and reread the Story.

The flickering lights didn't help. Neither did the storm.

"It's like living in a Boris Karloff horror movie," Delanie reflected. She lifted uneasy eyes to the high windows. Jagged forks of lightning streaked through the night sky. Could the professor see them?

"Oh, please, God," she whispered. "Let him still be alive. I do care, no matter what Ingrid Hoffman thinks."

Delanie's fingers tightened on the papers she held. Dr. Hoffman, now there was a puzzling woman. "Vindictive," she mused out loud. "Consumed. But by what?"

Nothing came to her. Thunder rattled the professor's test tubes and with a sigh Delanie returned her attention to the Story.

"'The angel only sees the horns of Lucifer, cast out, reborn to rule the Underworld of fire and brimstone.'" She paused. "Rondel and I saw horns." She shook her head.

"'Six demons called,'" she read, "'and four sent forth. But two remain in Satan's lair, this earthly world of wind and air, of woods and mountain caves and lore and somber superstition. More than myth begins to unfold here. Walpurgis breaks, the night of fear.'"

Her fingers shook. Yes, fear. What was that ungodly thing they'd seen in the fire? "My brother is dead," it had said. "Think of Aric Bellal as a demon," Mahira had told them. They wouldn't survive the Game any other way.

Delanie's stomach twisted itself into knots. "I hate this Game," she whispered to the rain.

Restlessly, she began to pace. The professor's scarf sat on the table. She wrapped it around her neck, rubbing her arms as much to ward off her fear as to fight the cold.

"Rondel, where are you?" she said through her teeth. She was about to head for the phone when she she spied the headlights that streaked wetly over the lab windows.

"Thank God." She ran down the stairs and pulled open the door. "Did Mahira say anything...?" She choked back a startled scream when a man's ghostly pale face emerged from the shadows.

"Good evening, *fräulein*," the caller said, lurching forward before she could slam the door. "I came to thank you for saving my life."

Adolph Schiller!

Delanie jumped back, her eyes searching automatically for an escape. But despite his pallor and unsteady gait, Schiller was very fast. His hand shot out to grab her wrist and haul her up against his sinewy body.

"Where are you going?" he demanded. His breath reeked of bourbon. Ingrid Hoffman must be some great doctor, Delanie thought with fleeting irony. She twisted ineffectually on her wrist.

"Let me go," she cried above the lash of rain and wind that blew through the door. "You shouldn't be walking around in your condition." She had to steel herself at the expression of malice that invaded his features.

"I owe my life to you," he snarled, pushing her back as he advanced. "You and that she-beast who has time for all men except me. Well, I will owe nothing to a woman." He shook Delanie roughly. "Do you understand? Nothing!"

Pain shot along her arm. She set her teeth to keep from crying out. "Go to hell, Herr Schiller," she retorted. She might as well be bold. He was going to hit her anyway.

He shook her again, hard. His skin had an unearthly white sheen to it, his eyes looked to be lit from inside his skull.

Delanie's heart rate tripled. Her throat muscles were frozen. But there was a chance. She gave her arm a fierce jerk, then brought her knee up hard between his legs. She hit something, she knew she did, but it didn't feel human.

The wind blasted through the watchtower, tearing at his hair, making it stick up. His grip strengthened. "Foolish woman," he shouted. "Do you think me defenseless against a puny thing like you?" He shoved her backward, as far as the stairs. "I will show you who is defenseless, *fräulein.*"

Her fingers clawed at his face and hands. He seemed not to notice. It was as if he were impervious to pain, even to the kicks she landed on his shins.

Drunk to the point of senselessness, or not human? She wasn't sure which.

"God will damn you for this," she managed to choke out. He faltered, and suddenly something flashed through Delanie's mind. Fear, a tremendous surge of fear. His fingers crawled up her neck. She held herself very still. This made no sense. What was he afraid of?

God!

It came to her on a blast of icy wind. The burgermeister was terrified of God.

It was the last thing she remembered thinking. The fear in him exploded. He tightened his grip. His fist came down like a club on her cheek.

She heard the blow before she felt it, a whip cracked across stone, and then a searing shaft of pain. It shot up one side of her face and down the other.

An alarm sounded in her brain. Don't fall! But he'd shoved her again and the hall was spinning, and he was laughing like a madman, his hair sticking straight up, his eyes tinged red by the watchtower lights and the flash of the storm behind him.

"First you," he growled. "And then I will deal with the other."

The other. Who else had said the other to her?

Delanie's head hit the stone floor. The burgermeister's laughter rose to a roar, then slowly began to die out. Blackness invaded her mind. Just ahead of it swam Roland Popporov, chortling as he held up a lighted match. "Oh, that the other should come up with such a plan."

But he spoke of a different "other," she realized through the deepening shadows in her mind. The other demon. Could Popporov's "other" be Adolph Schiller?

The question dissolved. The breath left her body. Darkness rushed in, and at the very last second, a double beam of light splitting it. Tunnel to heaven, maybe?

Her eyes fell closed. No more lights. No more burgermeister. Thank God, no more pain.

"WAKE UP, Delanie," a far-off voice commanded. "It is time we talked, you and I."

Delanie awoke with a start to a welter of shadows, tinged red by an unseen fire. Her fingers curled on the floor. Not stone, she realized, dirt, packed hard from use.

"Who are you?" she whispered. "Where am I?"

The red tinge spread. Walls appeared, earthen walls. In a cave, a tunnel, what? She climbed shakily to her feet. "What is this place?"

"So many questions," the voice chided.

Delanie went rigid. The snake's voice! The vision in the fire! She looked around in desperation. There was no fire visible now. "Who are you?"

"Think, child," Mahira said. But it hadn't been her speaking before.

Delanie backed away from the seeping red glow. "I can't think," she said with a tremor. "I don't understand."

"That," Mahira accused, "is your problem."

The other voice broke in. "Come to me, Delanie."

A claw appeared through the black mist ahead. She forced her eyes away from it, down to the ground. "A dream," she told herself. "It's a dream."

She felt the claw stroke her cheek. "So close," the snake's voice murmured. "You passed the third temptation, yes, but how would your angel feel about your reasons? Come. Come to me now, and I will set the angel free. You have the promise of The Visitor."

"Which is no promise at all," a third voice supplied.

Delanie's head came swiftly up. "Professor!"

The red glow began to shift. It made her dizzy to look, and she continued to back away from it. Something evil in the red.

"Professor?" she called, taking a tentative look at her surroundings. This didn't feel like a cave. It was too hot, too dense.

"You cheat, professor," the Visitor accused. "You cannot come here."

"*I* cheat?" The professor chuckled. "Pity your poor demon, Visitor, for what he doesn't know of your nature."

Delanie cringed as The Visitor's tail snapped. She saw the tail, the claws and the horns, but no sinuous limbs. It seemed those other things were embedded within the red glow. The illusion lent an aspect of enormity to the creature.

Huge yellow eyes opened above her.

"Go away, professor," the Visitor whispered.

A great rush of hot air poured over Delanie. Sulphurous, but with an underlying sweetness. Flies to honey, she thought, then shuddered and retreated as far as the walls would permit.

"Let her go," the professor warned.

He sounded huge now himself.

Red and gold. Two colors filled the cave.

"Tunnel," Mahira corrected. "Use your senses, girl."

"Leave here, Mahira," The Visitor ordered.

The wind roared up, catching Delanie's hair, whipping it across her face. The ground shook.

"Shut it out, Delanie," the professor told her.

"Cheat," The Visitor hissed. "So like your sister when she killed my brother Aric."

"She played the Game. He cheated. He lost."

The Visitor's snarl made Delanie's blood turn to ice. "You are not Anna, professor. You are a pathetic reflection of her wisdom and guile. You are as your doomed brother was. You have chosen poorly. You terrify my demon number five, but you do not terrify me."

"Shall I tell you about your demon number five?" the professor challenged. "Or shall we talk about number six, instead?"

The ground rose up as if something moved beneath it. The sudden swell threw Delanie against the wall, almost into the red mist. She pulled away at the last second, lost her balance and fell to her knees.

"Enough!" The Visitor roared. "You're nothing, professor, an ant for me to crush."

"What about your sixth demon, Visitor?"

"I said enough."

The hot claw slid along Delanie's spine. She scrambled away from it, toward the twin pools of golden light that appeared before her.

The ground trembled. Her body trembled. The wind still tore at her hair.

She felt a hand on her face, turning her head. A gentle touch. She sensed love, tenderness. Rondel?

The golden light bathed her eyelids. Heat and cold mingled.

"Three temptations," she heard the Visitor predict. Fiery breath grazed her cheeks. The pain began to creep back in. The claw touched her neck, right over the pulse. "Two more to face, and then the Game."

But this is the Game, Delanie wanted to protest.

"A Game within a Game," the professor said directly into her head.

She opened her eyes to the yellow eyes far up on the roof of the tunnel.

''For the death of my brother, Aric Bellal, you will die,''
The Visitor promised. ''The pure see no treachery. The
treacherous cannot pass my tests. You are trapped, Delanie
Morgen. You will not live to see Walpurgis end.''

Chapter Twelve

Rondel recognized the burgermeister's car as soon as he saw it in the courtyard outside the watchtower.

Swearing, he slammed on the brakes and jumped out. The front door was open. A shadow moved inside. It made a spasmodic motion, then vanished.

Shoving the hair from his forehead, Rondel ran for the porch. He could see a silhouette in his mind. It was laughing. The burgermeister!

He caught the edge of the door for balance and ran inside. Adolph Schiller was crouched at the base of the stairs. He looked up at Rondel's rushed entry. One hand rested on the side of Delanie's neck.

"Delanie!" A growl formed in Rondel's throat. "What have you done to her!" he shouted at the startled-looking man.

The burgermeister didn't answer. His eyes located the door. Clambering to his feet, he charged toward it. Rondel would have called his reaction fearful, except he knew Adolph wasn't afraid of anyone, or so he claimed.

He flung a wild arm out to knock Rondel away. Rondel caught it and twisted him around.

"What did you do?" he demanded.

The burgermeister cried out. "Nothing! She fell and hit her head."

"Liar." Rondel jerked his arm up higher. He was tempted to break it.

Gurgling in pain, Adolph dropped to his knees. "Don't," he begged.

"Why not? You deserve more than a broken arm."

Delanie moaned behind him. He glanced back. Alive, he thought with tremendous relief. He faltered, slackening his grip. He should have checked on her first.

"Revenge. Pain. Make him pay."

Words sliced through Rondel's head; the snake's voice! Adolph squirmed and almost broke away. Rondel caught him.

The wind blasted rain and leaves into his face. "She saved your life," he said to the flailing burgermeister.

"Make him hurt... End his life." The voice seemed a part of the wind. It swept into the watchtower, descending on Rondel like a cloud.

He must have loosened his grip again. Adolph's elbow plunged hard into his stomach. Rondel let out a sharp cry of pain, then gnashed his teeth and thrust the burgermeister up against the wall.

"Bastard," he snarled.

"Fiend," the snake's voice added. *"Monster, brute. He is mine already. Give his worthless soul to me, Rondel, and accept Gerda's gratitude. For Gerda, for the baroness, for Delanie, you do all of these women a favor if you kill him."*

Adolph's eyes were glazed, his face a sickly shade of white. Rondel smelled stale bourbon on his breath. Yes, he should be dead.

A strange sensation passed through him then. He felt lifted out of his body somehow, a watcher high above himself, looking down.

"Let your temper go," the voice entreated. *"One twist of his neck and it is done."*

Rondel looked sideways. He was floating on the ceiling, and beside him hung a circle of golden light. He needed to reach that light. His eyes went down to the sight of his own hands pinning Adolph to the wall. Delanie stirred. Her eyelids fluttered.

"What...?" she began, then sat up with a startled gasp.

She seemed disoriented. He wanted to go to her. Forget Adolph.

The wind pierced him. Suddenly, the golden light was everywhere. He felt his mind return to his body.

"No, do it," the silky voice persuaded. *"Send him to me."*

But Rondel had lost interest. His muscles relaxed. "Scum," he spat in the burgermeister's face. "Get out."

He thrust the man aside and turned to Delanie.

"Very good," someone congratulated, but it wasn't the snake's voice this time. *"Another loss for you, Visitor."*

"Rondel, what's going on?" Delanie asked. "Why am I on the floor?"

He fell to his knees beside her. He saw Adolph rushing out the door. It didn't matter. "Are you all right?"

"Yes. No, wait!" She clutched his arm, her eyes going wide. "I had a dream. I was in a tunnel, and the professor was there." She peered past his shoulder. "The burgermeister! I remember now. He hit me."

"I can see that." Lightly Rondel brushed her cheek. Anger almost overwhelmed him. He snatched his head around. "The voice was right. I should have killed him."

Delanie pulled on his jacket. "Voice?"

He nodded, then forced back his anger and turned her head gently so he could see the bruise on her cheekbone. "I thought someone was talking to me."

She winced as he touched a sore spot. "Rondel, there's no one here."

"I had tea with Mahira," he mused. "Herbs, potions." Then he dismissed the whole thing. "It doesn't matter. You're alive, that's all I care about."

She smiled, and he absorbed the delicacy of her features in that moment. "Alive," he whispered, and hungrily covered her mouth with his.

DELANIE DIDN'T remember much about that night, beyond the fact that Rondel carried her upstairs, set her on the bed and undressed her as carefully as he might a doll.

The storm raged all night. She dreamed of horned Visitors and Adolph Schiller running like a scared jackrabbit from Rondel's outstretched hands.

"I should kill you!" Rondel shouted after him.

Mahira's face appeared to her. "You see? I knew you would endanger my Rondel's life. For what is this if not a temptation?"

It felt like a temptation. Delanie kicked at the blankets. Thunder shook the old stone walls. Something wet touched her sore cheek.

"Relax, Delanie," Rondel said. "It's only me."

Only him, in jeans and no shirt. No bulging muscles, only smooth tanned skin and a smattering of chest hair. Very Latin. Sexy. Why couldn't this nightmare Game stop for one night?

She awoke to gray skies, and a clock that read four-thirty. On her stomach, she propped herself up and pushed the hair from her eyes. Four-thirty p.m.? "It can't be," she whispered.

"Yes, it can," Rondel told her when she staggered downstairs in her robe. "Don't feel bad, Delanie. I only woke up half an hour ago myself."

He sat at the table in black sweats, a cup of coffee in hand. His feet were bare, his hair rumpled. He poured a second cup for her and grimaced.

"A man from Interpol called."

She regarded him expectantly. "And?"

"They have no information on Aric Bellal."

"What?" Delanie was stunned. "How is that possible? What about Anna Nagel?"

"Nothing."

"But that's ridiculous. There must be something somewhere."

Rondel leaned forward. "Not necessarily. The Visitor could have gotten into the Interpol computer. You said Aric Bellal's family was extremely powerful."

"Well, yes, but... Nothing?" Carefully, she fingered her injured cheek. It felt better. "This is very strange, Rondel." She paused. "Why are you staring at me?"

A faint smile played on his lips. "You're beautiful, Delanie."

"Thank you. But I see more than 'beautiful' in your eyes. What's wrong?"

"What isn't?" He studied her, then relented and reached down on to the chair beside him.

When he brought his hand up, she drew instinctively back. "The mandragora!"

He set it on the table between them. "It seems we passed the fourth temptation."

Delanie stared at the ugly, hairy root. A shiver started deep inside her. "Why don't I feel relieved?"

"IT'S A GOOD IDEA," Rondel insisted, pulling Delanie from the car. "It's the only idea. Springfest in Klausberg is tradition. Anyway, we can't just sit around waiting for another temptation."

"We could sneak into the castle," she suggested, buttoning her black jacket.

"Not before dark, we couldn't."

"What about the tunnels into the cellar? You got in that way yesterday."

"After an hour of blind stumbling. Dex's dog untangled himself before I did." Rondel set a patient hand over her mouth, forestalling her protest. "When it gets dark, Delanie. Until then, let's have some beer and sausages in the music hall. I'm hungry."

The hall was typically Bavarian, with long wooden tables and benches, oompah music and waiters dressed in old German costumes. Delanie seemed surprised by the loudness of the noise and laughter.

"The villagers always seem so somber to me. Why the change?"

Rondel collected a pitcher of beer and two steins from one of the stalls. "It's a facade, Delanie. They're still scared. Well, superstitious anyway."

"Of the Visitor?"

"A lot of people here believe in the Story."

"And fear Mahira?"

He shrugged. "She leads the Sisterhood. She looks and acts like a witch. What else are they going to think? Here's a table."

She slid onto a bench by the wall, well removed from the stage and the folk dancers performing on it. With her head she indicated the door. "Company," she said. "John Kessler and the baroness."

Rondel didn't bother to look. "No Harry or Ingrid?"

"Not that I can see." Delanie raised her voice. "Good evening, Herr Kessler, baroness."

"Alicia, please," the baroness murmured. She wore a blue silk dress and a tiny pout on her lips. "You haven't seen Harry, have you? He's disappeared again."

"Probably searching for a crooked painter," Rondel said into his beer stein.

"A what?" Kessler asked.

"Nothing. Would you like to join us?"

Alicia sat with a movement that conveyed both irritation and elegance. A frown marred her features. "I should marry my rich count, I think. What happened to your cheek, *fräulein?*"

Delanie's smile was deceptively serene. "The burgermeister."

"Of course." Alicia revealed a bruise directly under the collar of her dress, between neck and shoulder. "He is a monster." She shuddered. "Never mind, he has been placid enough today."

"Yes," Kessler said with a humorous look in Rondel's direction. "So placid, in fact, that we thought someone might have hit him back for a change."

Rondel merely sipped his beer.

The baroness managed a smile. "Enough of this. I will make one more search for Harry, then I must return to the castle and prepare for the night of Robes and Riddles. This is an intriguing little ritual we have where we all wear hoods and skull masks and walk around like corpses trying to confound each other with clever verbal stratagems."

Delanie rested her chin in her hand. "You mean it's a guessing game?" she asked. "A mystery?"

"Very much," the baroness said. "A bit darker than any game of mystery you would play, but the idea is the same. One of us becomes the symbolic Visitor. The choice is made by lot. Whoever determines the identity of this person first, or solves the most significant riddles, is declared the winner."

"Sounds fascinating."

"Oh, it is, *fräulein*," Kessler assured.

Rondel didn't like the way the hypnotist's eyes seemed to be stripping off Delanie's jacket and blouse, but then again, what right did he have to object? He drank his beer and forced himself not to snarl.

The baroness tapped Kessler's hand. "Tell them about the other thing," she urged. "You know, what Roland did last night. John hypnotized many of us," she explained briefly. "He instructed us to reveal our deepest fears. For example, mine is a fear of domination. I do not like men who think they can control me. Dr. Hoffman's was a fear of falling from high places."

Delanie stared at the stage. "Adolph Schiller fears God," she murmured.

Rondel frowned but it was John Kessler who laughed and said, "I beg your pardon, *fräulein?*"

She pressed her lips together. "Nothing. I'm sorry. Please, go on."

The Baroness blinked. "Where was I? Oh, yes. Well, Gerda said she feared fire, but of course we know that is a lie, so perhaps the hypnosis did not work on her." Kessler seemed mildly offended, but she ignored him. "Then it was Roland Popporov's turn," she said, linking her fingers. "Now can you guess what his deepest fear was?"

"The Visitor?" Delanie suggested.

"No. The professor."

Rondel glanced at Delanie. "It is true," the baroness maintained. "He is most afraid of Professor Gerald Nagel. And as the professor has disappeared and you two are concerned with finding him, I thought you would be interested to know this."

"Are you sure Popporov was under?" Rondel asked, not quite trusting the information. Or maybe it was Kessler he didn't trust. If that man looked at Delanie's breasts one more time, Rondel was going to haul off and hit him.

Kessler stared evenly from beneath his black widow's peak. "He was most definitely under."

"And yet I have to ask myself," the baroness said with a bewildered shake of her head, "why on earth would Roland fear the professor? I find this most intriguing."

"It is," Delanie agreed. "But the other question is even more intriguing." She sent Rondel a significant look. "Why would Roland Popporov let himself be hypnotized in the first place?"

DARKNESS DESCENDED like an evil black wing over Klausberg. The night of Robes and Riddles had commenced. All of the club members were present, suitably masked and hooded—anonymous shuffling monks, playing a frivolous game. If only they knew the truth.

Roland Popporov was sweating as he crept down to the cellar for his meeting with The Visitor.

"Come in," The Visitor invited when he arrived.

Roland hid his annoyance. What was the other demon doing here, and looking so smug about?

"Sit, Roland," The Visitor said. His eyes were cold. He was very angry. Roland's counterpart merely smirked.

The Visitor approached like a stalking tiger. "Afraid of the professor?" he challenged, and Roland cringed.

"I'm sorry," he said. "I didn't mean to let myself be hypnotized. I didn't think it could happen."

The other chuckled nastily. Roland glared, then lifted his eyes to The Visitor's stony face. "It won't happen again," he promised.

"It had better not." A cold finger slid under Roland's chin, bringing his head up farther. "You will stay with the professor tonight, I think. Number six will remain with me."

"But . . ."

"You must face your fear, Roland," the other chided. "Although, personally, I would think it wiser to fear The Visitor than the angel."

"You are a sniveling coward," Roland charged. "What have you done in all of this?"

"My part," the other answered with a self-satisfied look at The Visitor's implacable profile. "Isn't that right?"

"We have both done our parts," The Visitor agreed. A sly smile formed on his lips. "Only you, Roland, are in danger of failure at this moment."

Treacherous devil, Roland charged, then quickly buried the thought. The Visitor could read any mind.

The other's smile widened. "Quaking little demon. No wonder the professor frightens you."

"Enough," said the Visitor. "Go to him, Roland. Number six and I will attend to matters upstairs."

What 'matters'? Roland wondered as he started off into the tunnels. But he knew better than to ask. Four of The Visitor's demons were already dead. He had no desire to become the fifth.

"THE BARONESS INVITED us for dinner tomorrow night," Delanie reminded Rondel as he worked at opening one of the locked castle windows. The kitchen, she suspected, but couldn't be sure. "Why don't we just wait until then to sneak around the castle, and search the tunnels tonight, instead?"

"Because the tunnels are a labyrinth, and I want to know what this Robes and Riddles game is all about."

"It's about identifying The Visitor," Delanie said, shifting her weight from foot to foot in an effort to keep warm.

Rondel sent her an expressive look over his shoulder. "Precisely."

"Symbolic, Rondel, not real."

He returned to his chore. "Did it ever occur to you that either Alicia or Kessler could have been setting us up by telling us about Popporov?"

"Maybe, but we're not likely to learn much by breaking in. Everyone will be wearing robes and masks, remember?"

He grinned back at her. "A perfect disguise, don't you think?"

Delanie paced restlessly, letting her eyes roam the woods behind them. Something snapped in the darkness. Straightening, she tugged on Rondel's jacket. "Did you hear that?"

"No."

Another sound reached her, closer this time, a soft rustle of leaves.

Rondel's head came up. "That I heard. Do you see anything?"

Wiping her damp palms on the legs of her jeans, Delanie shook her head. "Are you almost finished?"

"Another minute."

Her chest constricted. "I know this is going to sound paranoid," she said, tapping her hands on her legs. "But I feel as though we're being..."

"Watched?" a man's smooth voice inserted.

Delanie backed nervously into Rondel's arm. "Who...?"

"It's just Harry," Rondel said in her ear. "Ignore him. He's probably been out treasure-hunting with Dex."

"Wrong, old man. I've been groping my way through the woods because Alicia's car broke down on the Klausberg Road." The man's eyes sparkled in the weak light from the castle. He couldn't have been more than thirty-five or so. He was also extremely handsome. "You must be Delanie," he said. "We haven't officially met. I'm Harry Bates, antique dealer."

She took the hand he offered, then tensed and waited for the words to come. Only one did. *Deceptive.*

"I say, are you trying to break in, Rondel?" Harry asked.

"No, I'm doing a security check. Of course I'm trying to break in."

The man grinned. "Well, there are easier ways, you know." He produced a set of keys from his jacket pocket. "Being as I'm late and Alicia has a fetish about tardiness, I think it might be a good idea for me to sneak in with you.

I'm not up to an argument tonight. That long walk really whacked me."

He didn't look particularly whacked, Delanie reflected as they started for the nearest door. And she'd sensed blatant deception in his nature. What did those two things together mean?

"This way." Harry indicated a small rear door. "You go your way, I'll go mine, and we never saw one another, right?"

"If you say so." Rondel pushed a reluctant Delanie across the threshold. "Where are we, by the way?" There was no answer. He glanced back. "Harry?"

"Gone," Delanie said, shivering lightly. "Like the Cheshire cat."

"Well, Harry has that quality." Rondel's hair brushed Delanie's cheek as he leaned over her. "I can't see anything. I think this is a hallway. Wait here. I'll try to figure out where it leads."

But Delanie's mind was still on Harry. How deceptive was he? He hadn't looked like a man who'd walked all the way through the woods from the Klausberg Road. He hadn't looked as if he'd walked any distance at all, except maybe down the stairs from his bedroom. That was it! He'd been too neat to have just groped his way through the forest.

"Rondel?" she whispered, reaching for him. "I think your friend Harry was lying." She frowned at the silence. "Rondel?"

Now, when had he wandered off?

She shrugged the question aside. It didn't matter. All she needed to do was follow the hall. She'd find him eventually.

Far ahead, through shadows as thick as the walls themselves, Delanie detected eerie strains of music. Devil worship, she thought grimly, but of course it wasn't. Only a harmless game of seek-out-the-symbolic-Visitor.

She closed her mind quickly to the memory that thought awakened. Yellow eyes opening above her and a persuasive snake's voice. *"Come to me, Delanie, and I will set the angel free. . . ."*

"No!" she said, pushing on her temples with her fingers.

The memory subsided. The shadows thinned. She could see other passageways now, and small sets of stairs with plank doors at the top.

"Rondel?" she tried softly, but received no response.

Her feet carried her cautiously forward. The night of Robes and Riddles. Skull masks. People in hoods. Which one of them was the Visitor, related to Aric Bellal? Would that person be a psychic as Aric had been? Probably.

"Oh, professor," she whispered. "I wish I understood this."

A door to her right opened, and a robed figure stepped out. Delanie started visibly.

"I'm sorry, *fräulein*," a man's muffled voice apologized. "I didn't mean to startle you."

She thought she almost recognized the voice, but the skull mask distorted it. "It's all right," she said. "I didn't expect to run into anyone."

"Nor did I." The figure pointed a gloved finger farther down the hall. "The Game is that way."

"I know."

Amusement entered his almost-familiar voice. "Ah, I see. You don't wish to play, merely to observe, unobserved."

She nodded. Who was this person? She felt she should know, and yet the voice wasn't quite a match for anyone she'd met. It lacked any trace of an accent to her ears.

"Are you American?" she asked with uncustomary candor.

"Not by birth. Tell me, *fräulein*, what is it that you don't understand?"

"Excuse me?"

"When I came out of the blue room, you were saying that you wished you understood something." He motioned behind him. "We can go inside and talk if you prefer."

"No, here's fine." Delanie shoved her hands into her pockets, studying the figure mistrustfully. "One thing I don't understand is why you haven't asked me what I'm doing here. Aren't you curious?"

"Yes. And that is why you're here. Curiosity. There was no need for me to ask."

She stayed well out of range. There was something vaguely compelling about talking to a man who looked to be a cross between a Franciscan monk and the Grim Reaper. She felt repelled, yet strangely drawn to him.

"Do I know you?" she asked.

"Perhaps."

"Would you take off your mask and let me see you?"

"That is not permitted."

"Why? I'm not part of your Game."

He came down one of the three steps. Delanie forced herself not to retreat. "Of Robes and Riddles, no," he agreed pleasantly. "Where is your friend?"

"Around."

"Are you sure you wouldn't like to come into the blue room with me?"

"Yes." Her eyes scanned the hallway to her left. Where was Rondel?

The figure descended another step. The shadows appeared to deepen. "You're nervous, *fräulein*," he observed. "Why are you nervous?"

She held her ground. "I don't like talking to masks."

"Is that all?" He laughed and came down the final step, arms out in an attitude of surrender. "In that case, be my guest."

He bowed his head to her. Delanie considered the idea, then removed her hand from her pocket.

"Come to me, Delanie Morgen," the voice in her memory commanded.

She hesitated. "Why the drama?" she asked in suspicion.

The man's hooded head came up. She couldn't see his eyes behind the mask. "Drama, *fräulein*? But I thought you wanted to know my identity."

"I did—I do." The darkness intensified. Illusion, she told herself, but felt a chill on her skin even so.

"Well?"

Her hand fell back to her side. "I've changed my mind," she said, edging away.

The man in the robe stood perfectly still. "As you wish. I had thought you were inquisitive. Tell me, do you still search for the professor?"

She stopped dead. "What do you know about him?"

He made a vague gesture, and Delanie could have sworn he floated closer. "What is there to know? He's the angel. You and Rondel are chosen. The Visitor's brother is dead. So is the angel's sister. The Story unfolds."

Although she tried desperately, Delanie couldn't move her feet. "Who are you?" she whispered, terror creating a lump in her throat.

The shadows shifted. Something in their texture altered. A cool breeze rippled across her cheeks. With it came more of the eerie music. She felt the unrelenting hardness of the stone wall against her spine.

The figure bowed his head again. "Remove the mask and see my face. I will tell you who I am then."

Why would he have to tell her anything once the mask was off? Anger began to simmer inside her. She didn't appreciate people who toyed with her. Not like this.

In one swift motion she brought her hand up. Her fingers caught the edge of the mask and ripped it free.

Immediately, the man raised his head. The hood fell back.

Delanie's entire body went numb with shock. No! her brain cried. This was impossible! She couldn't scream, she could only stare in disbelief at the face before her. Empty eye sockets stared back at her, and teeth with no lips to cover them. Bones, all bones. But this was no skull mask, it was a skull! A human skull!

Slowly, theatrically, the figure removed his gloves. More bones emerged.

Her limbs felt like rubber. The thing leaned closer. Its mouth opened. There was nothing but darkness inside.

"See me, Delanie Morgen," it commanded. "See what you will soon be."

The hood fell back farther still. Delanie stopped breathing. Run, her brain ordered. Escape!

"Death," the skeleton whispered. "That's what I am. The reflection of your death." Bony fingers reached for her. "Come to me, Delanie Morgen."

"No!"

She wasn't aware that she moved. She had no idea how she eluded the fingers. But suddenly, she was running down the hall, and the skeleton was laughing in her wake. Laughing and calling her name.

"Delanie..."

She collided hard with someone in her path. The impact tore the scream from her throat. With her fists she beat at the obstructing body.

"Delanie!"

Something in the sound of her name quelled her panic. She stopped pounding and looked up.

"Rondel!" She almost fainted with relief.

He gripped her arms. "Delanie, what was it? What happened?"

She dropped her head onto his chest, then recalled the laughing skeleton and twisted around.

"There," she exclaimed. "It's all bones and..." She stopped, unbelieving. "It's gone!"

Rondel turned her back to face him. "What's gone?"

"The skeleton. It was there. It said it was Death. *My* death." Her body went rigid with fear. "My God, Rondel, what if we've been wrong? What if the devil *is* here?" Dizziness pressed in on her. "What if The Visitor's real?"

Chapter Thirteen

"Not real? A trick? Is this what you want me to say?"

Mahira hobbled around the cottage, collecting bits of herbs from every box and jar she passed. Rondel watched both her and Delanie at the same time.

The previous night at the watchtower had passed like a nightmare. Three days now remained until Walpurgis ended. It might as well be three centuries. Rondel was exhausted and out of patience with this Game. And concerned about Delanie. She couldn't get the skeleton out of her mind.

"I saw it," she insisted stubbornly.

"Of course you did," Mahira said. She went to the window and surveyed the black afternoon sky. "More thunder will come. It is the sign. One hundred years." She glanced at Delanie's pale face. "Did this skeleton say he was The Visitor?"

Delanie sat erect in her chair. Rondel wanted to hold her, but knew better than to do it now.

"He said he was Death. He said that Aric Bellal was The Visitor's brother."

"Then accept that as truth and move forward."

"But skeletons don't walk around," Delanie argued. "They can't. It has to have been a trick."

Mahira shrugged. "Such tricks are possible. So are false visions." Her eyes touched on Rondel's guarded face. "I cannot say that all you have seen and heard is real. But all is not false, either."

"You're talking in riddles, Mahira," Rondel said with an edge of impatience.

"I told you when you came to me two nights ago that I am not permitted to say more. I stand between The Visitor and the angel, that is my place. You are chosen, that is your place. You must play the Game."

"A Game within a Game," Delanie murmured. "That's what the professor said."

Did a bitter smile cross Mahira's lips? Rondel saw no hint of it when he looked again.

"It is on weakness that The Visitor preys," she said sadly to Rondel. He felt her hands stroking his hair. "Beautiful child, I did not want you involved. You must keep your mind strong."

The fire in the wood stove flared up. Mahira looked but didn't stop talking.

"Weak minds fall victim to The Visitor's mental strength. Trust no one, for their actions may not be their own."

The fire roared up this time. Delanie watched it; Rondel didn't want to. Mahira bent over, setting her mouth close to his ear. "Demons deceive," she whispered, then straightened and regarded the flames in defiance.

"That is all," she said. "You and the girl must leave. Do what is expected of you. If you do not, the angel will die. And so will you."

FRIDAY AFTERNOON flowed into Friday night. Rain fell in sheets, driven by cold winds from the east. Gerda hadn't wanted to come to the castle tonight, so she'd drunk three glasses of cognac. Now she didn't care where she was.

She walked into the great hall, where a banquet table had been set up. A gloomy atmosphere prevailed. A full three-quarters of the people wearing their robes. Only the guests didn't, two of them being Delanie Morgen and Rondel Marcos.

Delanie looked lovely, Gerda thought distantly, stunning in a simple black dress with long sleeves, a drop waist and a sweeping hem that almost skimmed her ankles. High-heeled boots and a strand of pearls completed the picture, setting off her loose fall of golden hair. No wonder Rondel stared at her so attentively.

Gerda glanced over and saw Roland Popporov approaching. She should run from him. He would only gloat, or taunt her.

But suddenly she couldn't move. The great hall had begun to blur around her. What an odd sensation. A red haze crept into her head, warm and soothing. It spoke to her, not with words she understood, but by some more nebulous means.

Her limbs grew heavy. Her face became a mask. People milled about. Roland and Delanie. What were they saying? Something about fear. Gerda felt no fear. She stared at them.

"I fear no one," Roland was saying.

"That's not what I heard," Delanie said.

Rondel and Dex joined them, and then the baroness, who seemed annoyed.

"I can't believe this," she exclaimed. "Harry has disappeared again. How does he do that? Have you seen him, Rondel? No? Fine, then let us dance."

Delanie wasn't pleased, but she hid it and started in again on Roland. "Tell me, Herr Popporov, why do you fear the professor?"

He glared at her.

"Forget it, Doc," Dex advised. "How about you and me taking a turn about the dance floor?"

Delanie cast a final dark look at Roland and left.

"Your husband is coming this way, Frau Schiller," Roland remarked in a sour voice.

"I see that," Gerda said without inflection. The red haze in her head thickened to the consistency of blood. "Do you know where Alicia keeps her port?"

"In the wine cellar," Roland replied. His smile grew sly. "Next to the weapons room."

"So, RONDEL, did you have a nice dance for—" Delanie checked her watch "—thirty minutes?"

His smile was faint. "Jealous?"

"Not at all." She took a glass of wine from the offered tray. "But just out of curiosity, where *is* Harry?"

"Probably off with one of the maids." Rondel raked a hand through his hair. "Is it hot in here?"

"Tolerable." Delanie lifted polite eyes to his. Maybe not jealous, but definitely defiant. She'd recovered from her skeleton fright. He wished he could. "Would you like a progress report?" she asked.

"Not really, but go ahead."

"Well, for starters, Roland Popporov hasn't left the window or taken his eyes off me for the last twenty-five minutes."

"A demon with good taste," Rondel said in mild amusement. "What else?"

"Ingrid Hoffman's with the burgermeister and they've cornered John Kessler. Gruesome threesome, don't you think?"

Rondel arched an eyebrow in surprise. "You don't like Kessler?"

"Not much. I think he's very cunning, like a rat." Taking his hand, she drew him into a dark corner. "The real mystery, however, is Dex and Gerda."

Rondel didn't understand, but he liked the corner. "Why Dex?"

"Because he very neatly handed me off to another partner on the dance floor, then slipped quietly out of the room."

Amusement curved Rondel's lips. "That's no mystery, Delanie. He's gone on a treasure hunt."

"Explain."

He slid an arm about her waist, bending his mouth to her ear. "The richest residents of Klausberg are here tonight. What better time for Dex to loot their barns and storage buildings."

She gave him a knowing look. "Basements, too?"

"Sometimes. What about Gerda?"

"Who? Oh, she left, just sort of drifted out the door. I'm not sure, but I think she had that same thick look about her that she did the day the burgermeister fell into the stream."

"Interesting." Rondel's eyes fastened on a point beyond Delanie's shoulder. "Don't," he said when she would have looked. "Pretend you're talking to me. I want to see where they go."

"Who?"

"Stop fidgeting. Ingrid, Adolph and Kessler."

"Not Popporov?"

"Popporov won't try anything with us watching him. But remember the Story, Delanie. The Visitor has two demons." He paused, then said, "They're going into the cellar."

"Are you sure?"

He nodded. "I wonder what's down there."

Delanie took his hand. "Tunnels. Come on, we'd better follow them."

Rondel considered the idea with uncharacteristic reluctance. Of course the tunnels would be the best place for The Visitor to be holding the professor. But something about all of this unsettled him. What had Mahira said? It was on the weakness of lesser souls that The Visitor preyed. A psychic would be stronger than most of the souls gathered here tonight. Maybe too strong even for him and Delanie.

He recalled the conversation he'd had with Mahira earlier that afternoon, before she'd headed off to her cave. She'd come up and put her old hands on him.

"That girl again," she'd snapped irritably. "Do you think of no one but her?"

"I think about lots of things," he'd told her patiently.

"But Delanie Morgen most of all. Why?" She trapped his chin between her fingers and thumb. "Do you love her?"

He didn't blink or look away. "Yes," he'd said, surprising himself, but possibly not her. "Is that what you wanted to hear, Mahira?"

"It is dangerous," she'd replied, her lips thinning. "Your mind cannot be clear."

"My mind's clear enough."

"No!" She stomped her foot. "It is tangled up, filled with uncertainty."

"I told you before, I'm not going to get involved with her."

"You had better not," she'd warned. "Or you will be destroyed."

The ominous prediction was stated with such conviction that Rondel half believed her. He'd been shaken after that, chilled by her words and frightened of feelings he felt powerless to defend. When had he fallen in love?

He brought his mind back, aware that Delanie was tugging hard on his hand.

She eased the cellar door open and peered down. "It's dark, but I see lights."

And heard voices, Rondel realized. From below he caught a sentence fragment.

"...forbidden to drink the devil's blood," John Kessler was saying.

Delanie recoiled, but didn't resist when Rondel took her hand and started down the stairs. They crept through the musty corridors, well behind the somber trio.

"First we will take the challenge," Kessler said quietly. "Then we will drink the blood. Agreed?"

Rondel led them through an archway into a huge chamber filled with kegs and a vatlike barrel that was half the size of Mahira's cottage. Stairs ascended to a wooden platform set on top. Through the gloom he could see a door behind the barrel, partially opened. A weapons display was visible inside.

"Come on." He pointed to the left. "We can hide behind that stack of beer kegs."

"I will fetch the knives," Kessler said while the other two mounted the stairs. "Ingrid, you draw the pentagram."

Delanie shrank back into Rondel as the hypnotist passed them. "They're Satanists."

"I don't think so." Wrapping an arm around her waist, Rondel pulled her closer. It wasn't necessary, but he did it anyway. "This is another game. Dex says they have a lot of occult pastimes. It's all right on the edge, but it falls short of satanic."

"No sacrifices?"

"No." He tucked her in behind him, nodding at a small patch of darkness beneath the staircase. "Stay here. I'm going to see if I can hear anything from under the stairs."

He was gone before she could object, and before John Kessler could return. When the hypnotist did come back, he brought with him six knives and a large bottle filled with a red liquid. Wine, Rondel hoped, because despite what he'd told Delanie, he wasn't sure just how real all of this was, and he certainly wasn't anxious to get mixed up with devil worshipers.

Releasing a deep breath, he crouched down, his back pressed against the huge barrel. Then he heard a tiny creak behind him and felt one of the barrel's panels give way. It happened in a split second. One minute he was under the platform, the next he'd fallen through a spring-loaded door, a hidden entrance into some sort of secret room.

Voices murmured above him. It sounded like a chant. He climbed slowly to his feet, rubbing the back of his head where he'd hit it and testing his weight on the floor.

It felt solid enough, but there was air coming up from somewhere, the moist air of an underground passageway. He must have fallen into the barrel.

Going down on his knees, he began searching for a trapdoor. Like the one in the cave, it wasn't difficult to locate. Unlike the one in the cave, however, there was a light in the darkness below. Someone was down there!

A quick glance over his shoulder revealed that the panel had snapped back into place. The chanting continued, so the three people up there couldn't have heard him fall. He'd go into the tunnel, see who was wandering around in it, then find Delanie and get out of here.

A frisson of unease slid down his spine as he descended. He ignored it and groped his way along the passage. The walls were mossy and more or less dry. The person with the light was heading toward the ruined part of the castle.

Around him, Rondel heard a warning clatter of tiny pebbles skidding down the walls. A fine coating of dust sprinkled his hair.

He stopped and listened, one hand pressed to the wall. Was it vibrating? He frowned and lightened his touch so he could feel the tremors better. They lacked the resonance of thunder, his instincts told him.

The person ahead had stopped, as well. The ground seemed to be rumbling, a dull roar, barely audible, yet in its own way deafening.

Get out, Rondel's senses warned. But he hesitated. What about the other person?

This time the rumble was a definite threat. More stones showered him. He coughed, straining to find the light, but it was gone. Only darkness remained and the choking fumes of some underground gas.

Rondel didn't trust the coincidence, didn't like it. Why would the tunnel cave in now? Who was down here with him?

He shot forward through the falling earth and stones to where the passageway was more stable. More tremors sounded behind him, then stopped as precipitously as they'd started.

No, he didn't trust this at all.

He walked on and a minute later located the light again. It was closer now, so close that he had to stop dead to keep from being spotted.

A big man stood in the middle of the tunnel. His flashlight was pointed at the ceiling.

Rondel's stomach gave a hard twist.

"Dex," he whispered in disbelief.

Mahira's warning rushed into his head. He squeezed his eyes closed but couldn't block it. "Trust no one," she'd said. "Demons deceive."

Another faint vibration shook the ground. Rondel opened his eyes. There was no light shining now, and no Dex. There was only blackness and silence, and a feeling of uneasiness that Rondel, for all his love and loyalty, couldn't shed.

THE CHANTING above her sounded like a mantra. From her hiding spot Delanie couldn't see a thing, not even Rondel, who must still be eavesdropping under the stairs.

Restlessly, she shifted position so that she faced the door to the weapons room. She shivered at the gruesome display, then did a double take and frowned.

Gerda Schiller was creeping past the door. Delanie was sure it was Gerda because the woman stopped and listened for a moment. Her eyes climbed to the top of the barrel, and lingered there for the longest time. Even in the poor light Delanie couldn't miss the blankness of her expression, or the unnatural whiteness of her features.

It was that same zombie look she'd had on the bridge!

She stared intently at her husband, then moved out of sight.

With a quick look up, Delanie inched along the wall, clinging to the shadows. The chant, though faster, had dropped to a whisper. She sensed malevolence in it, but refused to dwell on the dark sounds or the fear that brought goose bumps to her skin.

She stole a glance into the room. Gerda was wandering about like a ghost. Her black robe trailed on the floor. Her fingers ran lightly over a set of knives.

"No," she whispered to the shadows. "Too messy."

Delanie fought a sudden memory of the skeleton, promising, "I am the reflection of your death."

"It was a trick," she told herself fiercely. "A deception."

Gerda drifted on, past maces and muskets, past the rifle cabinet to the guns. She paused there, her hand resting on a small pistol. "Fast," she murmured. "Painless. Good."

No! The word screamed in Delanie's head, yet she remained absolutely still, a shadow beside the door.

"Die!" she heard herself shout at her father. Yes, abusers deserved to die.

She saw the gun again. It disappeared into the pocket of Gerda's robe. Her head fell back for a moment, then suddenly snapped up. Her eyes located Delanie in the shadows, as if she'd been expecting her.

"Go away," she snarled.

Delanie's fingers curled behind her back. Zombie, her senses whispered. Weak minds fall victim to the Visitor's mental strength.

"Gerda . . ." she began.

"Go! Mahira would not kill him for me, so I will do it."

Taking a deep breath, Delanie started cautiously forward. "Don't do it, Gerda," she said. She touched Gerda's arm, hesitated, then whispered, "Can't you feel it?"

Gerda's face contorted. She snatched her arm away. "Feel what?"

Something in her mind. Delanie couldn't breathe. She pressed her fingers to her temples to keep her head from spinning. "Evil . . ."

"*You* are the evil," Gerda hissed. She sounded like a snake. She brought the gun from her robe. "You bring death when it suits you, yet you give life back to Adolph. You are evil to me!"

"No," Delanie denied.

The gun came up. Gerda's hand shook. Her breathing was labored.

"Yes!" she spat. Then her eyes cleared slightly. She stared at the gun. "No! What am I doing?" She looked around in sudden distrust. "Who's there? I hear you talking. Who are you?"

The room darkened. A cold breeze touched Delanie's neck. Words flowed in with it, muffled, not meant for her. More illusion?

Gerda stood by the wall, a marble statue. Her eyes had glazed over. Delanie collected her courage and stepped forward once again. Her fingers found Gerda's arm.

"*Kill her,*" she heard the snake's voice command. Then it laughed. "*Death to the evil witch.*"

Delanie's heart pounded in her ears. I am not a witch, she thought desperately. I am not evil.

"I hope you die!" the child cried.

"Cheat!" she accused The Visitor through Gerda. "You know I can hear you. You want me to run."

"*Kill the evil witch!*"

Gerda started, her body convulsing as if she'd been yanked from a trance. "Kill the witch," she repeated, and obediently swung the gun around. "Kill her."

Delanie couldn't move. She saw red limbs in her mind, and a skeleton. She saw her father's face. *I didn't kill him!*

Gerda's features shone white in the eerie light. The chanting from the other room grew louder. The tempo had increased to a tribal throb, like the voodoo songs Delanie had heard in Haiti.

Blood still pounded in her ears. "Listen to me, Gerda," she pleaded, tightening her grip despite the waving gun.

"No," Gerda snapped. "Kill the witch. Kill Adolph."

Delanie wished the macabre humming behind them would stop. The gun barrel rose to her throat.

"You're not a murderer, Gerda," she whispered. "Think."

Gerda's hands were shaking badly. So were Delanie's. She fixed her eyes on Gerda's face. "Don't do it, Gerda."

"Do it!" The Visitor's voice roared.

Gerda jerked in reaction. But Delanie's reaction was quicker. Her fingers closed about the barrel of the gun and yanked it free. The weapon clattered to the floor.

The chanting sounded like a feral heartbeat now. "Kill!" Gerda choked. Then her eyes rolled back in her head and she fell to the ground in a silent faint.

TIME AND EVENTS fused after that. Warily, Delanie revived Gerda and took her back upstairs, careful not to disturb the three people in the other room.

"What happened?" Gerda mumbled as if waking from a dream. "Where am I?"

"Safe," Delanie promised. She found the baroness and asked her to stay with Gerda—"Too much cognac," she lied—then returned to the cellar to look for Rondel.

Thankfully, the chanting had ceased. Whatever the devil's blood was, it must have been potent. Adolph and John and Ingrid were thoroughly drunk when Delanie got there.

She ducked under the staircase first. Nothing. She checked the other nooks. Still nothing. A fearful shiver engulfed her. Where could he have gone?

The other rooms she entered all proved to be empty, and the one marked "The Visitor's Game" was locked. Her stomach curled into a painful knot. Had The Visitor taken him?

Roland Popporov hadn't, of that she was certain. When she returned to the great hall, he was sitting in the same chair he'd been in when she and Rondel had first gone into the cellar. And he was scowling, not smiling in triumph.

She went to the salon. "Please, Delanie," Gerda said, touching her arm. "Take me to Mahira. I feel so very strange. Perhaps she can explain."

"Don't count on it," Delanie muttered, but Gerda was adamant and terrified, so she left a message with the baroness and took Gerda in Rondel's car to Mahira's cottage.

"Mahira will understand," Gerda insisted as they drove.

Delanie glanced at her. "How much do you remember?" she asked.

"About what?"

"The gun, the cellar. The voice in your head."

"Voice?" Gerda pressed her fingers to her mouth. "Yes, there was a voice. It said I should kill Adolph. And kill Mahira. No, wait, that's wrong. Kill the evil witch, it said." Her eyes went wide with fright. She flung herself against the door, staring at Delanie in horror. "It spoke your name. Kill Delanie, it told me. Destroy the evil witch!"

THERE WAS ONLY a trace of thunder tonight, far to the east.

"It hovers over the Brocken," Mahira revealed ten minutes later. On her knees, she stared into the fire of her wood stove. "Forces of darkness begin to stir as Walpurgis draws near."

"Night of power," Gerda murmured, still regarding Delanie with misgivings. "This is the year, isn't it, Mahira? The time of evil."

Delanie wanted to return to the castle to search for Rondel, but her curiosity held her at the cottage a moment longer. "What year?" she asked.

Mahira made an impatient gesture. "The one hundredth anniversary of The Visitor's time on earth. Did you not read the Story?"

"I read it."

"Then you should know. For the past one hundred years, The Visitor has been free to come and go from hell."

"That's not in the Story," Delanie said flatly. "It says, '*If the Visitor should win, a reign of darkness shall begin.*' It doesn't say anything about him coming and going for the past century."

"That's true," Gerda agreed, calmer now. "But every one hundred years, this happens, whether The Visitor wins or loses."

Mahira sent Delanie a harsh look. "Think, girl. You are chosen. Why are you chosen? The Game is played once every century."

"But The Visitor can't be real," Delanie protested. "The skeleton was a trick, a clever disguise. I believe that now. None of this is real."

Mahira's fist pounded the hearth. "It does not matter what you believe. The Visitor acts in the hundredth year."

Her gaze returned to the flames. Her voice rose above the crackle of wood and the rain on the roof.

"In the century of your American Revolution, the angel was successful. She was clever in the way that is necessary to defeat The Visitor. My great-grandmother met this angel, whose family has for hundreds of years been involved in the Story of the Visitor. She was very strong. She won. But the next angel was not so clever. He was her brother and filled with goodness, but too easily deceived. He did not choose well. He was destroyed." Mahira's ancient eyes fastened on Delanie's pale face. "In the last century, The Visitor did not return to hell."

Chapter Fourteen

Delanie was shaking by the time she left Mahira and Gerda at the cottage.

The professor's sister and brother had both played the Game. Female and male angels alike had played it, according to Mahira. But there was no connection, there couldn't be. The angels were myths. Anna and the professor's brother were real. Besides, the female angel had played the Game two hundred years ago. Aric Bellal had only died thirty years ago. The times didn't correspond.

On the other hand, the professor had told her that Aric escaped. Anna had had to track him down twice. And by the time she'd done it the second time, their brother was already dead, a premature victim of vengeance, courtesy of Aric's powerful family. So in that sense, the stories were consistent.

"Oh, don't be ridiculous," she reproached herself as she drove through the slanting rain. It was a coincidence, nothing more. Finding Rondel was all that mattered now.

Lightning bolts flickered over the Brocken. Walpurgis was on Sunday. That meant tomorrow, Saturday, was Walpurgis Eve.

She let out an agitated breath. "Where are you, Rondel?"

He wasn't at the castle, she discovered. And he hadn't gone back to the cottage, because she phoned and was flatly told so by Mahira.

"Maybe he's at the watchtower," Harry suggested, having returned from wherever he'd been. "Or he and Dex could be off together somewhere."

Delanie smiled but didn't believe that. Rondel wouldn't have left her without an explanation. Something was wrong.

She drove back through the rain to the watchtower. He would be all right, she told herself with conviction. He had to be, because . . .

Unexpected tears shimmered in her eyes. "Because I love him," she whispered to the empty car. "I shouldn't, but I do." She closed her eyes for a brief moment. "Oh, damn."

The simple admission both astonished and disturbed her. It was like a revelation, a thing she'd never believed would happen. Loving Rondel, loving the professor, it was a double miracle, and a dangerous one at that.

At the watchtower she changed quickly into warm clothes and rain gear. She had no idea where to start looking, but she was determined to search for him. She could begin in Mahira's cave, or the one by the stream where Rondel had found the tunnel entrance.

Pulling on her hat, she started out into the wet night. She'd try the tunnels first. And she wouldn't stop looking until she found him.

HE WASN'T DRESSED for this, Rondel reflected as he made his way through the thick black woods. It was cold and raining and he was soaked to the skin. He'd lost Dex over two hours ago in the tunnels, but it didn't matter. He refused to mistrust Dex.

For a good sixty minutes he'd wandered through the passageway. It had taken another sixty for him to untangle himself. He'd finally emerged in the briar hollow, which was about as far from anywhere warm and dry as you could get.

His watch told him it was almost midnight. Would Delanie have stayed at the castle all this time? Maybe. She would have looked for him, that much he knew. She might even have given in and gone to Mahira.

Since the watchtower was closest, he started for it, cutting through the densest section of the forest to the Klausberg Road. He could dry off and phone around from there.

The wind sliced through him like an icy knife. His teeth were chattering by the time the watchtower came into sight. Were the lights on? He pushed hair and water from his eyes and squinted through the rain. Yes, two lights, one upstairs, one down. That meant power and hot water and, he hoped, Delanie's warm, soft body.

He started to jog, so cold now that he couldn't feel his fingers. What had he learned tonight? That he loved Delanie and that Dex had been wandering around in the tunnels under the castle. All in all a disturbing evening.

"Two witches," he muttered, squeezing his eyes closed. What a nightmare.

He slowed to a walk when he reached the courtyard. He noticed his car, then saw the front door open and Delanie in the professor's raincoat outlined against a glare of light.

"Rondel!" She shouted his name, darting across the muddy driveway. He felt her arms around his neck, her face pressing into his shoulder. "I thought something horrible had happened to you." Her head came up. She gave his shin a light, accusing kick. "Where have you been? I was worried sick about you."

He managed a distracted smile, but his eyes were fixed on her lips. They looked so soft and kissable in the shadows. "I'll tell you all about it," he promised, lowering his head. His mouth found hers in a hungry kiss. "Later."

THE PROFESSOR was sitting cross-legged on his cot, playing solitaire of all things, when Roland arrived.

"Five temptations, Herr Popporov," he said, not lifting his shaggy brown head. "Your boss must be getting worried."

Roland kept his distance. "I haven't spoken to The Visitor tonight, but I assure you, there's nothing to worry about."

"No?" The professor looked up, his expression one of amusement. "Well."

"What do you mean, 'well'?"

"What I said, of course," the professor retorted. "Oh, don't be obtuse, man. Gerda Schiller's not the sort of woman who'd pull a gun on an innocent bystander. On her husband possibly, but not on Delanie. The Visitor put that thought in her head, and that's a definite breach of rules. However—" his smile become affable "—since everything turned out well in the end, I'm willing to let it go."

From a safe distance, Roland challenged, "You are so sure of yourself, professor, and so sure of them. But I think you underestimate The Visitor."

"As do you, Herr Popporov." The Professor returned to his game.

"What do you mean?"

"Oh, nothing." Uncrossing his legs, the professor came over to the bars. "A word of advice," he said calmly, hanging his arms through the bars. "Don't try any more little tricks like the one you played at the Cemetery Rocks, hmm? You might get caught, and you know what The Visitor does to demons in distress."

Roland felt a stab of fear in his stomach. "Do not try to trick me with clever words, professor," he retorted. "Your cunning is nothing by comparison to The Visitor's."

The professor's grin broadened. "Precisely."

DELANIE HAD NEVER thought that she would react so eagerly to a kiss. But she reacted to Rondel, and in a way that would normally have shocked her.

The rain did nothing to dampen the heat that passed between them. Rondel's body was hard against hers. But he was shivering and the rain was coming down in buckets.

She dragged her mouth from his. "We can't stay here," she said. "It's too cold."

"I know."

He fed on her neck, a sweet sucking motion that almost made her knees give out.

"Stand still," he murmured.

But it was difficult to stand at all when he did that.

The next thing Delanie knew, he'd scooped her up into his arms. He continued to kiss her all the way into the watchtower. Her whole body shook from wanting him, but she suspected his reasons for shaking stemmed more from being cold and wet than anything else.

Disentangling her mouth from his, she kicked her legs. "Put me down."

His smile was beautiful in the pale light. "I will," he promised. "When we get where we're going."

"Bathroom," she ordered, loving the way his mouth looked in shadow. So sexy.

His hooded eyes watched her. "I don't make love in bathrooms."

She teased the corners of his lips with hers. "You should try it."

His teeth closed on her earlobe, biting gently. "Voice of experience, Delanie?"

"No," she admitted, then waited for him to set her away from him.

He didn't. His only response was to tighten his hold on her and say, "That's what I thought." Then he kissed her so thoroughly that she forgot to be insulted.

"Bathroom," she whispered without conviction while he explored her throat and neck. "No arguments, Rondel, or this won't happen."

She felt his mouth curve against her neck. "This has to happen, Delanie. I need to be with you tonight."

His tongue came into her mouth, a warm, wet tease that was giving and demanding, too arousing for her to care about anything else. She didn't utter another sound. A hot bath could wait. The chill was gone anyway. Delanie meant to see that it stayed gone all night.

RONDEL MADE no effort to understand the clamor in his head. He wanted to make love to Delanie, and to hell with the consequences.

To kiss her wasn't enough, but it excited him, took him right to the edge. His mouth traveled over her face and neck, her cheeks and eyelids and chin. Her nipples were hard when his hand moved beneath her clothes. Her breasts were soft and lush and so beautiful to caress that he groaned against her.

She pushed up against his palm so that he longed to rip off her bra, but he waited, using his other hand to strip away her raincoat and hat while his thumb ran over the tip of her nipple, making it as hard as he was.

The slowness of the act aroused him. He whispered tenderly in her ear.

"Love me, Delanie," he murmured. "Touch me."

And she did. Her fingers tugged at his belt and the wet zipper of his pants. Were they in her bedroom? He wasn't sure, didn't care. His arms and legs trembled as he picked her up and started for the bed. They tumbled down onto it and the feel of the cotton sheets and quilt beneath him brought a groan to his throat. His whole body throbbed with the fever of anticipation.

One by one he discarded her clothes, her sweater, her boots, her jeans.

"No, wait," she begged when he would have continued, and obediently he stopped, his eyes half-closed as he watched her work at his pants. "You're all wet," she complained.

"That's not the problem, Delanie," he murmured with a trace of a smile.

Her smile was far more telling. With both hands she touched him, and he hissed in a sharp breath of response, not expecting the contact. "I know," she whispered softly.

He caught her mouth again, drawing her tongue against his while his hands stroked her damp breasts and the round softness of her backside. She was long-limbed and slender, a delicate creature who was driving him out of his mind.

He loved the scent of her beautifully tousled hair, her flushed skin. He loved the taste of her, the warmth of her breath when he kissed her, the tender hardness of her nipples when he suckled them.

She ran her hands over his chest, then across his ribs and around his back. She was so ready, and yet he waited, enjoying the exquisite torture that had the power to make him shudder.

"Masochist," she whispered, then gasped and arched up into him as his mouth strayed lower, to the heat between her legs.

Her voice, her cries of pleasure were a delicious echo in his head. She seemed to understand what he wanted. Maybe there was something to witchcraft, after all.

She clung to him for only a moment more, then set her lips on his chest, his nipples, his chest and stomach. Her hands held him, but only until her mouth took over.

Then it was Rondel who cried her name, whose hips arched against her. Enough, he thought. He couldn't hold back any longer.

Reaching down, he tugged her away and laid her down gently, covering her body with his. His fingers ran through her damp hair, brushing the silky tendrils from her face. He came into her with a thrust that was both insistent and intense.

Maybe he talked to her, he couldn't remember. He only knew what his mind and body needed, what they received. It was everything in that one hectic moment, better than it had ever been before. It was a memory he would cling to for the rest of his life.

DELANIE SAVORED every minute of the long, exquisite night. She wouldn't consider tomorrow or what feelings the light of day might bring. She would only think about the present, and that meant Rondel.

They ended up making love in the bathtub, after all. Clawed feet, no lights, bubbles everywhere—it was heaven.

"I'm going to be bruised from head to foot tomorrow," Rondel said in amusement, while Delanie played with the bubbles.

She kissed his chest, letting her mouth linger on his hard nipples. "It'll be worth it."

It was worth it, so much so that they'd gotten adventuresome and gone up to the professor's lab.

Thunder crashed outside. Little forks of lightning turned the room an eerie shade of violet. By two a.m. the storm had grown fierce and, in the way nature could be sometimes, highly erotic.

"No lights," Delanie said when Rondel would have gone over to the panel. "The switch isn't grounded. Besides, storms are better in the dark."

Clad in his white T-shirt, she leaned back into him, watching as a bolt of lightning shot across the sky. "I used to think God got mad and made thunderstorms. Now I think they're a reflection of The Visitor's rage. It's Walpurgis Eve, you know."

Rondel rested his chin on the top of her head. "And Monday's May Day. If we make it until midnight tomorrow, it's over. Or it should be." She glanced up and saw his eyes shift to the window. "Fair play will depend on our particular Visitor. The real one would automatically return to hell. A homicidal maniac might have other ideas."

Delanie trembled. It was all so grisly, so macabre, so totally beyond their control.

The harsher elements of the storm came and went. But Delanie hardly noticed that. They went downstairs and built a fire in the blackest part of the night. No visions, please, she prayed, and God must have heard, because no monsters roared out of the flames.

She gazed into the warming fire and thought of Snow White. "I wish we had a poison apple for The Visitor," she said softly.

Rondel's fingers turned her face back until she was looking into his eyes. "We do." He kissed her. "We'll pass the sixth temptation and find the professor."

"A Game within a Game," she murmured. "The professor said that to me in a dream. I wonder what it means."

She felt his mouth move against her hair. "'If they cleave,'" he said, reciting from the Story, "'to their beliefs and persevere, do not submit or bow to fear for five tests, if they play the Game, and that survive and win, defame the devil's demons six and five, they'll find the angel still alive.'"

"Yes, but we've only passed four temptations," she reminded him. Then she shivered. "Although that horrible thing I went through with Gerda tonight felt a lot like a test to me."

"Maybe it was. In any event, it sounds like the last temptation might be six tests rolled into one."

"Game within a Game?" Delanie asked, not wanting to accept that. She hunched her shoulders. "If it is, it's a cheat," she said. "Like having three wishes and asking for three more on your last wish." She paused, then turned to look back at him. "Do you think it means we have to play the Game at the castle? Is that the Game the Story's talking about?"

"I don't know," Rondel said. "But if it is, we'll have to do what no one in The Visitor's Club has ever done. We'll have to win."

ROLAND STEPPED over the sleeping burgermeister's outstretched legs and walked to the cold fireplace where The Visitor stood.

"Aftereffects of the devil's blood?" he asked with a smug smile, and The Visitor nodded.

"Some cannot handle its potency. It doesn't matter. What concerns me are the chosen two. They're doing too well. Did you take the mandragora to the watchtower?"

"Yes, Master."

"And did you take care of that other matter?"

Roland held up a sharp knife. "All done."

The Visitor's eyes passed over the burgermeister, who scowled even in his sleep. "What about the professor?"

Roland squirmed. "He is well. Silver-tongued as always," he added in a tentative tone. "He thinks you're very cunning."

The Visitor's chuckle sent a chill down Roland's spine, as did his ominous, "He's right." The chuckle became a cold smile. "I believe I'll go below for a time, Roland, where the earth is warm and I can think. Do you know what to do next?"

Roland's nerves calmed slightly. "Yes, I'm going to scare them to death."

"Not to death," The Visitor warned. "They must not be killed. Do you understand?"

"Treacherous, Roland," the professor had said. "The Visitor is very treacherous. Don't ever forget that."

Roland nodded, aware that he'd begun to perspire.

"Good." The Visitor started off. "Do it properly," he said over his shoulder. "And remember how I deal with my failures." He stopped to look back. "We'll all go to hell together if we don't succeed. It's up to you, Roland, and demon number six to make sure that doesn't happen. For were we three to go down, rest assured, I wouldn't be happy." He smiled. "And you may also be assured that 'rest' would be the very last thing either of you would ever have again."

"CAR TIRES SLASHED, power out, one storm gone, another moving in, and it's Walpurgis Eve." Delanie leaned against the watchtower door, watching as Rondel fingered the cut tires of his car.

It was barely seven a.m., dark and gloomy and threatening rain. The tires must have been slashed by Popporov, she reasoned. But why? Closing her eyes, she jammed her hands into her jacket pockets. What else could go wrong?

Last night certainly hadn't been wrong. Well, maybe it had, but she'd loved every minute of it. Two witches, neither one evil, and wave after wave of sensation.

She relaxed against the door for a minute, then frowned as something jabbed her in the back. It felt hard, unpleasant. Turning, she looked down—and promptly scrambled away.

Her hand went to her throat. "The mandragora," she whispered. "Gerda and the gun. I was right. It must have been the fifth temptation."

Rondel came up behind her. He tore the hairy root from the doorknob where it had been hung.

"Popporov," he muttered.

"Or the other demon." Delanie shuddered. "So what do we do now? Walk to Mahira's?"

Rondel nodded. "I wonder if he cut the phone line."

Delanie shoved her hands back in her pockets. "I wish you hadn't said that."

"So do I." His eyes scanned the forbidding forest around the watchtower. Then he kissed the back of her head and started down the steps. "Come on."

But Delanie didn't want to go. And neither did Rondel, she suspected. There was something sinister about the woods today, some malevolent aspect to the trees that made their limbs appear almost human.

"The trees look like they're going to grab us," she said, nudging Rondel's arm with her shoulder. "Do you feel it?"

He managed a small smile. "No."

"Liar."

"Just keep walking, Delanie, and try not to think about what's ahead."

What was ahead was an even denser patch of forest. Thick vines all but choked off the daylight. Not that there was much of that, with the mass of black clouds suspended directly overhead. The wind blew in circles around Delanie's ankles. It swirled through the branches, rousing the crows. A pair of them glided past, their black eyes cold and beady, their outstretched wings barely missing Rondel's cheek.

More wind gusted up in their wake. Strands of Delanie's hair blew across her eyes. She was perspiring. Why? There was nothing to fear here. The Visitor would want them alive for the sixth temptation, wouldn't he?

"Alive, but maybe not unharmed," she said.

With a somber look past her, Rondel reached for her hand.

"Don't dwell on it," he advised. But he sounded distracted, as if he too sensed something in the air.

The silence deepened. Rondel stared into the trees. Delanie's muscles tensed. "What is it?" she asked.

"Nothing. I thought I heard a twig snap back there."

She glanced uncertainly over her shoulder. Nothing stirred in the shadows. The wind only came at intervals and even then it seemed to be blowing very low. The trees didn't move at all.

Naked limbs loomed over them, like raised human arms frozen in a cartoon-ghost stance.

"Sleeping Beauty meets Frankenstein," she said, fighting a shudder. "I feel as though we're walking deeper and deeper into a gigantic spiderweb."

"We are," Rondel said, which didn't calm her fears at all. "Mahira told us we'd have to do what was expected of us. I think The Visitor has this day planned down to the last detail."

"That's not very reassuring," Delanie said, then she twisted her head around. "Another twig! Did you hear it?"

He nodded, setting his hand lightly over her mouth. "Keep going," he whispered. "I thought I saw a flash of metal to your left."

Metal as in gun? Delanie wanted to ask, but didn't. Panicking would get her nowhere. A lump formed in her stomach. Her feet dragged. The wind gusted up again, whistling eerily through the branches. She heard the skeleton's warning in her head. "I am the reflection of your death."

She plodded on, glad that Rondel was with her. But could they defeat The Visitor, even together?

Leaves crunched behind them. Delanie caught back a startled breath and snatched her head around.

"Popporov," she whispered. A sliver of dread ran down her spine. "Rondel, he's stalking us."

The words were scarcely out of her mouth when another sound reached her from the opposite direction. She dug her fingers into Rondel's arm to alert him.

"Stay calm," he said, and she nodded, straining to see who the second person was.

From the shadows between the trees, a man emerged. Black overcoat, white hair, a scowl on his lips...

"It's the burgermeister," she said with a gasp. She looked swiftly back. "And I'm positive that's Popporov behind us. We're trapped."

"Shh," Rondel said in her ear. He stared at Adolph Schiller, not protesting as Delanie pulled him into the shelter of an old oak tree. "I don't think he sees us."

She twisted her head from side to side, still pulling on him. "Which one?"

"Adolph."

"That's fine," she hissed, giving his arm a final tug. "But at least we know where he is. Popporov's disappeared."

"What?" Rondel frowned and squinted into the woods. "He must be hiding. Wait here."

"No." She refused to let him go. "Let him find us."

"So he can shoot us?" Rondel pushed on her shoulders. "Stay down. I'll circle around and..."

Delanie caught his sleeve. "Rondel, look," she interrupted. "The burgermeister's coming this way. But look at his face, his eyes. They're...I think they're glowing."

"They can't be glowing. It's a trick of the light."

"There is no light," she said through her teeth.

A cautious footstep disturbed the vegetation on the forest floor behind them. Hugging the tree trunk, Delanie risked a fearful look.

"Popporov?" Rondel asked.

She nodded. "I think he has a rifle."

"Is he coming closer?"

"Yes."

He grabbed her hand. "Then we'll have to take our chances with Adolph."

They ran from the tree just as Popporov stepped into view and aimed at them. Not with a rifle, Delanie realized, but a crossbow. Seconds later, a metal bolt embedded itself into the trunk of the old oak.

Shock and anger coursed through her, but she had no time to act on her feelings.

A gurgle of laughter rang out from behind. "Run, chosen two," Roland taunted. "Run to the witch who is the link. Run to the Game at the castle. Or run straight to hell, for that's where you'll wind up in the end."

Delanie tried to shut the words out. The forest became a blur as they ran. The wind grew stronger, blowing hard in their faces. She glanced back and saw Popporov raise the crossbow again, then looked forward and watched in surprise as the burgermeister came to a halt on the path. His eyes went past them briefly, then lifted to the blackened sky.

"Forces of evil," he cried. "The Visitor is here!" His arms rose. "He commands us. We are his slaves." He impaled Rondel and Delanie with his glassy stare. "You think you can escape, but you cannot. He is Death and Treachery. He is Evil. He plays the Game. I thought Aric was my friend, but he deceived me. That is the way of his family. Aric was brother to The Visitor, but she who hunted him did not care. She was the angel. She—"

He broke off sharply, his eyes widening with shock. Delanie wasn't sure how she noticed that, because she was busy watching Popporov take aim with his crossbow again.

"Run away," Popporov mocked them, and it occurred to her that he couldn't see or hear Adolph.

With a panicky motion, she grabbed Rondel's arm and dragged him sideways.

A loud whoosh filled the air. The arrow shot past their heads.

"No, stay down," she whispered, holding on to Rondel. He seemed transfixed. His eyes were locked on the burgermeister, or they had been until she'd hauled him from the path.

A strangled cry echoed through the air, followed by a startled "Oh no!" that could only have come from Roland Popporov's throat.

Delanie levered herself up, looked back, then forward, then scrambled to a crouch beside Rondel. She pointed a horrified finger at the last metal bolt Popporov had fired. "Rondel," she whispered. "He shot the burgermeister in the chest!"

Chapter Fifteen

Popporov's face registered shock. He stumbled backward, caught his foot on a vine and landed on his back on the dirt path.

Rondel saw the crossbow fly from his fingers. With a quick directive to Delanie to check on Adolph, he took off.

An image came to him as he ran, hazy and undefined, but he wiped it from his mind, or tried to. He'd seen something just for a moment behind the burgermeister. A flash of red, like an enormous pair of clawed hands cupped around Adolph Schiller's body.

He fought a shudder and ran to where Popporov sat, desperately struggling to free himself from the vine that had twisted itself around his ankle.

"No!" the demon shouted. He made an attempt to kick Rondel away. "I can't be caught. Don't you understand?"

Rondel understood only that the man's foot had landed on his shin and it hurt. Reaching down, he pulled Popporov up by his coat and shoved him face-first into a chestnut tree.

"Who's the Visitor, Popporov?" he demanded.

The demon's eyes bulged. "No, no, you must let me go! You must. He'll kill me!"

"Who'll kill you?"

"Oh, no," Roland denied hastily. He was sweating. "You can't trick me, Rondel Marcos. I'll never tell. I'm loyal." He raised his voice and his head. "Do you hear me, Master? Your number five demon is loyal."

Or crazy, Rondel thought. A picture of enormous red hands appeared in his mind, and for a moment he closed his eyes, leaning his weight on Popporov, suddenly dizzy.

Crazy, he repeated to himself. Popporov had to be insane. The alternative was unacceptable to him. The Visitor could not be real!

FROM THE PATH, Delanie studied Adolph Schiller's body, a motionless heap on the forest floor. The black storm clouds seemed to watch him, and her. She forced herself to move closer.

He lay half on his side, his eyes wide and staring. He didn't stir. Nothing did, not even the wind in the woods around her.

Be safe, Rondel, she prayed, but her gaze was fastened on the burgermeister. She bent to touch his wrist. Dead, her senses told her instantly. Beyond revival.

She brought her fingers back, kneeling beside the corpse, her hands clammy and cold, her body trembling.

The skeleton in her memory laughed at her. *"I am Death, Delanie Morgen. Death!"*

She flinched at the words. A cool breeze ruffled her hair. From inside it, another voice seemed to speak. "Trust no one."

Confused, Delanie lifted her head. "Mahira?"

The voice swirled around her like the air. "Do not forget, girl, demons deceive."

With unsteady hands Delanie reached out and closed Adolph Schiller's eyes. It felt strangely like the end of something to her. And the beginning.

ROLAND POPPOROV SAT in his jail cell, too terrified to move. In his mind he kept going over his capture. How could it all have gone so wrong? He hadn't meant to kill Adolph. He hadn't meant to kill anyone. He had never intended to get caught.

The day wore on slowly. His abject fear mounted with each hour that passed. They came from the castle to see him—Harry and the baroness, Dexter Solomon, John Kessler, Ingrid Hoffman, even Gerda, whose husband he had accidentally killed.

"All an accident," Roland said over and over again. He knew he sounded desperate. Who wouldn't, in his position? The Visitor had been among the parade of curious callers from the club. He had not looked pleased. The other demon had merely looked amused.

Roland hung his head and stared at the floor. What would The Visitor do to him? What did he do to any demon who got caught?

"But I didn't talk," Roland protested weakly to his empty cell. "I would never betray you, Master. I was doing what you wanted me to do. 'Scare them,' you said. 'I want them nervous before I thrust them into the sixth temptation.' And I did shake them up," Roland defended himself to the silence around him. "Adolph simply got in the way. I didn't see him. But, you know, his death could be used to advantage. Rondel and Delanie think he might have been your demon number six. So, you see, I might have done you a favor, don't you think...?"

His voice trailed nervously off. Clasping his hands, he lowered his head once more.

There was a guard in the hall outside his cell and three officers on duty in the front.

"Lights out in five minutes," the guard said as he strolled past.

Roland sat like a broken doll on his cot. He had no watch. He'd been strip-searched. All of his personal effects had been taken away. He didn't even have his shoelaces.

The clock ticked on. As predicted, the lights in the cells went out. Only the corridor remained lit.

Roland heard a soft sound and looked up. He was going to say something, but in a split second the words in his head vanished.

"No!" he whispered, his dread so swift and immediate that he wasn't even aware of rising.

He plastered himself to the wall, his gaze locked on the eyes that stared serenely back at him. Yellow-tinged, he was sure of it. And now a weapon was being extended to him through the bars.

He swallowed hard, his mind working feverishly. Treacherous, as the professor had said. How could he have been so blind?

"Please," he begged, gaping first at The Visitor, then at the knife. "I didn't mean any... I didn't know... I thought... You!"

A smile curved The Visitor's lips. No compassion in it. The knife blade gleamed in the dull light as it was thrust forward.

Shakily, Roland reached for the weapon.

"Visitor, please," he tried one last time, but The Visitor's expression remained unaffected.

"You failed me, number five."

The words resounded in Roland's head. The last of his hopes died. "Oh, professor," he whispered. "I should have listened."

Releasing a wail of anguish, he plunged the blade deep into his heart.

"AS FAR AS I KNOW, Mahira's down at the caves with the Sisters," Dex said when Rondel and Delanie came into the cottage late that evening. "And stop glaring at me, Rondel. I told you this afternoon why I was in the tunnel Friday night. I've been nicking a few things from the castle. That's hardly on the same level as murder."

Rondel said nothing, just gave him a dark look and started for the door. On the porch he stroked Delanie's cheek. "Wait for me here, okay?"

She nodded, not bothering to ask for details. He appreciated that. Explanations were beyond him right then, even the obvious ones.

He half climbed, half slid over the rocks that led down to the caves. How did Mahira do this?

"Probably has a broomstick," he muttered, then smiled a little, picturing it. Good or evil, at least she loved him, he could always count on that.

He sought information tonight, or rather confirmation of what he thought he already knew. The Story said that if the chosen two survived five tests, then played the Game, they would find the angel. A Game within a Game, Delanie called it. He wondered if that meant they had to play the club Game at the castle. Mahira might be the only person who would know for sure.

He navigated a particularly slippery portion of the slope. The dwarf trees loomed below, squat shadows with no moon to illuminate them. The first raindrops of the day splashed on his cheeks, and the wind caught at his hair. He thought of Popporov and the burgermeister. Had Adolph been the other demon? Maybe, but there was no way to know. Popporov wouldn't talk. All he did was sit in his cell and repeat, "It was an accident. I didn't mean to shoot him."

Rondel believed that. The man was too distraught to be lying, too worried about the repercussions of his "mistake."

Climbing over the final boulder, he hopped down. Other memories crowded in, more profound ones.

As hard as he tried, he couldn't block the image of those huge clawed hands cupped around the burgermeister in the forest, like a giant shepherd guiding his lost sheep. Except that this was a shepherd from hell, and Rondel had no idea what that made the late Adolph Schiller.

Shuddering, he pushed aside the curtain of dead vines and weeds and stuck his head into the cave. "Mahira?"

No answer. Except for the glow of a dying fire, the cave was dark. She must have left some time ago.

He pushed his way inside anyway, tossed his flashlight down and shook the rain from his hair and jacket. Something Delanie had told him after they'd left the jail that afternoon disturbed him. She hadn't seemed to have much faith in the bars of Popporov's cell.

"Maybe he can't get out," she'd conceded. "But he's still a demon, so to speak. Two of the other demons that the professor tracked down died in jail. The police and doctors said it was suicide.''

But neither the police nor the doctors could explain how such a thing was possible. One demon had set himself on fire. Where had the matches come from? Another had ingested poison. How had he obtained it? Both men had been heavily guarded, as Popporov was.

Rondel's eyes stung from the residual smoke. It curled up from the coals in long tendrils. Medusa snakes, he thought idly, then shook the thought away and knelt to warm his hands.

Rain pelted the valley floor beyond the cave opening. A feeling of inordinate tiredness washed through him. The orange glow from the fire seemed more a thing inside his head than before his eyes. He felt the glow spreading, drawing him closer to it.

Wisdom told him to move, break the spell before it began. Morbid curiosity held him there, unmoving.

His eyes located the center of the stone circle, where the coals were brightest. Heat enveloped him, tremendous heat, an inferno consuming him.

Something touched his cheek. He couldn't see it. *"Play the Game,"* the familiar snake's voice whispered. *"One Game inside another. You understand."*

A flash of sinuous red limbs cut across Rondel's line of vision. A small, darting creature with horns and spiked tail laughed, then darted past him again.

Demon or Visitor? he wondered, too fuzzy now to try to rationalize this.

The little creature shot forward and poked Rondel's foot with a tiny hoof. Its skin was red and scaly, its beard small and pointed, its eyes a sickly shade of yellow.

''See number five,'' it said, then darted away, laughing.

The red color in Rondel's mind intensified. He saw black metal bars and a cot. On the floor lay a man's body. It was Popporov. But why was he on the floor?

''One demon set himself on fire, the other took poison...''

He heard Delanie's voice in memory and drew swiftly back from the unfolding scene. Shut it out, his brain ordered. Stop it before...

His eyes fell on the knife handle. His stomach lurched. Blood on the knife, and on Popporov's shirt. Blood on the floor.

Rondel recoiled, denying all of it. Not there! It wasn't possible!

The coals came back into focus. He closed his eyes, felt the dampness of his skin under his clothes. "Gone," he breathed, feeling numb all over. "Thank God."

Then he heard the voice high above him bellowing, larger than life. *"The Game at the castle, Rondel Marcos. You and the other chosen one must play the Game. Wait for my message...."*

The voice faded away. The glow died. Exhausted, Rondel pushed himself to his feet. He felt dizzy, disoriented. Play the Game, he thought. Play it and win.

"But remember, Rondel," a less ominous voice whispered. The professor's? "Demons deceive. So does The Visitor."

RONDEL FELT SICK that night, in his heart, in his head, in his body. He'd seen Roland Popporov, dead. He'd heard The Visitor's voice. He'd stared at the blood....

Safe and dry now at the watchtower, he shivered. It was a constant thing, involuntary, he couldn't stop. He squeezed his eyes tightly shut. Delanie...

He'd collected her from the cottage in a daze and told her everything. He didn't know if he'd explained it clearly, or if she'd understood. "Fire... Visitor... Deception... Professor!"

He felt Delanie beside him on the bed, her hands in his hair and on his shoulders. She pulled off his coat, then his shirt, his boots and his jeans. She somehow got the covers pulled up over him.

"Don't go," he said to her, turning his head on the pillow.

She ran her fingers through his hair, then bent and kissed him. "I won't."

There was no violence in the storm that night, no thunder or lightning, only the wind and the rain and broken black clouds. But even that wasn't a promising sight. If anything, the effect was eerier than the electrical storms of the previous nights. The wind howled beyond the tower walls, and so for some reason did one of Dex's wolf-dogs. And sometimes, when the clouds separated, they took on the aspect of huge hands, reaching out for him and Delanie....

"Don't think about it," Delanie said, curling her soft, warm body around his trembling one.

Rondel moved closer, his face pressed into her neck. "Popporov's dead. I saw him. It shouldn't have been possible."

"I know," she said. She didn't try to rationalize it, but then she of all people would understand, wouldn't she?

Far away in Klausberg, the village clock began to strike. "Midnight," Rondel murmured when it finished. "Walpurgis and the sixth temptation." Another shudder tore through him. "We have to play the Game."

A PONDEROUS KNOCK sounded on the watchtower door at eleven o'clock on Sunday morning. Delanie didn't want to answer it, but she had to. Rondel was on the telephone with the Klausberg police.

The day was the blackest she'd seen so far. No breeze stirred, no rain fell, no thunder disturbed the unnatural silence.

"Who is it?" she called from the entry hall.

The only response was another heavy knock.

She pressed her head to the wood for a moment, then took a deep bolstering breath and turned the bolt.

A robed and hooded figure greeted her. Its head was bent so that the hood concealed the wearer's face. Both hands were folded into the large sleeves.

She recalled the skeleton at the castle and kept herself carefully distant as she ventured a tentative, "Yes?"

"Message for Delanie Morgen and Rondel Marcos," a muffled voice revealed. She couldn't discern who or what this was. A gloved hand brought a small ivory envelope from inside one of the sleeves. "From The Visitor."

The messenger's head remained bent downward. Delanie had a sudden impulse to throw the hood back, but better judgment prevailed. She didn't need to be shocked this early on Walpurgis. No doubt she'd have plenty of that later.

"Anything else?" she asked, accepting the envelope without touching the gloved fingers.

"Obey," the figure said simply.

It sounded amused, and when she thought about it, not quite real. The voice had a husky aspect to it, but it wasn't terribly deep. She studied the robes closely. Could this messenger possibly be a woman?

A tiny sound that might have been a chuckle came from beneath the hood. "Until tonight," the figure said, then it turned and started into the courtyard.

Delanie glanced at the envelope, then up again. She should have been shocked. She wasn't. The figure was gone. Like Popporov at the Cemetery Rocks, it had vanished into the gloom.

Come to the castle at 9:00 p.m. Use the entrance in the cave by the stream. You will be led to your destination....

"Led to your doom would be more appropriate," Delanie said to Rondel after they'd read the message. Her eyes strayed to the dismal black sky. "It's like there's no light left in the world. Is there anything we can do to prepare for this Game?"

He joined her at the window, his hands running lightly up and down her arms. "Nothing."

She looked up at his implacable features. "We could take a weapon," she suggested, but he shook his head.

"And then what?" he challenged softly. "Wait for The Visitor or his last demon to turn it on us? I don't want to believe in a corporeal devil, Delanie, but there's some kind of exceptional mental power involved here. Someone's manipulating people and circumstances. How do we know we can fight that?"

"Manipulation," Delanie murmured. She stared at the eastern sky, where intermittent bolts of lightning flashed over the Brocken. "The way Gerda seems to have been manipulated on the bridge that day with the baroness and the burgermeister, and in the cellar with me on Friday night." She leaned into his chest. "But what about Adolph? You said The Visitor's 'last' demon might turn a weapon on us. Since Popporov must have been a demon and he's—" she shuddered "—dead, then what does that make Adolph? Dead demon, or human victim?"

Rondel rested his cheek against her hair. "You tell me. You're the sensitive."

"Evil and cold," she said. "No soul—or a forfeited soul, I'm not sure which—but those are the things I felt in him. He could have been a demon. Maybe that's why Popporov was eliminated."

"Or it could be that demons who get caught have to die."

"Some kind of pact, you mean. They commit suicide if they're captured?"

"You said it happened twice before."

"Well, yes, but—how did Popporov get the knife he used? The guard said no one could have come in after hours, and before that, he was being watched constantly. We were there. I don't see how anyone could have slipped anything to him."

"Neither do I," Rondel said.

She felt the tightness of fear slide through his body. It wasn't in his voice or his touch, but it was there inside him, and that frightened her. Rondel had grown up with Mahira. He was familiar with her powers, he accepted them. For Delanie this was a new and terrifying experience, a deep involvement in matters she could barely begin to understand.

The sky darkened, casting thicker shadows over the watchtower. No fire burned in the grate. "No more visions," Rondel said flatly, but Delanie wasn't sure it really made a difference. When she looked up at the clouds, she swore she saw two paler patches, like slashes of sulphur laid over black pitch.

Like a pair of enormous slanted eyes watching their every move.

DELANIE'S FEET wouldn't budge. "I can't go in there," she whispered to Rondel at the mouth of the cave. "I can't do it."

"Yes you can." He stood behind her, staring into the gloom.

Night had fallen, and the lightning from the Brocken had crept closer. Thunder rumbled over the castle. Each time the sky lit up, Delanie saw those grotesque yellow eyes.

"Chimera," Rondel called it. "The picture's being placed in your mind."

Of course that had to be the case, but it frightened Delanie that she couldn't repel it. Now her frustration mounted. Why couldn't she bring herself to enter the cave?

"I will do this," she said out loud. She hunched her shoulders in defiance of whatever force had invaded her mind. "For the professor. For all of us."

"That is your decision, then?" a voice from the shadows before them inquired.

Startled, Delanie slammed back into Rondel. "It's the messenger," she exclaimed in a barely audible whisper.

The robed and hooded figure emerged from the depths of the cave. No part of its face or body was visible. The hood hung forward so far that only blackness could be seen inside it.

"That's our decision," Rondel answered.

"Then come, chosen two." With a gloved hand, the messenger beckoned to them. "Come and face the final temptation. The six tests of the Game within a Game await you. I am selected to be your guide. I am the eyes and ears of The Visitor. I lead you now into the tunnels. Fail one test, and I will lead both you and your angel into hell."

The figure chanted the Story as it led them through the cavernous darkness of the underground tunnel.

" 'For so the ancient Story tells, four demons will return to hell, sent there by one from heaven's door.... ' "

"The professor," Rondel said under his breath.

"Angel," the figure corrected, then continued, " 'who'll catch these demons one to four. But not the demons five and six, and not The Visitor whose tricks cannot be faced by one so pure. Two humans must these trials endure.' "

"Guess what?" Delanie murmured with a meaningful glance at Rondel.

Truthfully she didn't know where the spark of sarcasm came from. She didn't feel sarcastic or even marginally confident. The figure unnerved her to the point of recklessness. It was all she could do not to rip off that hood and see who hid beneath it. If only the figure would stop its morbid chanting and let her think.

" 'So this is it,' " the figure intoned. It seemed to glide rather than walk through the shadows. " 'The Story told, related to us long ago. Of Lucifer, the devil, or the evil one, The Visitor.' "

"Lucifer," Delanie repeated to Rondel. She tried very hard not to notice the feeling she had that the walls were watching them. "The fallen angel, supreme master in hell."

"Doesn't seem fair, does it?" Rondel returned, his eyes trained on the now-silent figure. "Humans against Satan."

Delanie thought the figure laughed softly, but she couldn't be sure. The only certainty here seemed to be that nothing was certain. Nothing was as it appeared or felt. Eyes in the clouds, visions in the fire, talking skeletons, demons—what was real?

Desperation and fear battled each other in her head. Despite her warm clothing, and Rondel's presence at her side, Delanie shivered. Darkness reigned inside and out, a horror movie come to life. The people of Klausberg would be huddled about their warm fires, telling the Story, while the chosen two lived it. And the angel, oh, God, where was he? How would this nightmare end for any of them?

From out of the black void, an archway slowly took shape. A set of barred double doors stood just inside. The figure glided soundlessly forward and lifted the heavy bar as though it weighed nothing at all. It opened both doors, then stood aside and tucked its gloved hands back into its sleeves.

"Enter here," it told them, gesturing into a new tunnel of darkness with its hooded head. "Once you pass through these doors, you may only go forward. The way back will be barred. The six tests await. Welcome to the world of The Visitor."

Chapter Sixteen

The Visitor's world was as close to hell as Delanie ever wanted to come. Through the blackness they walked, to a smaller wooden door. The figure followed at a discreet distance. It said nothing, merely stood and waited while Rondel turned the iron handle.

Delanie drew back from the glare that greeted them. The chamber was blue-white, alive with fluorescent lights, so many of them that for a moment she felt physically sick. The room was empty and cold—and moving, she realized with a start.

"Rondel, where are we, what is this?" she asked. Her skin had gone ice-cold. She pressed her palms to her cheeks and took a deep breath. "Why do I feel so strange?"

"It's an illusion." His warm body against hers helped her maintain her balance. "The walls are giant screens. They give the impression of motion."

"But it's so stark." Delanie widened her eyes briefly, fighting to adjust her vision. "How can you see motion in that?"

"This is the entry chamber of The Visitor's Game," the figure said.

It had followed them inside and positioned itself in the corner, seeming to move as the walls did. Delanie fought a wave of dizziness and ordered herself to concentrate.

"You have thirty seconds upon completion to answer The Visitor's Question. As the seconds pass, the intensity of the light will increase and the temperature will drop. Fail this test, and you will be sealed within these walls until you die."

Delanie turned from the figure. "This can't be the same Game the club members play."

Rondel leaned over her to whisper, "Close your eyes for a second. It'll help."

Delanie tipped her head back. She would have complied, except that something had begun to stain the wall ahead of them. She stared with a blend of horror and disbelief as a long white finger seemed to paint words across it in red. Deep red, the exact color of blood.

She heard Rondel's sharply indrawn breath, and told herself what she was seeing was all a trick.

A horrible coppery odor filled the room. Delanie swallowed hard, forcing herself to breathe through her mouth. She focused on the words, not the blood scent or the finger, which looked as though it belonged on the skeleton she'd met in the castle corridor.

"Time begins now," the figure stated. "Twenty-nine, twenty-eight, twenty-seven."

Think, Delanie ordered herself, scanning the blood-written words. But the words were a riddle, they made no sense.

"'What is the beginning of eternity, the end of time and space, the beginning of every end and the end of every race?'" she read out loud. Frustration set her nerves on edge. "That doesn't mean anything!"

Rondel stared at the wall. "It must. Think."

She was, but the room was getting cold now. She could see her breath. At least, she could until the light grew so harsh that she had to squint just to see the shimmering red words.

Teeth chattering, she inched closer. "I am the reflection of your death," the skeleton had predicted. Was that it? Death? The beginning and the end? "Beginning of eternity," she murmured. "End of time and space." She raised her voice. "Is it death?"

The figure chuckled. "Nineteen, eighteen, seventeen . . ."

Not death.

"What about God?" Rondel questioned softly.

"Twelve, eleven, ten . . ."

Delanie couldn't feel her fingers anymore. "Well, it can't be The Visitor," she said with rising panic. "End of time, end of space, beginning of every end, end of . . ." She stopped suddenly and grabbed Rondel's arm. "Spelling!" she exclaimed. "Letters, Rondel. The word *time* ends with the letter E. End of space, beginning of end . . ." She appealed to the glowing white walls. "Is it the letter E?"

For the longest time, nothing happened. Then, slowly, the words began to fade away. The walls stopped moving, the temperature rose. Behind them the figure dipped its head farther. "The Visitor's Question has been answered," it conceded in a monotone. A panel to their left slid open. "You may live, chosen two. For now."

PASS THIS TEST, then you will lose. Fail and pass. Now you must choose.

"More riddles," Delanie remarked with a tremor that had nothing to do with cold this time. Cautiously, she brushed aside a stringy cobweb.

This second room was not white. It was an Addams world of real and rubber spiders, of dust and cobwebs and cheerless brown shadows. Along the walls sat two glass cases, each with several snakes curled up inside. Three minutes the figure had given them here. Then the cases would be opened.

Right now they faced the third of three rhymes offered to them in this room. All had been presented on scrolls and set out on the floor for them to decipher. Another cheat, to Delanie's mind.

"Three riddles in one test. That's not fair."

"Devil and demons deceive," Rondel reminded her. He glanced at his watch, bending over the last scroll. "Forty-seven seconds left."

Delanie's skin had been crawling ever since they'd entered this wretched stone chamber. A big black spider crept across the scroll, but Rondel merely brushed it off. He read the opening rhyme, then the evil-looking script below it.

"'Start with the numbers four and six, but be warned that the wrong answer to the following question is the right one— Which of the numbers above cannot be divided by two?'"

Sitting back, Rondel swept a cobweb from his dark hair. "Which cannot be divided by two," he repeated, then he frowned. "Neither, right?"

Delanie knelt beside him, struggling not to think about the spider that had just crawled over her foot. "'Neither' is the right answer," she said. "But the scroll says that the wrong answer is the right one. So if the right answer is 'neither,' the wrong one must be 'both,' which in this case would be the right answer—

"No, wait!" she interrupted herself. "That's not right, either, because the rhyme above the question says that if we pass the test, we lose. We have to fail it to win. So if 'both' is the answer to the second part of the riddle, then 'neither' must be the answer to the whole thing." She snatched her hand away from a particularly grotesque spider. "Like a triple negative."

Rondel stared at her. "I'd ask you to repeat that, but we're out of time. Try it."

She regarded the figure in the dusty corner. "The answer is 'neither.'"

Again there was a long empty silence, stretched-out seconds when nothing happened. The glass cases remained closed, but the snakes seemed to be slithering impatiently. Then a door beside them creaked open and the shadowy lights overhead were extinguished.

The figure's head moved. "The chosen two do not die in the Chamber of Spiders and Snakes. Proceed to the Mouth of the Dragon."

RONDEL'S HEAD was starting to hurt. He knew enough about Mahira's power to know that the pain was being induced, either mentally or through a burned powder.

Beside him, Delanie pushed the hair from her cheeks and stared at the enormous dragon facing them. "You mean we have to walk into its mouth?" she asked, dismayed.

Rondel squinted at the tongues of flame inside. The heat was increasing, making him dizzy. Perspiration slid down his neck.

Gently, he pulled off Delanie's jacket and his own. Not real, his mind kept insisting, but that didn't help much. It felt all too real at this point.

They crept carefully into the dragon's fanged mouth. Smoke and fire swirled around them. The ground felt spongy beneath Rondel's feet. He saw Delanie close her eyes.

"We're walking on the dragon's tongue," she whispered in revulsion.

"At least there's no blood," he said, waving at the smoke that stung his eyes.

"Walk through the fire," the figure following them instructed. Did it sound amused? Rondel glanced back but couldn't see it.

"We can't walk through fire," Delanie said, halting. "Rondel, we can't do that!"

"It's a passage of faith," he said, studying the wall of flames directly before them.

"But I—" she started to object, then broke off and squared her shoulders. "All right. Let's do it."

With a quick silent prayer, Rondel took her hand and stepped into the flames.

It was a thin barrier, he realized, easily penetrated.

Delanie stepped out. "Not real," she said, smiling in relief. Then she gave the fire a suspicious look. "But it felt real."

Rondel squinted through a thick curtain of smoke. He caught a rustle of rope and, glancing up, saw a human effigy being lowered into the same wall of fire through which they'd just passed. Seconds later, the smoldering rope was all that remained.

Delanie stood still, lifting only her eyes to his face.

"Real," Rondel said, baffled.

"I don't want to think about it," Delanie told him. "Let's just go on, shall we?"

Still puzzled, Rondel led the way cautiously through the dragon, past more fires and finally into the belly, which very much resembled a painting of Dante's *Inferno* that Rondel had seen in Lisbon. Before them stood a low table. On the table sat a strand of beads and a scale. High above, a hundred or more metal spikes hung ready to impale them.

The figure materialized behind them. "For this test you are given two minutes," it revealed. "During that time, the fangs of the dragon will begin to descend. Fail this test and you will be pierced by the dragon's teeth."

Was the figure's voice growing more malevolent? Rondel couldn't be sure. His head had begun to hurt quite badly now.

"On this table is a strand of nine pearls, painted black," the figure said. "Among them is a fake, which weighs less than the others. The scales may be used two times only. Find the fake pearl and place it in the tray beside the dragon's rib."

Delanie stared at the table in horror, but Rondel knew she was thinking. He risked a look up. As promised, the metal fangs were descending. The teeth of death.

He forced his mind to function. "Math," he murmured. "Logic." He knelt and picked up the black strand. Concentrate, he ordered himself. Break the string. Was that allowed? He looked back at Delanie, then broke the sturdy thread.

"Eight loose pearls," she whispered, "and one fake. But they all feel like they're the same weight." On her knees now, too, she set the beads down, glanced at the descending spikes. "They're getting closer."

"I know." For sixty of the precious one hundred and twenty seconds, Rondel considered the matter. Holding the hair away from his forehead with one hand, he told her, "Take six of the pearls, Delanie, any six, and put three on each side of the scale."

He refused to look at the spikes, which would stab them now if they stood. His eyes flicked to the balance needle. "Okay, they're even."

Delanie nodded. "So the fake isn't among these six pearls."

"Right." Rondel scooped up the remaining three, while she emptied the scales. "How much time?"

"Eighteen seconds."

The robed figure watched in silence. Rondel swore softly and set two of the three pearls in either pan.

"There!" Delanie pointed. "The left one's lighter. That's the fake." She scrambled over and dropped the false pearl in the appropriate tray. Then she backed away until she collided with Rondel's leg.

Did the fangs stop inching downward? With all the smoke swirling through the dragon's belly, it was difficult to see, but they must have. Their time was up.

It took forever for the figure to stir. When it spoke, it sounded dangerous. Its voice echoed around the dragon's smoldering stomach as the spikes slowly began to rise.

"You have walked through fire and found the false pearl. Leave by the dragon's wing and do not look back. If you do, you will be destroyed by the Fork of The Visitor."

IT WAS a nightmare, pure and simple. Screams erupted behind them, hideous cries of pain. Rondel even thought he heard Roland Popporov calling out to him.

"It is torture down here," the dead demon wailed. "Please, someone, help me!"

And then the burgermeister let out an agonized wail. "I am sorry, Fräulein Morgen, truly sorry for what I have done. Help me, please!"

Rondel saw flames in his mind, towering walls of orange. "Run from the fires of hell," the robed figure urged him. "Run from the two who call to you."

"It's a lie," Rondel said, shaking the damp hair from his face. "Mental manipulation."

Delanie appeared to be fighting off the same dreadful sights and sounds. Fingers pressed to her temples, she peered into the darkness ahead. "Fork of the Visitor," she said, echoing the figure's words. "That's behind us. I hate to think what's in front. Is that a door up there?"

It looked like three doors to Rondel, but only until he forced the imaginary flames away and focused his eyes. He opened his mouth to speak, then snapped it shut again as a new voice reached his ears.

"Rondel, stop! You cannot win."

"Mahira!"

He almost lost control and looked back, but Delanie stopped him, setting her hands firmly on his face. "No," she said, her tone frantic. "It's a trick. She's not here. Fight it, Rondel. Use your mind."

It took all of Rondel's willpower and more to resist Mahira's cries.

"Rondel, no," Mahira pleaded. "Do not go through that door. It is—"

Her voice broke off abruptly. A hot wind began to blow down the stone corridor. Out of the darkness, a pair of yellow eyes opened. The figure glided past them. Raising its gloved hands, it made a silent motion. Immediately, an invisible door swung back.

"Go then," it said with deep contempt. "Go into the Chamber of Icons. Let your religion serve you."

Rondel ignored the cold tone and the yellow eyes and the hot air that blasted them as they stepped inside. A long red carpet led to an altar upon which stood a golden statue.

Delanie's eyes were wide with confusion. "A statue of Jesus in the middle of all this?" Suspicion tinged her voice. "What kind of a test is this?"

Rondel's gaze combed the room. In the opposite corner stood a statue of the devil, complete with horns and a beard, also made of gold. The other two corners contained wooden crosses, one inverted, the other properly hung.

The robed figure went to stand beside the devil. "Choose your God," it commanded. "Approach the proper altar, kneel and call Him by name."

"It's too easy," Rondel said softly, taking Delanie's hand. "Do you sense anything?"

"No, but Satan's no god. That only leaves the statue of Jesus."

The figure spoke again. "Be warned," it said. Did it sound vaguely smug? "Each altar has a kneeling pad, yet only one of these pads will bear the weight of your prayers. Choose unwisely, and you will be sent to the depths of hell." Gloved fingers spread wide. "Do not choose at all, and you will meet the same fate."

"Sent to hell," Delanie echoed dully. Her cheeks were pale, her eyes large and frightened. "You mean we're not already there? It can't be the Satan statue, Rondel. It has to be Jesus. Maybe the trick's in the simplicity."

Mistrustfully, Rondel surveyed the golden statue of Jesus. "It's not right," he said again.

"You have forty seconds," the figure told them, and Rondel swore to himself. He was sick to death of this Game.

Cautiously, he approached the statue. Sandals on Jesus' feet, loose robes on his body, in his hands a loaf of bread, and around his neck... Rondel's stomach muscles tightened.

"No!" He held Delanie back. "Look at his neck. He's wearing an inverted cross. It's not Jesus!"

"Twenty seconds," the figure informed them.

Rondel grabbed Delanie's hand. "It's the Ten Commandments," he said, dragging her off the carpet. "'Thou shalt have no other gods before Me.' That statue's made of gold, and it's not in the image of God."

"A golden idol. Then what...?"

"The cross. That's our altar."

They ran for the corner where the wooden cross was suspended, fell to their knees and addressed it as they'd been instructed.

Nothing happened. They waited in silence for the figure to speak. It seemed a longer interval each time, as if The Visitor wanted to make them sweat.

"I don't think we're supposed to have made it this far," Delanie whispered.

Rondel shook his head. He could feel the hostility in the air and the heat which was still rising. He said nothing. If

The Visitor expected impatience at the delay, he was going to be disappointed. They had knelt at the proper altar.

"You may proceed," the figure finally announced. The words were muffled, the tone displeased. It motioned to another door. "You now enter the Chamber of One Question. It is doubtful that you will exit alive."

"IT'S LIKE an old burial chamber," Delanie said as they crossed the next threshold. She shoved the damp hair from her face with an impatient hand. "I just know there are going to be skeletons in here."

Rondel played his flashlight beam carefully around the room.

Something snapped beneath Delanie's heel. It managed to sound brittle despite the must of half a dozen centuries. This was getting more macabre by the minute. And yet, one thing puzzled her.

Why wasn't The Visitor playing more with their minds, bombarding them with images and voices as he had done in the beginning? Unless, of course, he felt they'd learned how to deal with that kind of mental assault.

Pushing her thoughts away, she looked down. The ground was rough and slippery in spots. Inset on the stone walls were a number of slabs, many of them occupied, if her eyes could be trusted.

The room was dark and still. It had a definite graveyard feel to it. They were obviously quite some distance underground, and yet the heat was stifling, as if they were approaching a giant furnace. Delanie hated to think what that meant.

Rondel nodded at two doors on the far wall. Two gray-robed figures stood guard before them. She caught a flash of dirty white bone under one of the hoods and had to grind her teeth to keep from screaming.

Rondel's fingers curled themselves around the nape of her neck. "Graveyard ghouls," he said quietly. "Centuries ago, they were placed in German cemeteries, as sentinels."

Delanie dug in her heels, unwilling to go closer. "I can't..." she began, then gasped. "It moved, Rondel! I saw one of the hands move!"

The figure behind them spoke before Rondel could respond.

"You are in the Chamber of One Question," it said. Its tone was decidedly menacing now. "The doors before you are passageways. One leads to heaven, the other to hell. Beside them stand two guardians. The guardian of heaven's door is ever-truthful. The guardian of hell's door will always lie. You have one minute in which to ask one question of one guardian. Pass through the door to heaven and you will be directed to the angel. Pass through the door to hell and you will die."

"I don't believe this," Delanie murmured. Then she marshaled her strength. "No, I won't give in. We're allowed one question, but we don't know which ghoul will answer truthfully, right?"

She felt Rondel's hands on her arms. He was silent for several seconds, then he said thoughtfully, "I have an idea."

Delanie slid her eyes to his face.

"One question," he said to the motionless guardian on the right. He glanced at the other, then back again. "If I asked this question of your companion, which door would he say led to heaven?"

A bony hand rose, its finger outstretched. Delanie ordered herself not to step back.

"He's pointing to the door on the left," she said and tried to understand what that signified. But it was difficult to concentrate with two black eye sockets staring at her and the word *death* racing around in her head. "A lie or the truth?"

Rondel reasoned it out. "Let's assume he's the guardian who tells the truth. He would point to the wrong door because that's the one his lying counterpart would point to."

"And if he's the guardian who lies..." Delanie continued.

"Then he would automatically lie about which door the guardian of truth would indicate, so the one he's indicating must still be the wrong door."

A frown touched Delanie's lips. "That sounds right," she agreed. She set her hand on the iron handle. "Please be right," she whispered. Squeezing her eyes closed, she gave the ring a twist.

TIME STOPPED for an endless stretch of seconds. Finally, the door swung open. Hell or heaven? Rondel wondered. He looked back. The figure that had been following them had disappeared. Was that a good sign?

They stepped across a pitch-black threshold that smelled like wet earth. A very gloomy place for heaven. On the other hand, they were still alive.

They entered a small stone room with two diagonal corridors branching off from it. At the juncture stood another ghoul in gray robes. Shadows fell across its skull face.

"Now what?" Delanie said nervously.

Rondel regarded the unmoving figure. "We wait."

It felt like hours before a man's voice, this one amplified and sounding as if it was all around them, grudgingly conceded, "You have passed through heaven's door. The Game is over. You have won. The final guardian points the way to the angel."

Rondel's head still throbbed, but at least the heat had subsided. He watched as the figure motioned toward the left tunnel.

"The way is shown," the amplified voice said in a tone of defeat. "The angel waits."

Delanie glanced up at the roof of the passage. "We win? As simple as that?"

No answer.

Rondel released a tired breath. "It looks like there's only one way to find out."

She compressed her lips. "I knew you were going to say that."

Somehow this didn't feel like a victory to Rondel. Nevertheless, they started down the darkened passageway, pushing cobwebs aside as they went.

"Delanie, Rondel, are you there?" a voice far ahead called out.

Delanie's fingers tightened on his wrist. "It's the professor!"

"Where are you, professor?" Rondel called back.

"In one of the tunnels. From the direction of your voice, I'd say you should keep going left. But hurry. There's a time limit they didn't tell you about, and you've almost reached the end of it."

"Time?" Delanie repeated. She slowed her steps. "How much time?"

"Judging from the height of the blade over my chest, I'd say—ahh—no more than thirty seconds. Run, Delanie. Run!"

She hesitated, then shook her head and halted. "No," she said firmly, although her expression was one of agitation. "This isn't right. It feels like—no! The professor wouldn't yell for help."

Rondel rubbed his pounding temple. Another trick? "He might if he had a knife over him."

He saw her brow furrow. She began counting on her fingers. "The white room, the spider room, the dragon with the pearls, the room with golden statues, the Chamber of One Question." Her head came up. "That's only five tests. The sixth—" She looked around as if expecting something to pounce. "The sixth must have something to do with where we are now." She tugged frantically on his hand. "Rondel, that ghoul back there sent us down the wrong corridor!"

BEHIND THEM, Rondel heard an ominous rumble, prelude to a cave-in, he realized with a jolt of recognition. They had to get out of here.

"Run!" he shouted to Delanie, giving her a push.

A huge chunk of the wall broke off, crashing to the ground at his feet. The shadows deepened. Dust clouds swirled around them. He heard the tiny explosions that preceded the collapse of various sections of the tunnel. He could see it happening in his mind. The archway was falling apart.

His lungs ached from the dust. The sixth test, he thought hazily. Fundamental oversight. Why hadn't he counted?

"There!" Delanie raced for the quivering stone arch that was all that remained of the opening. Already, rocks had piled up beneath it. One hit Rondel's shoulder and another his leg as they scrambled over the top.

Grabbing Delanie around the waist, he hauled her sideways to the juncture. Seconds later, the entire arch collapsed.

"The guardian's gone," Delanie said, choking on the dust that followed them out. She climbed to her feet, waving at the thick cloud. "I wonder if that's good or bad?"

Standing with difficulty, Rondel took her hand. "It couldn't be any worse than what we've just been through. Come on."

They entered a cleaner tunnel this time, shadowy, but not draped with cobwebs. And yet something here didn't feel right, either.

They passed several doors as they walked, all bolted from the inside. Nothing stirred in the gloom. No sound broke the silence. Too easy, his brain warned. His feet dragged. His skin felt damp and chilled.

The tunnel gradually widened. Dark forks appeared, branching off in all directions. From one of them a hot breath of wind blew across his face.

"No," Delanie protested when he would have walked toward it. "I feel something. Evil. Treachery."

Behind them, one of the bolted doors creaked open. The robed and hooded figure that had been with them earlier glided out.

Delanie pressed herself against Rondel's arm. "What do you want?" she asked in distrust. "We passed The Visitor's tests. All six of them."

The figure drew closer.

"What are you?" Rondel challenged when it didn't respond. "A demon?"

The robed shoulders shook with silent laughter. "Demon?" it questioned in amusement. Then its voice roughened. "Can your mind not see me for what I am, Rondel? Do you not feel my presence, Delanie?"

It took another step, then stopped and lifted an arm. Light flared around it, an aureole of deep red light. Dust particles rose and swirled as the figure touched its hands to the folds of its hood.

"Am I Death, Delanie Morgen?" it taunted. The voice became louder, clearer, nearly recognizable. Gloved fingers eased the hood back. "No, not Death, not a demon," it answered itself. The hood fell away. The head lifted. Triumph lit its smile. "I am your nemesis, chosen two. I am the Visitor!"

Chapter Seventeen

"Nothing to say?" the unhooded figure challenged. It let out a delighted laugh. "No comments, Rondel? I am the supreme demon in hell. Does that not surprise you?"

The robe swished as The Visitor spun about in the tunnel. Threads of red light burnished the edges, creating an evil glow. Delanie felt breathless, off balance. This was The Visitor?

"Yes," the figure answered, stopping to fix her with an amused stare. "I am The Visitor. I am Satan. And you, chosen two, are at my mercy." The amusement faded. An outstretched finger pointed accusingly at them. "You would have prevented me from having my revenge, so I took matters into my own hands. I did not send an underling demon to do the devil's work. I came to you myself. I watched you play the Game."

Win the Game, Delanie couldn't resist thinking. She still had trouble accepting the truth. And yet why should it seem farfetched to her? Because she hadn't *felt* it?

"Ah, yes." The Visitor, smiling again, began to strip off the encumbering robes. "You felt no evil in me, did you, Delanie? And that bothers you. Maybe you're not so 'sensitive' after all. Don't move, Rondel." A gun appeared, drawn out of the robe pocket. The Visitor's teeth gleamed in the bloodred light. "Bullets kill humans most effectively."

Rondel stared. "Why not kill us with your mind, instead?" he challenged cautiously. "You are a psychic, aren't you?"

"And you are extremely insolent, considering that this gun is pointed at your throat." The Visitor's eyes narrowed. "I'm also a much better shot than my number five demon. Arrogant little being."

Delanie's heart pounded. She felt the pulse beneath her throat racing. Crazy, she thought. Why hadn't she sensed that? Had Aric Bellal been insane, as well?

The Visitor's amused eyes turned to her pale face. "Very dangerous thought, Delanie. I would watch my mind if I were you. You have powers, yes, but they are insignificant compared to those which I possess. I'm the strongest in my family. That is why I am supreme. Aric couldn't rival me. Oh, he tried, of course, many times, but he was no match for me."

Rondel studied The Visitor's serene features. "Aric Bellal died thirty years ago. You wouldn't have been old enough to challenge him."

The Visitor's lips curved into a smug smile. "Illusion, Rondel. Clever artifice. I'm not as young as I look. But the gender you see, now that is quite correct. And how would your male-dominated human world react to that truth, I wonder?"

Laughter rang out in the tunnel. The rush of hot air increased. Sulphurous. Fiery.

Delanie couldn't quite catch her breath. A deranged psychic. Powerful. And yes, against all stereotypes, female. She hadn't expected this.

"Ah, but you should have foreseen the possibility," The Visitor's voice seemed to whisper into her head.

Delanie's mind blurred. Snatches of a conversation came to her through the inexorable din. A woman said, "Dr. Hoffman fears falling from high places."

"Lucifer fell," The Visitor said out loud, still laughing. Then she whispered a mocking, "But you're on the right track, Delanie." She turned the gun. "Come one step closer,

Rondel, and I will shoot. Now, think, Delanie. What else was said that night?''

Fire, Delanie thought faintly, aware of The Visitor's mind in hers, yet unable to shut it out. Gerda feared fire.

"Hell is fire," The Visitor reminded in an evil hiss. "Continue."

She heard Rondel's voice. "What are you doing to her?" he demanded. He sounded very far away.

Delanie pressed her hands to the sides of her head. Concentrate. John Kessler, hypnotizing the club members—the answer resided partly in that act. Or did it? Could The Visitor be manipulating her?

"Think," the Visitor commanded, drawing closer.

Rondel shook her shoulders. "Stop it, Delanie."

No, there was something in this. Domination, that was it. Control. "I do not like men who think they can control me."

She could see the woman who spoke, hear the music that swelled behind her. Beer hall music, loud, people everywhere. Then she saw a mane of long chestnut hair, a blue silk dress. "Where is Harry?" Hazel eyes blinked innocently. Small pout on her lips; wistful sigh. "My last husband's relatives owned this castle."

Delanie heard laughter in her ears, endless laughter, then caught a distant cry of warning. "Demons deceive!"

She pictured the hazel eyes again, saw them slowly turn yellow. Around them, a woman's face took on definite shape. Owner of the castle. The woman who'd confessed, "I do not like men who think they can control me!" The liar who had said, "I did not know Aric Bellal personally."

The face emerged completely from the shadows now. Angular features, older than they looked. They were the features of The Visitor, the Baroness Alicia von Peldt!

MAHIRA'S BONY HANDS passed through the flames in the cave. The Sisters rocked back and forth on their knees, a silent force of minds from which she drew an added measure of energy.

Smoke circled her head. She looked through it, straight to the center of the fire. An image was born, as dark as blood on black tar. The smell of brimstone reached her.

She half closed her eyes, rocking as the Sisters did now. Softly she began to incant, "'For so the ancient Story tells, four demons will return to hell, sent there by one from heaven's door, who'll catch these demons one to four. But not the demons five and six, and not The Visitor whose tricks cannot be faced by one so pure. Two humans must these trials endure....'"

Hazy faces took shape within the smoke. She saw horns, then slanted yellow eyes, and sinuous limbs. A tiny demon danced through the fire, flicking its tail. Its beard was flame, its laughter audible above the crackle of the wood. "Play the Game," it teased, then laughed and darted away.

Mahira's eyes closed.

"What is it, Leader?" one of the sisters cried out.

"Trickery," the old witch answered. She passed her hand through the flames again. The smoke stirred. Faces appeared, cloaked in shadow. The chosen two. The Game continued. Did they know that? Did they understand?

Leaning forward, she directed her words to the fire. "Demons deceive!"

THE PICTURES in Delanie's mind shattered, as if the baroness had placed them there, then sharply withdrawn them. Delanie opened her eyes. "Gone," she whispered to Rondel, who still held her arms. "Words and images...she wanted me to remember. Fear of domination."

"Poorly put," the baroness said calmly. She slipped a cigarette and lighter from the pocket of her red silk dress. "As you might imagine, I don't fear domination so much as I refuse to be dominated."

Delanie's mind still felt vaguely invaded, unsure. The hot air continued to pour through the tunnel. The red light deepened, as if they had passed into hell, she thought hazily. But wasn't this supposed to be the passageway to heaven?

The Baroness lit her cigarette.

"Rondel," Delanie shook herself, forcing her thoughts into order. "What about the Game?"

He nodded. "You sure you're all right?"

"No—yes. But the Game, we won, didn't we?"

With an elegant arch of her neck, the baroness exhaled a stream of smoke. "You're forgetting the Story, Delanie. I quote, '. . . if they play the Game and that survive and win, defame the devil's demons six and five, they'll find the angel still alive.'"

Delanie watched the gun with uncertain eyes. "But we did all of that."

"No, you did not," the Baroness said flatly. The gun and her eyes flashed in the red light. "Adolph Schiller was not a demon."

"Then who . . . ?"

The Baroness took a step closer. Menace lit her features. "That is for you to determine." Her smile became one of pure malevolence. Her voice rose. "My power on this earth shall be decided for a century. But only if my demons lose." Cigarette smoke spiraled around Delanie's head. She edged closer to Rondel as the baroness advanced on them. "My demons did not lose, Delanie. Number six is alive and well. It is you who have lost. You and your precious angel, brother to Anna, who took the life of my brother, Aric."

Delanie pressed a hand to the tunnel wall for support. Her head and her senses reeled. *Evil!* Now the word crashed over her.

"Yes, evil," the Baroness confirmed. "Quintessential evil. Death to those who oppose me." Amusement lurked in her eyes. "It gives me pleasure to torment lesser creatures, to manipulate minds with nothing more than a simple thought. 'Hate,' I said silently to Gerda, and the floodgates opened wide."

Gerda, Delanie recalled distantly. Yes, of course.

The hot air was affecting her balance badly now. And Rondel's. But his eyes were focused on the gun in Alicia's slender hand.

Think, Delanie ordered herself. Gerda. The bridge. The Baroness had been there. She'd exploited Gerda's feelings to set up a temptation. And later at the castle, she must have used Gerda again, to threaten her in the cellar.

"Yes," the baroness said. "All true, Delanie." The hot wind caught and lifted strands of her chestnut hair. The gun shone black in the unearthly light. Delanie felt Rondel tense. What was he planning?

No! Don't do that. Hold The Visitor's attention. Distract her. Think of other questions. Had Adolph been manipulated, too?

"Only through his fear," the baroness replied. "Of God."

She laughed. Her feet carried her smoothly forward. There was no sound to her steps. Delanie looked down. Had she seen hooves?

The illusion dissolved. More laughter echoed through the tunnels. Rondel touched her back, then eased away. A signal? No, she must not think about him. Create a diversion.

Eyes closing briefly, Delanie collected her resistance to this woman's mental strength. The red light shimmered. *Evil!* And yet . . .

She opened her eyes. "You're putting these thoughts in my head," she whispered, her terror deepening. "Why?"

"Why not?" the baroness returned. A shadow fell across her shoulder. Did she see it, sense it?

"What," Delanie said hastily, "are you going to do with us?"

"What," the Baroness mocked, "would you suggest? You failed to defeat my demon number six. But even if you had, who's to say that I would have played fair with you. Only one rule in this Game is truly unbreakable."

The shadow shifted. Delanie kept her mind blank as she held the baroness's gaze. "Which rule?"

"Walpurgis."

"I don't understand."

"It is 10:53 p.m. If before midnight you were to learn the identity of my number six demon, I would have to—" her smile widened "—well, concede defeat is I suppose the best way to put it."

"You mean you'd take us to the professor?"

The baroness gave an eloquent shrug. An affirmation?

She glided forward another step. The gun was trained on Delanie's chest. The heat was almost unbearable.

"Blond like an angel," she murmured, so close now that Delanie could see the flecks of yellow in her hazel eyes. "But a poor choice, I think. Still, Aric might enjoy you."

The shadow fell across the baroness's arm. Delanie saw it. The baroness didn't appear to.

"Aric's in hell?" Delanie asked. Blood roared in her ears. The wind rushed over her

The Baroness smiled. "Aric is where he belongs, but most unhappy in his confinement. I will give you to him as an amusement. For myself, I might take Rondel."

Her gaze slid sideways. The gun jerked. Her eyes snapped back, boring into Delanie's. "Where is he?"

A sudden fiery pain burst through Delanie's head.

"Where!"

Delanie's groping hand found the baroness's arm. The shadow resolved itself into a man. Rondel . . .

With a snarl, the baroness ripped her arm free. Delanie sprawled facedown on the ground. The baroness's cigarette smoldered in the dirt. The smoke revived her somewhat.

She felt no pain now, but her head still spun. She scrambled to her knees. Where was Rondel?

Sounds of a struggle reached her. The gun thudded, then was kicked away. Delanie looked for it, but something else intruded.

What had she felt when she touched the baroness? Evil, yes, and treachery. *Deceit.*

What did that last thing mean?

She saw the discarded robe in the dirt, heard the baroness above her. "You would dare to strike a woman?"

Delanie almost laughed. Her cold fingers latched onto the robe. She struggled to her feet.

"Let me go!" the baroness shrieked.

Delanie caught a movement in the gloom near one of the archways. She stumbled to the door from which the baroness had emerged. Small cell, bolts on both sides. Good.

She fought an attack of vertigo. "Rondel, here!" she cried, leaning heavily on the tunnel wall.

He swung the angry baroness around. Pushing off, De-lanie threw the robe over her head. "In there!" she panted, motioning at the tiny room.

The baroness kicked and screamed. "I will kill you for this!"

Rondel shoved her into the cell. Delanie slammed the door.

"You will suffer," the baroness shouted. "Feel great pain!"

"Block her mind, Delanie," Rondel warned above the woman's pounding fists.

He bolted the door, then dragged Delanie from the wall. Confusion filled her mind. "Demons deceive," she whis-pered, no longer sure where the words in her head came from.

"I am The Visitor!" the baroness screamed. "You will release me!"

Her rage was an invisible force in the tunnel. It ham-mered at Delanie's control, twisted it. She dug her fingers into Rondel's skin. "No," she whispered. "Something's wrong. Can't you feel it's all wrong?"

He drew her to the other side away from the light and the burning wind. "What's wrong, Delanie?"

"She is." Delanie searched her tangled thoughts. "I can't explain it. She's not telling us the truth. I mean she is, but she isn't. There's something else, something devious hap-pening here."

He stared at her, uncomprehending. "You mean the bar-oness isn't The Visitor?"

"No—yes—no. I don't know. The skeleton I saw at the castle, it was a man. I know it was. It said it was Death. The devil is Death. The devil is also treacherous, and strong. And yet the baroness does have some kind of mental power, I can feel it. That much is real."

"I'm real!" the baroness shouted angrily. "I am The Visitor. I am supreme. I will not be defeated. I will have re-venge for my brother Aric's death. Do you understand me, chosen two? I am indomitable. I am . . ."

"A liar," a man's quiet voice interrupted.

Something clicked behind them. The tiny sound echoed down the tunnel. Delanie twisted her head to look. She heard Rondel's hissed breath of surprise.

The shadows parted. The wind died down. The pounding of fists stopped. A man came slowly into view.

"Professor!" Delanie gasped in relief. "You're alive. But who...?"

Her voice trailed off as a second man suddenly appeared. He wore black, all black. She hadn't seen him in the darkness. Her eyes fastened on the gun he held. Fear strangled her throat muscles. "Rondel," she whispered.

He eased her sideways. "You?" he asked, and the man smiled.

"Me," he agreed. He pushed the professor roughly forward. Delanie closed her eyes. The baroness *was* a demon. Number six. It had all been a lie, a clever, cunning lie. Demons truly did deceive. Here was the real Visitor, this man with his slicked-back hair and pointed black beard. John Kessler! The devil incarnate. On earth a mere hypnotist. In hell...?

Laughter resounded through the tunnel, hideous peals of laughter. "Did you really think you could trap The Visitor so easily?" John Kessler challenged in a roar that echoed loudly in Rondel's head.

"Yes, well..." the professor began, but the man holding him sent him a dark look and he lapsed into obedient silence.

"The Game is ended," Kessler said.

The shadows emphasized the lean angles of his face. He had a Satanic look to him, but there was more to it than that, something Rondel sensed rather than saw.

"Lies," Delanie whispered to him and he put his arms around her instinctively, as much to reassure himself as her.

They'd walked straight into the center of hell, that's what it was. The Visitor's evil surrounded them. These people, Kessler and the now-silent baroness, were crazy. Beyond that, they had no connection to Satan.

"You think not, Rondel?" Kessler asked, arching a dark eyebrow at him.

Rondel lifted resentful eyes to the man's shadowed face. "You're a psychic, Kessler, we all accept that. It doesn't make you the devil."

Kessler seemed unperturbed by the remark, and yet the tunnel air temperature seemed to drop by several degrees. The wind that had blown so hot before started up again, a frigid breeze. It ruffled Delanie's hair, plastering strands of it across Rondel's cheeks and neck.

Thrusting the professor forward a step, Kessler said, "I am whatever you believe me to be, Rondel. Truth is transitory. When you are in hell with Roland Popporov, ask him to define truth for you."

"Then ask him to define treachery," the professor added.

Kessler brought the gun up sharply under his chin. "Pretend you have no voice, professor," he advised. "I am sure your chosen two do not wish to die here in the dampness of this rat-infested tunnel." His black eyes slid to Rondel. "Move back," he said. "Away from the door. I wish to speak with Alicia."

"You mean she's still alive?" Delanie muttered. She sounded angry, but Rondel knew she was terrified. He could feel the fear and tension radiating from her body. He tightened his hold on her as Kessler shoved the professor forward and tapped with the gun handle against the planks.

"That was very sloppy of you, number six," he declared. His voice had a taunting edge, but there was something beneath that, some dark emotion Rondel couldn't define.

And now he could see it, or at least the beginnings of it. A force gaining strength in the tunnel, swirling about them, like the residue of red light that lingered at the periphery of his mind.

He concentrated on the door where Kessler stood. Behind it, he caught the baroness's petulant response. "The girl, Delanie, tricked me."

An outline formed on the old planks. Huge yellow eyes stared at him. Across them, something scuttled back and

forth, a tiny demon whose flaming beard and tail fluctu-
ated with its erratic movements.

"*Tricks and lies,*" it said, laughing. "*Game within a
Game, lie within a lie. You do not know with whom you
deal.*"

A silvery hiss shot through Rondel's head. The yellow
eyes glared at him. His thoughts grew hazy. Lie within a lie,
he told himself, but the words were being sucked away. By
Kessler?

He struggled to focus the demon image, but the yellow
eyes refused to let him win. The mind behind them was
stronger than his. "*Forget,*" it instructed him. Then it
laughed, mimicking the fiery demon's words. "*You know
not with whom you deal.*"

Rondel came back to reality with a jolt that carried deep
into his bones. Kessler was smiling at him, but he spoke to
the baroness. "I think I will leave you here for now," he
said. "To reflect upon your failure, hmm?"

Around them the tunnel grew cold. The remnants of the
red light turned a dull shade of yellow, like the eyes of The
Visitor. Rondel concealed a shudder and pulled Delanie
closer to his chilled body. What had the little demon said?
Something about lies?

He wanted to remember that part, but it was gone. And
now the yellow light was filling the tunnel, bringing with it
the pungent smell of sulphur.

With a final look at the bolted door, Kessler slid his gaze
to Rondel's face. "Do not fight battles you cannot hope to
win," he advised. "You felt the power of my number six
demon's mind, but I assure you, her power is nothing compared to mine. Did Mahira teach you nothing about The
Visitor?"

"Enough," Rondel said, still trying to recall the image.

"Did she tell you about Aric Bellal?" the professor inquired.

Kessler's gun jabbed his neck. "Mahira never met Aric,
professor," he reminded. "Aric had no time for witches."

"Why not?" Delanie challenged. "Was he afraid of
her?"

Kessler laughed. The yellow mist thickened, obscuring his sharp features. "Hardly. Aric was simply too busy eluding a certain angel, persistent above and beyond the call of duty, to waste time playing witch games."

"Anna," Delanie murmured.

Kessler nodded. "Of course, after the first capture, none of us realized that Aric was still..."

"Alive?" the Professor supplied.

"Alive," Kessler agreed. "We thought Anna had destroyed him the first time around, and of course, Aric, being the deviant demon of the family, never saw fit to inform anyone of his escape. It wasn't until she recaptured him that we learned the truth."

"And so because you thought he was dead initially, and because you couldn't get to Anna, your family had the professor's brother killed, instead," Delanie accused.

"He played the Game," Kessler said, sending the professor a vicious little smile. "Played and lost. It all evened out in the end. Anna is gone, and now two of her brothers pay for her crime. She did not know with whom she dealt when she went after Aric."

"With whom she dealt," Rondel repeated softly. He couldn't think why that phrase sounded familiar to him. Who were they dealing with?

Kessler's voice rose to a triumphant level. His eyes shone. "Ah, Aric, now he was no ordinary demon. He was special, even more special than a number six demon usually is. For Aric's soul had never been mortal. He was family, brother to the one known as Lucifer. And like Lucifer and several others, he was cast out of heaven. An entire family of angels exiled." Kessler's face hardened. "Those who remained in heaven called it a judgment, but they were fools, all of them. The family simply made a new home for themselves. The underworld became their domain. And I, Satan, became their leader."

Delanie went rigid. "You mean, you really believe that you're..."

Kessler's laughter rang out. "The Visitor?" His eyes lifted to the roof of the tunnel. "Yes! Supreme demon. Most powerful member of the family."

Mad, Rondel thought. The mist stung his eyes. He squinted through it, unsure what to say as Kessler shoved the professor forward again.

"It is done," the man said. "The only thing left is for the angel and his chosen two to die." Kessler's teeth gleamed yellow in the swirling light. "Do you have a preference, professor, as to the location?"

They had a choice? Rondel thought, fighting the disorienting effects of the mist.

"Oh, yes," Kessler assured him. Then he smiled and tapped his temple. "You may consider me mad, Rondel, but crazy or not, I am still a psychic, and a formidable hypnotist. In fact, I'm often better than I intend to be." His smile widened. "Popporov was not supposed to go under. However, I was able to turn that little mistake into an advantage."

"So you did bait us," Delanie charged. "You wanted Rondel and me to go to the castle that night. You wanted me to see that skeleton."

"Yes, Delanie Morgen," Kessler replied with an evil chuckle. "It was time that you came face-to-face with Death, don't you think? You've lived with the ghost of it long enough." Before she could respond, Kessler returned his attention to the professor. "Where?" he asked simply.

The professor's eyes, trained on the floor for several minutes now, came up only slightly. A faint smile curved his lips. "The watchtower?"

Kessler gave a small nod. "As you wish." The aura of malice surrounding him intensified. The mist curled into a dozen demonic shapes. Kessler's eyebrows arched. "Something to say, Delanie?"

Rondel felt the tremor that ran through her. "You're taking us to the watchtower to kill us," she said. "So this whole Game has been a cheat."

Kessler's shoulders shook with silent laughter. "Not a cheat, Delanie. Not if you really know the Story." He began to quote, "' . . . if they play the Game and that survive and win, defame the devil's demons six and five, they'll find the angel still alive.'" He sent them a triumphant look. The point of his beard lengthened with the wicked smile that spread across his face. "The angel, as you see, is still alive. I have brought him here for you to find. It is as the Story says. You are here, and he is here. But no mention was ever made in the Story of your release."

Throwing back his head, he began to laugh.

Chapter Eighteen

"I sense great disbelief in your chosen two," Kessler remarked as they approached the watchtower in the professor's Vauxhall. "Considering their attitudes, it is amazing to me that they did so well."

"I'm impressed," the professor agreed, then he held up his hand. "Do you mind, Herr Kessler? That gun's very distracting. I'm not likely to jump out and leave my chosen two in the lurch."

A clap of thunder shook the tiny car. Delanie glanced through the window at the rain that enveloped them like a black curtain. In a small voice she said, "You tell us your mind is stronger than your sixth demon's, Herr Kessler. So why do you need a gun? Why not turn us all into mindless zombies and be done with it?"

Kessler chuckled. "You are unwise to put ideas like that into my head, Delanie. If I wanted to, I could make you all commit suicide, but I prefer to reserve that punishment for my demons."

"You must have very weak-minded demons," Rondel remarked.

"I prefer to call them loyal." Kessler motioned with the gun. "Park over there, professor, close to the door. I do not like to be wet."

"Fire and water don't mix," Rondel murmured. He let his head fall back against the seat.

Lightning shot through the sky, mirror image of the night they'd arrived in this horrible place, Delanie thought, rubbing her temple where her head hurt the most. Kessler might be stronger, but the baroness had more than her share of mental power.

She frowned in frustration. "I can't see her killing herself," she said to Rondel.

"The baroness?" He gave his head a small shake.

"Neither can I," the professor put in.

Kessler merely smiled. "Number six will do what is necessary, assuming it becomes necessary. Walpurgis is almost ended. In seventeen minutes, it will be midnight."

Delanie got no sense of madness from him, but it had to be there. This was insanity, all of it. Mad Visitor, mad demons—what kind of a family did Aric Bellal have?

In the front seat, Kessler laughed. "Your thoughts betray you, Delanie. What you think, I hear."

"Unless you put a guard around your mind," the professor said over his shoulder.

Kessler's eyes narrowed. "Enjoy yourself, professor. Fifteen minutes are all that remain to you on this earth." He raised the gun. "We will get out of the car now, one at a time. And if you wish to live without great pain for the next fifteen minutes, there will be no tricks."

His black eyes gleamed in the eerie flashes of lightning, and his widow's peak seemed to grow more pronounced. Delanie suppressed her terror. How was it all going to end?

She stepped from the car. Kessler motioned for her to remain by the door. Thunder shook the ground.

"Good," Kessler said calmly when the professor climbed out. "Now we go inside together."

Delanie stayed close to Rondel as they crossed the muddy courtyard and entered the watchtower. The air was cold tonight. She imagined great clouds of evil pressing in on her.

"No lights," the professor announced, unlocking the front door and pushing the switch. "The panel in my lab must be on the blink again. Do you mind, Herr Kessler?"

He smiled and removed a flashlight from the cupboard. "If I'm going to die, I would prefer it not be in the dark."

Humor, at a time like this? Delanie looked at Rondel, who merely shrugged and shook his head.

A thunderbolt underscored Kessler's reply. "Stall if you must, professor."

The lightning momentarily illuminated his narrow features. Yes, Delanie thought, her panic mounting, he was the devil to behold, all right. But why be so smug about it all? He had no right to be. This whole Game had been one big fake.

"You didn't win anything, you know," she couldn't resist telling him as they climbed the shadowy stone staircase to the professor's lab. "We survived your temptations and the Game. We trapped your sixth demon. If you really were The Visitor, you'd be back in hell by now."

The professor halted at the top of the stairs, using the scarf Delanie had left draped over the railing to wipe his wet face. "She does have a point there, Herr Kessler. How does the Story go again, Rondel?"

Rondel's eyes looked very dark in the light of the storm. Delanie watched him in profile as he replied, " 'The devil waits, The Visitor in guise whose fate, whose power on this earth shall be decided for a century. But only if the demons lose.' "

"Yes, lose," the professor repeated. "Unless I'm mistaken, your demons have done precisely that."

"I would watch myself, if I were you," Kessler warned, shifting the gun to the professor's chest. "The angel is a mere pawn in this Game. You have interfered more than enough as it is."

"And you haven't?" the professor returned benignly.

Lightning forked through the sky. The storm was centered over the watchtower now. Delanie's teeth began to chatter. Her terrified mind wandered. The Story, real or not? No, of course not. She'd already established that.

But what about the female angel who'd played the Game two hundred years ago and won? And the male angel who'd played it one hundred years ago and lost? Could these myths possibly have anything to do with Anna and the professor's dead brother?

John Kessler, or whatever his real name was, said that Aric Bellal had been cast out of heaven, a fallen angel as Lucifer was. The "family" ruled in hell now. Did Kessler really believe that, or was he just tormenting them?

Delanie squeezed her eyes closed. Lightning flashed against her eyelids.

Vibrations from the thunder slid up the stone walls. The professor wandered over to the electrical panel and played his dying flashlight beam over the switches. "Which lever is it?" he wondered out loud, then he raised his voice. "What was that other part of the Story, Rondel? The part about the Visitor losing."

Rondel stood against the wall next to Delanie. "'But if the angel chooses well,'" he said, "'The Visitor returns to hell.'"

"Ah, there it is, the light bar." The professor removed his gaze from the panel, a smile and another thunderbolt illuminating his narrow features. "Why aren't you in hell, Herr Kessler?" he asked in a guileless voice. "Demons all gone, May Day not yet upon us, don't you think it's time you admitted defeat? I know Aric didn't want to, but then, Aric was a rebel. I would think Satan should set a better example."

"Would you really, Professor?" Kessler retorted calmly. "I suppose you will now try to tell me that your own behavior in all of this has been above reproach, hmm?"

A blast of cold, wet air suddenly rushed up the stairwell. It swept across Delanie's face like icy fingers on her skin. She jerked back, then stopped.

Anger. The word burst through her head, and with it the sense that something more than air had just swirled into the laboratory. There was a presence housed within it, a distinct mental force.

"Mahira?" she whispered uncertainly.

No one heard her, and the wind didn't answer.

"What about the visions?" the professor was challenging Kessler, "and the dreams? Did those things just happen?"

"And we already know that Gerda was manipulated," Rondel said.

Delanie felt him move. Toward Kessler? She couldn't see much with all the flashes of lightning, or feel much, for that matter.

But something had come in on the wind. Didn't anyone else sense it? Palms pressed to the wall, she looked up and waited for the next lightning bolt.

"All of this is unimportant," Kessler stated. "We all have some degree of mental ability. Where such things exist, naturally there will be manipulation and trickery. That is accepted."

"Not by me, it isn't," the professor said.

"I grow tired of this conversation," Kessler told him. Then he swung the gun around. "Stand still," he ordered Rondel, who had indeed been working his way toward the panel. "Professor, shine what is left of that light over here. It is time the male half of your chosen two died."

That brought Delanie swiftly out of her trance. "No!" she cried above the thunder. She launched herself at Kessler. "You can't. I won't let you!"

It was like throwing herself against a stone statue. Kessler tossed her aside with one fling of his arm. With his gloved thumb he cocked the hammer, but the professor forestalled him. "Listen to me, Kessler," he said in an urgent tone. "You can't do this."

"Why? Because it is unfair?" Kessler shot back.

Delanie scrambled to her feet, but the professor prevented her from running to Rondel.

"There are rules, Kessler," he said. "You can't ignore them."

"Rules?" Kessler laughed. "Oh, come now, professor. Is that the best you can do, quote rules to me? There are only two minutes left until midnight. I can wait if I must. But the one who is related to the interfering witch will die first."

Did he feel the presence, too? Was it Mahira?

Delanie squirmed free. A streak of lightning snaked through the window. She saw threads of blackness in the air. No shape or substance, but she wasn't wrong. Someone else was here.

She ran to Rondel, who seemed to be transfixed by something. "No," she whispered, pushing him backward. "Don't touch the lever."

Staring at a point well above her head, he gave no indication that he heard her. Did he see even more than she had in the air?

She continued to hold him back. Kessler was beside the panel now. His hand reached for the bar.

"Do not try to be clever like your sister, professor," he warned with a humorless chuckle. "Rules!"

"Speaking of sisters…" the professor began, but a branch crashing against the watchtower's outer wall drowned him out.

"No!" a voice in the wind seemed to scream.

The flashlight had long since gone dead, but there was enough electricity outside that Delanie could see Kessler's fingers hovering over the metal lever. Ungrounded, she recalled with a grimace.

The gun moved.

"Stop, stop, stop!" the wind shrieked.

Delanie sensed fury in the hidden voice. Kessler paid no attention to it. Was it Mahira? Was she trying to distract him, keep him from killing Rondel?

One of the windows suddenly blew open, and Delanie jumped.

"What…" Rondel began, but she clapped a hand over his mouth. The crash must have penetrated his trance.

"Don't say anything," she whispered.

"Thirty seconds now," Kessler announced. "Walpurgis draws to a close. May Day arrives. My victory is complete."

High above them, one of the windows shattered. Slivers of glass showered the floor. A new torrent of wind poured through.

Delanie glanced at the professor. His eyes were closed, as if he were deep in thought. Garbled words came to her now, nothing that made sense.

"Twenty seconds," Kessler said.

The lightning flashed. Was his hand on the bar? What if he shot one of them before he pulled the lever?

Rondel set his hands on her arms. "We have to get the gun," he told her.

"Revenge," Kessler said. "Three deaths tonight for Aric." He raised the gun. "Say goodbye to Mahira, Rondel."

Rondel's muscles constricted.

"No, don't!" Delanie protested, but he was already gone, and she couldn't see or hear anything except the lash of the wind.

"Fool!" the wind hissed.

Desperately, Delanie groped her way down the wall. Pull the lever, she prayed.

Thunder rattled the remaining windows. Again the lightning flashed. The wind caught at her hair, momentarily blinding her. Shoving the wet strands from her eyes, she caught a glimpse of Rondel in silhouette. He'd almost reached Kessler, but the man was quick. He stepped back at the last second, still holding the gun, counting off the seconds now. "Nine, eight, seven . . ."

Another bolt of lightning revealed his hand on the electrical bar. "Four, three, two . . ."

With a laugh he yanked it down.

Delanie cringed.

She heard the sizzle of current as it flowed into the man's body. A crackle of blue-and-white sparks showered the immediate area. He let out a scream of pain. His arms and legs went stiff. His head fell backward. His teeth were bared and clenched.

The lights faded, then flared, then faded again. Rondel snatched the gun from his hand, and stood back. All Delanie could do was stare.

The wind around them died. So did the thunder. With a final strangled cry, Kessler fell slowly to his knees.

"So close," he managed to whisper, but then his throat muscles tensed and the words stopped.

He toppled facedown on the cold stone floor.

Endless moments passed before any of them reacted. The lights flickered, the rain continued to fall. But the thunder and the wind had both receded, as if they'd been centered within Kessler.

Delanie made her way across the floor. Her skin felt as if it were encased in ice. She dropped to her knees beside Rondel, who was already bending over the body.

"Dead?" he asked her. She put out a reluctant hand to check.

She got no sensations from him. Nothing. But there was a pulse.

The professor joined them. "Well?"

"Unconscious," Delanie said, glad for Rondel's arm around her and his cheek pressed to the side of her head.

Sitting back on his heels, the professor smiled a little. "It doesn't pay to cheat," he murmured. Then he pushed back his hat and squinted at the electrical panel. "You know, I really must remember to fix that one of these days."

THE NEXT twelve hours were total chaos, but better than the nightmare Rondel had been living for the past week. Except for meeting Delanie, of course. No nightmares in that.

A revived John Kessler was taken away to jail. So was the baroness. Dex showed up in the village just after dawn to say that Mahira had spent the night in the caves. And how, Rondel asked, did he know that?

"Well," Dex confessed. "Me and Harry have been stashing a few things down in those caves. Questionably acquired merchandise, you might call it. You see, once the professor and Delanie showed up in Klausberg, we had to find a new hiding place quick.''

''The old one being the watchtower cellar?'' Rondel assumed, and Dex grinned.

''So it was Dex and Harry we saw the night you fell through the cellar door,'' Rondel explained to Delanie as they drove to the cottage.

She still seemed distracted. ''But Popporov was there at some point, too,'' she said. ''I felt him.'' She paused. ''Rondel, did you sense anything in the watchtower last night—you know, when the wind rushed in?''

''Maybe.'' He fought a shudder. ''I thought I saw something for a minute, up near the ceiling, but I couldn't quite make out who or what it was.''

''Mahira?''

''Do you want me to ask her?''

''Would she admit it?''

''Probably not.''

''Then let's just leave it a mystery.''

They could leave the whole thing a mystery as far as Rondel was concerned. Demon visions, demon dreams, sinister warnings, tests, temptations, he wanted no part of them anymore. Except he was curious about the professor. Where had he been held?

''In the tunnels,'' he told them when they arrived at the cottage. ''Popporov ambushed me that first night. All part of the master plan.''

''But it's over,'' Delanie said. ''It really is over, right?''

The professor smiled. ''Yes.''

''So why wasn't it over when we caught the baroness?''

''Because demons deceive.'' Rondel mouthed the words as the professor responded. Then he added a humorous, ''It has been mentioned, professor.''

''And it's not much of an answer,'' Delanie maintained.

But it was all she got. And Rondel seemed to accept it.

''Kessler cheated,'' he said to Delanie a few minutes later. ''He wasn't really the devil. The real Visitor would have had to concede defeat the minute we caught his sixth demon. That's The Visitor's Game.''

"Some Game.'' Delanie shuddered. Then she frowned. "Where are we going?''

"To the caves.'' He helped her around a boulder. "Mahira left her cingulam there.''

"Her what?''

"Cord. Belt.'' He touched her waist. "Part of her witch equipment.''

She climbed over a clump of rocks. "Let's not talk about witches, huh?''

"Sore point?'' he teased, pushing into the cave.

"Very. Two witches, Rondel?''

"I know.'' He ran his fingers through her hair from behind. "But two careful witches?''

She looked over her shoulder at him. She wanted to give in, he could see it in her face. But she shook her head and knelt in front of the dying fire, instead. "What if I did kill my father with a thought?''

"I can't believe you could have done that.''

"You say that, but you don't know.''

"Don't I?'' He knelt beside her. "Don't you?''

He saw her hand hover above the remaining flames. For the longest time, she stared into the coals. Finally, she said, "Maybe I do.''

Rondel followed her gaze, and for a moment thought he glimpsed something deep within the ashes. Drunk driver on a wet highway, laughing as he tipped back a whiskey bottle...

"I bet he knows The Visitor better than anyone,'' Delanie murmured to the fire.

The image faded. Rondel took her hand, turning her gently away from the stone circle. "Let it go, Delanie,'' he said softly. With his thumb he stroked her lower lip. "I love you. We'll make the rest of it work.''

She gave him a grudging smile. He felt her arms slide about his waist. "I love you, too, Rondel. But it's going to be a lot of work.''

"Worthwhile work."

Her smile widened, lighting her face. With a quick motion she reached up and kissed him thoroughly, then pushed back and glanced around the cave floor. "I don't see any belt."

He pulled her back into his arms. "Does that tell you something?" he said with a small smile.

"We have Mahira's blessing?"

"Stranger things have happened."

She glanced at the fire, then tapped his arm. "Maybe stranger than we want to believe."

He returned his gaze to the coals. A man's face had formed within them. "Professor?" he said in mild surprise.

The image shimmered for a second, then disappeared.

Delanie brought her eyes slowly back to Rondel's face. "I wonder..."

But Rondel merely shook his head. "Take my advice, Delanie," he said solemnly. "Don't." Smiling, he reached hungrily for her mouth.

IN THE COTTAGE with Mahira, the professor looked away from the fire.

The old witch rocked in her chair, her eyes hooded as she stared at him. "You've done well, professor, to defeat The Visitor."

His lips curved slightly. "Thank you, Mahira."

"It was meant as a small compliment only." Her fingers worked the braided cingulam around her waist. "I am not happy that you chose Rondel."

"I think I chose very well."

"You knew that I would be upset."

The professor sat back, angling his hat over one eye. "Don't forget, Mahira, it was you who called for me in the first place."

"We asked for an angel to be sent. After your brother's failure, I wanted another woman. I had hoped for your sister Margaret."

The professor's eyes sparkled. "Why? Because she wouldn't have chosen Rondel?"

"I could have shielded him from her, it is true. Rondel is all that will remain of my blood when I am gone on to a higher place."

"He might have children," the Professor suggested.

Mahira snorted. "With the female you chose? She is a witch."

"So is Rondel."

"She could have gotten him killed."

"But she didn't. And while we're on the subject of death, I must say I appreciate your efforts on my behalf."

Mahira waved a bony hand. "The Sisterhood protects the one they call. That is accepted." "What will you do now, professor?"

"I don't know."

"Of course you do," she snapped. "You are the angel."

The professor sent her a big smile. "Professor Nagel," he corrected.

"One and the same. Will I see you again soon?"

He patted her wrinkled hand. "You know you will. Goodbye, Mahira."

"Goodbye, professor. And thank you, for defeating The Visitor."

"Thank Delanie and Rondel," he reminded her softly. "They won the Game."

"YOU WANT US to explore Berlin?" Delanie asked Rondel as they neared Mahira's cottage. "Why Berlin? Why not Moscow?"

"Do you speak Russian?" he asked.

"Well, that's a point." She looked ahead through the gray midday light. "Hello, professor. Did you have a nice talk with Mahira?"

"Interesting." The professor adjusted his hat. "Everything settled between you?"

Delanie smiled. "Not quite. Rondel doesn't want to go work at that museum in Lisbon, and I don't want to go back to the hospital in Portland, so we've been thinking about doing some traveling, just to see what's out there. Unless of course you still need us for something."

The Professor smiled. "What a splendid idea. We can always do with more angels."

"I beg your pardon?"

"Nothing." He arched an inquisitive eyebrow. "Something troubling you, Rondel?"

A frown marred Rondel's forehead. "I just remembered something I saw in a vision. A little demon with a pointed beard."

"John Kessler has a pointed beard," Delanie said absently. Then she frowned. "But he wasn't a demon, was he?"

"Must have been a false vision," the professor remarked.

Rondel gave him a suspicious look. "Must have been."

"Well." Grinning, the professor looked away. "I have to be off now."

"More demons to catch?" Delanie asked.

"Evil spirits." He glanced at his watch. "Let's see, it's the first of May. How about if I come back for you in say, two weeks? There's going to be a wedding, I trust. And I am invited."

Delanie reached up and kissed his cheek. "Yes and yes." She stood back. "Two weeks, professor. No more."

"I promise." He started for his car. "I'll send you a present," he called over his shoulder. His eyes rose to the lightening sky. "A rainbow, maybe. Over the baroness's castle. Kiss the bride, Rondel."

Rondel laughed and complied, his mouth hot and promising on hers.

"Two weeks," Delanie murmured when he finally lifted his head. "Remember that, professor." She looked around when he didn't respond. "Professor? Where did he go?"

Rondel glanced toward the cottage, but there was nothing. No Vauxhall, no professor, only silence, and the first hint of sunlight they'd had in weeks. "Did you hear his car?" he asked.

But Delanie's gaze was no longer on the cottage or the woods. Touching Rondel's arm, she pointed north. "Look," she said in astonishment. "Over the castle." Her disbelieving eyes returned to his. "It's a rainbow."

Epilogue

John Kessler sat alone in his jail cell, waiting. He knew what would come. It was only a matter of time. The Game was over. He had made a mistake, a big one.

He heard the quiet clank of a metal door opening, and then closing. He heard footsteps on the floor and he looked up.

There she stood in all her deadly regal glory. Her features were calm. Nothing showed in her hazel eyes, except that tinge of yellow around the edges that reminded him unpleasantly of sulphur.

Had Roland felt this way when he'd learned the truth about her identity? Had he regretted all the nasty remarks he had made to the one he'd thought was number six?

Kessler stood, shoulders squared. "I am sorry." He offered the useless apology, and she shrugged.

"It is done. You have failed me. My brother Aric's death will not be avenged in this century. The Visitor must return to hell, as the Story says." Her yellow-tinged eyes hardened. A cold smile spread across her mouth. "And with her she will take her demons. All of them, number six."

He nodded. "I am truly sorry," he said again.

She came up to the bars. "Not as sorry as you very soon will be, I promise you that."

John Kessler's fingers shook, but he did what he had to do. He took the length of rope now in his possession and threw it over a sturdy ceiling beam. Meticulously, he made a noose for his neck. Then, stepping up on his cot, the demon hanged himself.

OUTSIDE HIS CELL, Baroness Alicia von Peldt watched the ritual without expression. When it was done, she lit a cigarette and stepped back. Number six was gone. The Game was lost. Yes, demons did deceive, but not well enough this time around. The rules must be obeyed. She had no alternative.

Turning slowly, she walked away, disappearing finally into the shadows in a long, sinuous trail of smoke.

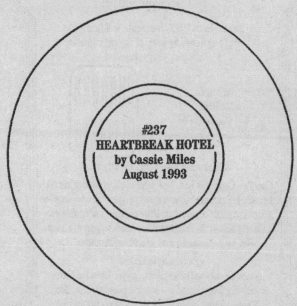

Harlequin is proud to present our
best authors and their best books.
Always the best for your
reading pleasure!

Throughout 1993, Harlequin will bring you
exciting books by some of the top names in
contemporary romance!

In August,
look for
Heat Wave by

BARBARA
DELINSKY

A heat wave hangs over the city....

Caroline Cooper is hot. And after dealing with crises all
day, she is frustrated. But throwing open her windows to
catch the night breeze does little to solve her problems.
Directly across the courtyard she catches sight of a man
who inspires steamy and unsettling thoughts....

Driven onto his fire
escape by the sweltering heat, lawyer Brendan Carr
is weaving fantasies, too—around gorgeous Caroline.
Fantasies that build as the days and nights go by.

Will Caroline and Brendan dare cross the dangerous
line between fantasy and reality?

Find out in HEAT WAVE by Barbara Delinsky...
wherever Harlequin books are sold.

BOB4

"I AM BETRAYED"

In the still of the night, those were the words spoken to
Emma Devlin by her husband, Frank . . . from beyond the
grave. She'd given him no cause to doubt her devotion, yet he
haunted her waking hours and disturbed her dreams.

Next month, Harlequin Intrigue brings you a chilling tale of
love and disloyalty . . .

#241 FLESH AND BLOOD
by Caroline Burnes
September 1993

In an antebellum mansion, Emma finds help from the oddest of
sources: in the aura of a benevolent ghost—and in the arms of
a gallant Confederate colonel.

For a spine-tingling story about a love that transcends time,
don't miss Harlequin Intrigue #241 FLESH AND BLOOD,
coming to you in September.

FAD1

**Relive the romance...
Harlequin and Silhouette
are proud to present**

by Request

A program of collections of three complete novels by the most
requested authors with the most requested themes. Be sure to
look for one volume each month with three complete novels by
top name authors.

In June: **NINE MONTHS** Penny Jordan
                              Stella Cameron
                              Janice Kaiser

**Three women pregnant and alone. But a lot can
happen in nine months!**

In July: **DADDY'S**   Kristin James
           HOME   Naomi Horton
                          Mary Lynn Baxter

**Daddy's Home... and his presence is long
overdue!**

In August: **FORGOTTEN** Barbara Kaye
           PAST   Pamela Browning
                          Nancy Martin

**Do you dare to create a future if you've forgotten
the past?**

Available at your favorite retail outlet.

HARLEQUIN®   *Silhouette*

Discover the glorious triumph of three
extraordinary couples fueled by a powerful
passion to defy the past in

Lingering Shadows

The dramatic story of six fascinating men and
women who find the strength to step out of the
shadows and into the light of a passionate future.

Linked by relentless ambition and by desire, each
must confront private demons in a riveting struggle
for power. Together they must find the strength to
emerge from the lingering shadows of the past, into
the dawning promise of the future.

Look for this powerful new blockbuster by *New
York Times* bestselling author

PENNY JORDAN

Calloway Corners

In September, Harlequin is proud to bring readers four involving, romantic stories about the Calloway sisters, set in Calloway Corners, Louisiana. Written by four of Harlequin's most popular and award-winning authors, you'll be enchanted by these sisters and the men they love!

MARIAH by Sandra Canfield
JO by Tracy Hughes
TESS by Katherine Burton
EDEN by Penny Richards

As an added bonus, you can enter a sweepstakes contest to win a trip to Calloway Corners, and meet all four authors. Watch for details in all Calloway Corners books in September.

CAL93

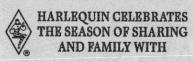

Fifty red-blooded, white-hot, true-blue hunks from every State in the Union!

Beginning in May, look for MEN MADE IN AMERICA! Written by some of our most popular authors, these stories feature fifty of the strongest, sexiest men, each from a different state in the union!

Two titles available every other month at your favorite retail outlet.

In September, look for:

DECEPTIONS by Annette Broadrick (California)
STORMWALKER by Dallas Schulze (Colorado)

In November, look for:

STRAIGHT FROM THE HEART by Barbara Delinsky (Connecticut)
AUTHOR'S CHOICE by Elizabeth August (Delaware)

You won't be able to resist MEN MADE IN AMERICA!